Escape

Ferguson Series Book 1

Authentic Stories of the Transgender Community Series

Helen Dale

ISBN 978-1-7397667-7-1

Cover illustrations

Background: ID 26048692 | Moonlight © Chatree988 | Dreamstime.com

Westland Lysander aircraft Martin Hatch / Alamy Stock Photo

Use of speech marks

As part of "Escape" is set in Germany and France during World War 2, significant parts of the conversations would be in French and German. I have used French speech marks: « and » to indicate where the conversation is in French, „ and " for German speech and " and " for English.

Acknowledgements

I am grateful to members of Manchester Women's Writers' group for their critiques of many of the chapters and to Joyce for her comments on the completed novel.

Also to the following for background information for Escape to try and make the story as authentic as possible. However, any oversights or errors are entirely mine.

RAF Flight Engineer & Air Engineer Association

https://raffeaea.com/

The Stirling Project

https://stirlingproject.org.uk/

RAFs ex-PoW Association
http://www.rafinfo.org.uk/rafexpow/

Bibliography

The following books were particularly useful in giving first-hand experiences:

A Stirling Effort: Short Stirling Operations at RAF Downham Market 1942-44 Steve Smith

A Thousand Shall Fall Murray Peden

Escape from Stalag Luft III: The True Story of My Successful Great Escape Bram Vanderstok, Simon Pearson

Into the Silk: The Dramatic True Stories of Airmen Who Bailed Out — And Lived Ian Mackersey

SECRET AGENT the true story of the Special Operations Executive David Stafford

The Long Road Home Adrian Vincent

The True Story of the Wooden Horse Robert J. Laplander

Wingless Victory: The Story of Sir Basil Embry's Escape from Occupied France Anthony Richardson

Authentic Stories of the Transgender Community Series

Authentic stories featuring transgender characters. The series are generally stand-alone books - though characters may well appear in more than one book (eg Jacqui is in both Summer Dreams and Operation Busted Flush). Most can be read in any order. The exceptions are the Impact Series which are planned as a trilogy.

The author identified as a cross dresser for decades before accepting that she needed to transition permanently in the mid-1990s. In that time, she has attended trans groups and met trans people from all over the UK (and abroad); she has run several trans and LGBT groups and has been a counsellor specialising in gender variant clients for twenty-five years.

She served on local and national diversity boards for the Probation and Prison Services, Police and Crown Prosecution Service and has provided trans awareness training for a diverse range of organisations. Socially she has met many hundreds, if not thousands, of trans individuals each with their own story.

This, together with her own experiences, has provided her with a wealth of details on which to base her novels and ensure that they are absolutely authentic.

Chapter 1.   Bored

August 1933

Simon was bored.

Bored, bored, bored.

He was also worried.

His mum wasn't well and he'd been sent to stay with his aunt and her family. Aunt Ida did her best to make him comfortable and stop him fretting.

"I'm sure your mum will be fine," she assured him as she handed him a freshly baked bun. "She just needs to rest until your new brother or sister is born. Your dad has to work at the forge so they can't look after you at the moment." She wasn't as confident as she tried to sound, however. It had been eight years since her sister, Emma, had given birth to Simon. Since then, she'd suffered two miscarriages and her latest pregnancy threatened the same result.

"I know," Simon said, "and it's nice here, but there's no one for me to play with."

The problem was his cousins were both girls and there were no other boys around. Not that he particularly liked football knockabouts that most boys played but he was interested in aeroplanes and loved reading stories of Biggles in 'The Modern Boy' magazine and had been given a copy of 'The Camels are Coming' last Christmas. He enjoyed playing 'dog fights' with other lads – pretending to be Billy Bishop or Alan Ball; both of whom had won Victoria Crosses for their exploits against the Hun. He'd watch aircraft like the Hawker Fury or the Bristol Bulldog from a Royal Air Force landing field not far from his home a few miles outside Andover.

'What would it be like to soar into the sky in the latest fighters?' he'd wondered as he'd watched their aerobatics.

Not that he'd ever have a chance to find out. People from his background didn't fly in aeroplanes let alone become pilots. The very best he could hope for would be working with the flying machines, perhaps as a mechanic. His father had followed in *his* father's footsteps as a blacksmith – indeed, there had been smiths for at least five generations. As motor cars and mechanical devices had replaced horses, Simon's father had learned how to repair them. Simon knew he was expected to follow the family tradition.

"Why don't you go and see if Daphne and Grace would like to go for a walk in the woods? They're up in the playroom with their friend Lucy," Aunt Ida suggested. "You might see a woodpecker, I'm sure I heard one earlier. Here, take these currant buns up with you."

It was true that walking through the woods was one activity that both Simon and his cousins all enjoyed.

The playroom had once been servants' quarters in the attic of the rectory. Whilst rectors may have previously been considered on a par with the gentry, his uncle, the Reverend Geoffrey Bartlett's income didn't stretch to more than a cleaner twice a week. Converting the attic did mean that the sound of the children playing didn't disturb his parish meetings or his concentration when he was trying to write his sermons in his study on the ground floor.

The door to the playroom was closed when he reached it but he could hear giggling from inside.

He knocked on the door – his cousins had made it very clear before that he wasn't to just enter their rooms which, he assumed, included the playroom. After a few seconds, the door was opened by Grace. At eight years old, she was the younger of the two sisters so usually had to do Daphne's bidding.

"Oh, it's you, Simon. Are those buns for us?" she asked, taking them from him. She took one and passed the other two to Daphne and Lucy. Seeing Simon was still standing in the doorway, she turned to him. "Was there something else?"

"Aunt Ida said to ask if you'd like to go for a walk in the woods. She said we might see a woodpecker."

"We were just about to rehearse a play that Daphne has written," Grace replied.

"Oh. Right then. It's just that I don't have anything to do or anyone to play with. Could I take part too?" Simon asked

"Not really, there isn't a boy in the story, only four girls," Daphne remarked.

"Unless you want to be a girl for the afternoon," Lucy interjected. Turning to Daphne and Grace, she continued "Girls, there are four roles so if Simon takes one, we don't need one of us to do two parts."

"That's true," Daphne confirmed "and men always took the female parts in Shakespeare."

"Well, Simon?" challenged Grace.

Simon considered the suggestion. It was only a play. It didn't mean anything.

"Why not?" He shrugged his shoulders – anything would be better than being bored on his own.

"Just a moment. If Simon is going to be a girl for the afternoon, he, or rather she, needs to dress as one," said Lucy. "You're about her size, Grace, have you got something you could lend her?"

Simon swallowed. He hadn't anticipated this. Reading out a girl's part in a play was one thing. Wearing a dress was something quite different. What if his aunt was to see him or, even worse, his uncle?

"Do I have to?" he asked.

"No, you don't," said Lucy. "You can go and play on your own if you like. But if you want to take part in our girls' play then you have to be a girl."

She and his cousins sat looking at him; waiting for him to make up his mind.

He really was bored with being on his own.

"All right then," he conceded.

Grace dashed down the stairs to her bedroom on the floor below before running back into the room a few minutes later.

"Here, put these on, you can get changed behind that screen," she said, handing Simon a bundle and pointing to a panel at the other end of the room.

Simon took the clothes Grace handed him and went behind the partition. He found that she'd given him a dress, petticoat, underwear, socks and shoes.

"Put them all on," Grace instructed.

There wasn't much difference in the style of the underwear or the socks compared with his own but they were lighter and coloured rather than plain white. When he drew them on, they felt softer against his skin. He wasn't sure which way round the petticoat went – but it seemed fine either way so he left it and pulled the dress over his head then did up the buttons. The shoes were slightly small but manageable.

He was self-conscious as he emerged from behind the partition to re-join the others, fully expecting them to laugh at him.

"You look lovely as a girl, Simon," remarked Daphne. "Doesn't she?"

"She certainly does, she can't be called Simon though, it'll need to be Simone," agreed Lucy.

Grace just smiled. "Here's your script, Simone," she said handing her the pages that Daphne had typed up on the Underwood machine her father used for parish business and writing his sermons. Simone's copy was the fourth set and with four sheets of paper and three of carbon paper to strike through, the keys had lost their impact and the words were barely legible.

Simone's self-consciousness dissipated as the four of them became engrossed in rehearsing the play. They were so absorbed that they didn't hear Mrs Bartlett entering the room.

"I've brought you all some orange squash," she announced as she came through the door. Then, realising what she was seeing, continued: "Can someone explain why Simon is dressed as a girl?"

"Mum!" cried Grace and Daphne in harmony.

"Aunt Ida!" exclaimed Simon and Lucy; the latter using the honorific title bestowed on parents' close friends. All four then started to explain about the play.

"One at a time! Daphne, you explain." She then listened while Daphne clarified why Simon was now Simone.

"Well, I don't suppose there is any harm in it. I'm not sure if your father would approve though so best not let him find out," she said.

Simon's mum gave birth to a daughter on 12th October 1933 and he was allowed to return home at the end of the month ready for the second half of the Christmas term at school. His mum still had to take things easy but, now nearly nine, Simon was considered old enough to help around the house – laying the fires, washing up, making cups of tea for his mum and watching over baby Mary while his mum rested.

At Christmas, Simon was presented with a parcel that he eagerly unwrapped. It contained a dark green pullover, a green cricket-style cap with yellow piping and a pair of garters with green tabs.

"You'll have to make do with your usual shorts and stockings for the rest of your Wolf Cub uniform," his mum told him. He'd been looking forward to joining the Young Scouts and had already been accepted for membership as soon as he was nine years old, now just two weeks away.

Chapter 2.   Camping

July 1936

Simon, now eleven, was preparing for his first summer camp. He'd moved up to the Boy Scouts from the Wolf Cubs immediately after his 11th birthday in January. In the Cubs, he'd been one of the senior boys, proudly wearing the two stripes of a Sixer. In the Scouts, he'd been the most junior until others had taken the low position on the totem pole. Now he was well on his way to gaining his 'Second Class' award after passing tests including knots, fire lighting, using a hand axe and knife and compass work.

As he pulled his rucksack over his shoulders, his father gave him a hand, checking that the straps weren't twisted while his mother stood there, holding his little sister in her arms.

"Ready son?"

"Yes, Dad."

"Got everything you need?"

"I think so."

"Right then, give your mum and sister a kiss and we'll be off."

It was a little under half a mile to the village hall where they were to board the lorry that would take them to a farm, owned by the Scoutmaster's cousin, near Frome. As they approached the hall, Simon could see the pantechnicon parked in front. Usually used for furniture removals, the tall lorry had ample space for all their personal kit as well as the large bell tents that would be their home for the next week.

Having loaded the lorry, the scouts paraded in front of the hall. The Scoutmaster inspected them, checking that their uniforms were complete – including their staves, whistles, sheath knives on their belts; their lemon squeezer hats squarely on their heads, stockings pulled up to just below their knees, their patrol flashes hanging from their shoulders: green and black for the Eagle patrol, plain black for the Ravens.

Satisfied everything was in order, he gave the command to board the lorry and settle themselves down on whatever they could find to absorb the bumps of the road. The tailgate was then lifted into place leaving the top half free to look out of.

The Scoutmaster then climbed into the cab. Dennis Slater, a Rover Scout, who usually drove the lorry as part of his job, started the engine; after expelling clouds of smoke, it settled into a steady beat and, with a jerk that threatened to dislodge several occupants in the rear, pulled away.

Clear of the village, the Raven's patrol second pulled out a mouth organ and started to play "She'll Be Coming Round the Mountain." The other scouts joined in with the words; they followed up with "Quartermaster's Store", "What Shall We Do with the Drunken Sailor" and other traditional campfire songs. Their route took them past Stonehenge and the Scoutmaster pulled the lorry off the road so the boys could take a break and explore the stone pillars. As they still had an hour's journey to the campsite, and would then have to erect the tents, gather firewood and start a fire before they could eat that evening, the Scoutmaster tapped out his pipe and told the scouts to reboard the lorry.

At the farm, the boys transferred the heavy tents and other equipment onto a trailer and followed as Mr Jacobs the farmer towed it with an elderly tractor that belched black smoke from the exhaust pipe sticking up from the side of the engine. The combination bumped its way down the valley on a rough track.

"Dennis would never get that lorry down 'ere, Wilfred," shouted Jacobs to his scoutmaster cousin over the noise of the tractor engine.

"Very true, Hector. It's kind of you to help us," his cousin replied.

"There's two quarts of fresh milk, a dozen eggs and a sack of spuds on the trailer – just send one of the boys up to the farm each day if you need any more."

Simon could hardly contain his excitement at this adventure. He could see there was a brook at the bottom of the hill which merged with a larger river downstream. A wooden footbridge across it led into some woods that stretched into the distance. Upstream from the footbridge, a railway also crossed the stream. As the scouts hiked down the track, a shrill whistle pierced even the din from the tractor and a tank engine pulling a single carriage came into view. It soon crossed the bridge and was hidden by the woods on the other side of the stream; although smoke and steam from the engine left a trail above the trees.

Farmer Jacobs stopped the tractor and trailer near the river.

"Come on lads, let's get unloaded. Patrol Leaders, get your patrol to set up your tents. Eagles over here, Ravens there," called Scoutmaster Dunn pointing out where he wanted the bell tents erected. "Send your Patrol Seconds here to set up the tent for Dennis and me," he added.

Before long, the scouts were spreading out the tents and assembling the tall central poles that held up the canvas. They then drove pegs into the ground to secure the guy lines, the sound of the mallets striking the wooden pegs ringing around the area.

Having sorted the tents, the patrol leaders sent part of their patrols into the woods to gather fuel for the campfires; some started peeling and dicing vegetables for the evening meal and others erected a flagpole and a shelter to provide cover while eating meals, then dug wet and dry pits for the rubbish.

The well-rehearsed routine enabled the scouts to set up the camp in a couple of hours. They were then able to cook their evening meal of a beef stew in three-gallon Dixies over the open fire.

Each morning, the troop paraded in front of the flagpole while one of their number raised the Union Flag then took a few paces backwards before saluting. The process was reversed before sunset to bring the flag down again. During the day, the scoutmaster and Dennis instructed the boys in various scouting skills such as tracking, tree felling, building shelters from natural materials and constructing a raft and other methods of crossing waterways without getting kit wet. They also supervised games including Capture the Flag, British Bulldog and Escape and Evasion – where two of the group had to get from across the woods without being caught by the others.

Waking up on the fourth morning, Simon was struck with a combination of excitement and dread. Today he and Martin, one of the other scouts, were taking their eight-mile hike test. They would be given a map and route to follow and be expected to answer questions about what they saw on their journey.

They wearily trudged back into camp four hours after setting off and immediately shrugged off their rucksacks before reporting to the Scoutmaster.

"Well, lads, did you find the answers to the questions?"

"Yes, sir," Simon replied handing him his notebook.

"Fine, well done. Now don't forget to write up the hike in your log book."

On the final night of their stay, the troop gathered around a large campfire for a traditional singsong with farmer Jacob and his wife as guests of honour. Each patrol was expected to do a skit. Eagle Patrol decided to do a Stanley Holloway song about a lion and a boy with a stick with a horse's head handle. The skit required someone to play the boy's mother. As one of the newest members of the patrol, Simon was appointed. Mrs Jacobs lent him a skirt, blouse and headscarf for the performance. Dressing as 'Mrs Ramsbottom' reminded Simon of the play with his cousins.

Over the next two years, Simon completed both his Second- and First-Class badges and was promoted to Patrol Second. He didn't realise how useful the bushcraft skills he'd learned would be in a few years.

Chapter 3.   Clouds Over Europe

January 1938

In January 1938, Simon celebrated his thirteenth birthday. He was now Patrol Second of the Eagles in the scouts and had completed nearly all of the tests required to qualify as a 'First Class' scout and at school he was top of the class in arithmetic.

One more year and he'd be allowed to leave school, possibly to join his father at the smithy. The problem was, his frame hadn't filled out as much as other lads and he was a good three inches shorter than his contemporaries.

"I'm not sure you're cut out to be a smith, Simon, you need more muscle and strength to work at forge. Perchance, you'd be more suited to mechanical work, repairing motors," his dad told him as Simon struggled to shape a horseshoe. "Your smaller hands may be better for getting at awkward parts. You have a quick mind at working out what the problem is with those mechanical contraptions in any case," his dad added. "I'm fit for repairing broken metalwork but figuring out what stops them engines working is beyond me."

"Yes, Dad, I like working on engines; seeing how they work and how to fix them."

"Aye, lad, happen you and me will make a good team together," his father replied, clapping him on the back.

Simon was relieved, his dad's suggestion fitted in with his own long-term goal of becoming involved in aircraft. He keenly devoured every page of 'Flight' and 'Practical Mechanics' magazines each month as well as the weekly 'Scout' magazine; paid for from the four shillings a week his father allowed him for helping around the smithy and in the workshop they'd built next to the forge.

As they trudged back, through the snow, from the smithy to the house, Simon felt confident of his future.

Newsreels at the cinema had shown action from the Spanish Civil War including the bombing of Guernica by the German Condor Legion the previous year – but that was in another country and unlikely to affect Simon. Or so he thought.

Two months later, the Germans marched into Austria and it seemed that the lessons of the Great War hadn't been learned after all.

"It'll be a'reet, you'll see. Herr Hitler don't have no argument with us. As the Daily Express do say, he only wants to reunite German-speaking people and he were born in Austria. That clever Mr Chamberlain will sort it right," Tom Ferguson told his wife.

When the Prime Minister returned from Munich and waved a piece of paper announcing that it bore Herr Hitler's and his own signatures and meant 'peace for our time', it seemed that Tom had been correct and the family celebrated a carefree Christmas with Simon bidding a final farewell to his teachers and fellow students at the end of term.

The first few months of 1939 were busy as Simon's reputation for repairing vehicles spread. Many customers were sceptical when they first saw him.

"'He be nowt but a boy," they'd say to his father. "Do he know what he be doing?"

When Hitler marched into Czechoslovakia, Tom Ferguson scratched his beard. He wondered if the newspapers were right to say that it was none of England's business what happened on the continent and we should stay out of any argument.

But the summer meant more work as horses needed shoeing and mechanical devices needed repairing as the harvest was gathered in. Simon and his father focussed on their own tasks; Tom spending long hours at the forge; while Simon was in the workshop or out at farms.

Chapter 4.   Blitzkrieg

May 1940

Simon's father joined up in September and, by the end of November, had been sent to France as part of the British Expeditionary Force. Some expected the war to be over by Christmas. Tom was not as certain. He knew that the Great War had been seen the same way and that had dragged on for four long years.

Dug in a few miles from Armentieres on the Franco-Belgian border, Tom's company had been told that any attack by the Germans was expected to come through Holland and Belgium and they would be on the front line. So far, however, apart from a few reconnaissance flights by Dornier aircraft, chased off by Hurricanes from the nearby RAF aerodrome, it was quiet and becoming known as the 'Phoney War'.

Christmas came and went and the war was still on, at least in theory.

Men in the trenches froze in the winter weather – protecting themselves as far as they could from the biting winds and driving sleet, warming themselves around braziers when allowed to take a break from the tedious hours of watching for the enemy to appear.

Sipping an enamel mug of tea, Tom, recently promoted to corporal, sat on a bench next to Private Fred Todd.

"Bloody cold enough to freeze the balls off a brass monkey," Fred remarked.

"Aye, it be that," Tom answered.

"So, what did you do before this lot, Corp?"

Tom packed his pipe with tobacco and held a match to the bowl, drawing the smoke in.

"I were a blacksmith, same as my father and his for five generations. Mine 'as taken the smithy on again while I'm over 'ere. He's got an old soldier to do the 'eavy work."

Tom reflected on the family he'd left. He prayed the war would be over before his son was old enough to be called up. He had no doubt that he would volunteer given the opportunity. He also prayed that he'd survive to return to his forge. If this war was like the last, his chances weren't good – few of the original volunteers of 1914 returned home after the armistice.

The Phoney War ended on 10th May with the German invasion of the Netherlands and Belgium and the Blitzkrieg offensive through the Ardennes.

After months of inactivity, Tom's company was ordered to stand to; an order quickly countered with one to move forward to attack the northern flank of the German thrust. That, in turn, was countered within hours by new instructions to withdraw to hold a bridge over the river Leie only two miles from where they'd been dug in.

As they took up their positions, clouds of Stuka dive bombers appeared overhead. Although outnumbered, a flight of three Hurricanes fell on the Germans as they prepared to attack troops and refugees below them. It was the first time the Huns had encountered modern opponents and several were shot down before the RAF fighters were attacked in turn by the protecting Messerschmitt 109s.

Having reached the bridge, Tom's company took up a position to guard the approaches. He wasn't sure how they were expected to stop tanks if they appeared. All they had was the Boys Anti-Tank Rifle which had already proved relatively ineffective against German armour – doing little more than knocking a few flakes of paint off the target even with a direct hit in many cases.

The company commander, Captain Harris, called the platoon subalterns and senior NCOs together. Tom's officer Second Lieutenant Seymour returned to his platoon, his face drawn, and called his men together.

"We've been tasked with holding the approach to the bridge while the remainder of the company withdraws towards Dunkirk," he told them.

Seeing the resigned looks of the platoon and the indecisiveness of the Second Lieutenant, Sergeant Miller, a regular soldier who'd seen action at the end of 1918, took command.

"Right, you shower. Corporals, deploy your sections. Ferguson you take the centre with the Boys and your section's Bren; Clarke take the right flank with the mortar; Morgan the left flank," he instructed. "If that's all right with you, sir?"

"Yes, carry on Sergeant," Seymour replied, thankful that Sergeant Miller had covered for his own hesitancy.

The German tanks appeared shortly after five o'clock, supported by infantry and the dreaded Stukas with their frightening sirens.

The first bombs hit fifty yards behind Clarke's section, causing them to flatten themselves even further into the foxholes that they'd dug. Seeing the Panzers appearing across the river, Clarke instructed the mortar crew to fire smoke shells to conceal their position and make it more difficult for the tank crews to take aim.

Tom instructed his Boys crew to hold fire until the tanks were within 300 yards before opening fire. They achieved a direct hit which penetrated the hull.

"Bloody hell," Tom exclaimed as the Panzer II suddenly stopped with smoke pouring from the turret. His joy was short-lived though as a second tank, a more heavily armoured model, fired its cannon directly at his section's position destroying the anti-tank weapon and killing the crew. It then turned its gun on the mortar and destroyed that in turn; Sergeant Miller, who had been directing its fire, was killed in the explosion together with Lieutenant Seymour and Corporal Clarke.

Without any other weapons effective against armour, the platoon's position was soon overwhelmed. Tom kept part of his section with him to allow Corporal Morgan to lead the others away to re-join the company. Four of them provided covering fire with two Bren Guns and two Lee Enfield rifles until the German tank found their position and fired again.

Chapter 5.   In Memoriam

May 1940

Simon was working on a tractor engine when he saw the telegram boy cycle up to the cottage gate, walk along the path and reach into his pouch before ringing the bell. Simon put down the spanner he'd been using. There could only be one reason why folks like them received telegrams.

Hoping against hope, he ran the few yards to the cottage, as his mother opened the door, put his arm around her and held her as she opened the envelope and drew out the flimsy sheet it contained.

'The War Office regrets to announce that your husband Corporal Thomas Ferguson has been killed in action. Letter to follow.'

His mother's weight fell on Simon's arms.

"Why did he volunteer?" she wept. "He didn't have to go. He could have waited. He would have been doing important work in the forge. Why, Simon? Why?"

Simon had no answer. He knew his father had been just too young to serve in the Great War but that one of his best friends had lied about his age to join up and Tom had felt guilty that he hadn't done the same.

Eli, Tom's father came into the house having heard his daughter-in-law's cries of anguish.

Simon handed him the telegraph then led his mother to a chair.

"Give her a tot of rum, Simon," Eli told him, "And pour me one too."

They sat together silently in the kitchen, each lost in their own thoughts. Emma was angry with her husband for leaving her – but proud that he had done his duty. She would miss that hulk of a man.

Simon wondered what implications his father's death would have for him. Would his mother want to continue living next to the forge? Neither of them could operate it and his grandfather had only stepped back in as a stopgap.

Eli had been happy to take on the smithy again for a short time – helped by Samuel Owen, an old soldier. But, at 58 years old, Eli knew he wouldn't be able to manage it for many more years. He'd argued with his son when he spoke of volunteering. Perhaps if he hadn't agreed to look after the forge, Tom would still be alive.

That night the only one of the family that slept normally was Mary who was too young to understand the implications of what had happened. As far as she was concerned, her daddy was away but would come home eventually.

Simon tossed and turned as he thought about the future. He wouldn't be able to run the forge himself even with his grandfather's help. His mother sobbed into the thick pullover she held close. She'd knitted it for Tom and it still carried his aroma. At times she was angry with Tom for having left her when he hadn't needed to – then in the next moment missing his arms around her and his scratchy kisses. She wondered how they'd manage.

The next morning, Emma made them all black armbands – then wrote to her sister Ida in Elmdene to give her the sad news. Simon made a notice announcing that the forge and workshop would be closed for the day. Eli met with Samuel to let him know the news – though he'd already guessed.

The vicar rode up to the cottage on his bicycle, leant it against the low wall separating the front garden from the lane, took off his cycle clips and removed his hat before knocking on the door. This was already his ninth such call since the phoney war had erupted into Blitzkrieg two weeks ago. Nearly one death reported each day in his own two parishes. He prayed that the present rate of attrition wouldn't continue but he feared it would.

Emma opened the door.

"Vicar, it's kind of you to call," she said.

"I'm so sorry for your loss, Mrs Ferguson. I hoped might be able to offer some comfort through our saviour, Jesus Christ."

Emme stood to one side, "Please come in vicar. Can I offer you a cup of tea? I've just made a pot. I'm afraid we don't have any sugar though."

"A cup of tea would be most welcome, Mrs Ferguson."

Once they had their drinks, they each took tentative sips.

"Shall we say a prayer?" the vicar suggested.

"Blessed Lord God, Father Almighty, giver of compassion and mercy, to those who trust in your Son, Our Saviour, Jesus Christ, take away our tears and lead us by still waters. Bring your faithful servant Thomas Ferguson into your presence where he shall have eternal life in your glorious presence. In the name of the Father Son and Holy Spirit. Amen."

"Amen," Emma echoed, wiping away a tear that had run down her cheek.

"Sadly, Mrs Ferguson, there are several families in your position where a father or son has fallen in the fields of France. All without a body for a funeral. I'm minded to hold a joint memorial service for Tom and the other local casualties. Would that be something you would wish?"

Emma agreed that it would be an appropriate gesture.

The service was arranged for Sunday 9th June and included giving thanks for the 'miracle of Dunkirk and the evacuation of more than 338,000 men'. By then, the number of local casualties remembered had grown to twelve.

Ida attended the service to support her sister Emma and persuade her to move into the rectory.

"There is plenty of room and you'll be safer in Elmdene than here with that RAF aerodrome down the road," she insisted as the family sat together after the service.

"What would I do about the smithy though?"

"I've been talking to Samuel. I'm getting too long in the tooth to carry on now Tom has gone. It was one thing to do so for a year or two – but not indefinitely. I don't think Simon wants to run it either, do you, boy?" Eli asked.

Simon hung his head as he replied. He knew the forge had been in the family for generations but running it wasn't his dream. "No grandad. I'm sorry but it's not what I want to do."

"That's all right, lad. As I said, I've had a word with Samuel and he'd be interested in buying the forge and the cottage. He can't pay the full value immediately but he could put down a deposit then the balance quarterly."

"There you are then Emma," said Ida. "And, Simon, there's a group of evacuee boys from South London who were scouts in Mitcham and have continued their meetings in Elmdene. Uncle Geoffrey has been appointed Scoutmaster as their original leaders had to stay in London."

Simon's face lit up at the thought of being able to carry on with scouting – he'd been dreading the idea of only having Daphne and Grace and their friend Lucy to spend time with.

It was all agreed and, three weeks later, the family packed up their personal possessions in three suitcases and a trunk and loaded it on a trap which would take them all to the local railway station. Simon followed the trap on his bicycle. Geoffrey Bartlett would meet them at Elmdene where one of his congregation would be waiting with a van to take them and their belongings to the rectory.

The day before the move, Emma heard from the Red Cross that Tom had been buried, with hundreds of his compatriots, by the German Army as it waited for the Luftwaffe to obliterate the remains of the BEF gathered on the beaches and in the surrounding dunes.

Chapter 6.   New Beginnings

1st July 1940

Eli stood on the platform next to their carriage window as the train was about to depart. Simon had lowered the door window on its strap; Mary's fingers were wrapped over the opening, her brother's arm around her back to steady her.

"You look after your mother and sister, Simon; you're the man of the family now," he called.

"I will, grandad. I promise." It was a promise that sat heavily on his shoulders.

The guard blew a shrill blast on his whistle and waved his green flag; the engine driver answered with two toots then fed steam to the pistons and released the brakes. The wheels span on the tracks for an instant before gripping and jerking the carriages into motion. A burst of steam mixed with smoke was expelled from the funnel, then another, the frequency increasing as the engine built up speed and clattered over the points.

Eli walked along the platform, staying level with their compartment as long as possible. He was soon unable to keep pace and Simon leaned out of the window and gave a final goodbye.

As the train left the town of Andover behind, it skirted the RAF aerodrome where Simon had watched Bristol Bulldog and Hawker Fury fighters practising. He watched as one of the latest Hawker Hurricanes flew a few feet above the train, drowning them in the roar of its Merlin engine as it left the ground for its natural element.

'If only I could be the pilot of one of those,' he thought. *'Or even work on them on the ground.'*

That wasn't an impossibility any longer. Provided the war lasted long enough, he'd be able to join the RAF as a mechanic when he was 18. He stared out of the window wondering what he'd need to do to improve his chances of being accepted.

At the next station, more passengers entered their compartment. Fortunately, the train had pulled up with the opposite side next to the platform and they didn't have to change seats – or move their legs for newcomers to squeeze between. A refreshment trolley was being wheeled along the platform but Emma had packed fish-paste sandwiches wrapped in greaseproof paper for them together with a bottle of diluted orange squash for Mary and Simon and a thermos flask of tea for herself.

It was mid-afternoon by the time their final train approached Elmdene station near Westchester having changed trains twice en route. They'd been held up several times for troop trains or expresses to take priority over their local services; the connecting train at Swindon had, itself, been delayed by half an hour – but that had given them the opportunity to use the station toilets.

In the absence of any porters at Elmdene, Simon found a trolley and collected their trunk and cases and his bicycle from the guard's van and wheeled it to the exit where his mother was already talking to his uncle Geoffrey and an elderly man he didn't recognize.

"Ah, Simon, well done. This is Mr Ellis who is kindly taking us to the rectory. The van is on the station forecourt."

"Good evening, Uncle Geoffrey, good evening, sir," Simon replied.

Mr Ellis led the way and Reverend Bartlett ushered Emma and Mary after him. Simon brought up the rear with the trolley.

"Bring the luggage round the back, lad," Ellis told Simon as he opened the rear door of his van.

"Put your trunk against the partition 'tween cab and here, lad. It'll give ye summut to sit on. We aren't going far but still."

Having secured the van's rear doors, Ellis went to the cab, switched on the ignition then took hold of the starting handle and swung it vigorously. The engine caught on the third attempt and Ellis jumped into the cab.

"Everyone ready?" he asked.

Mary was sitting on her mother's lap next to him with Reverend Bartlett half-twisted in his seat to give Emma as much space as possible.

Ellis clamped down on his pipe, forced the engine into gear with a worrying grating sound and drove off the station forecourt.

Elmdene station wasn't actually in the village – it had been built at the closest point that the railway came to the settlement; a distance of about a mile and a half.

"We weren't sure what time you'd get here with all the delays, so Ida has prepared a stew for dinner. She's also made some scones in case you needed something to keep you going."

"That's very kind of her, Geoffrey."

"Not at all, we're delighted you agreed to come and stay."

Ida, Grace and Daphne were waiting at the door when they pulled up outside the rectory and ushered Emma and Mary into their new home leaving Simon to drag the trunk and cases out of the van and into the hallway.

"Leave them there for the moment, Simon," his uncle instructed, as Ellis drove off with a cheery wave from his van; leaving a cloud of exhaust smoke in his wake. "Come and have a drink and a scone, I'm sure you could do with one after that journey."

Simon was well aware his aunt was a very good baker and her plum jam won many prizes at village fêtes.

After tea and scones, Simon and his uncle carried the cases up to the family's bedrooms on the top floor. Daphne and Grace took Mary to their playroom while Ida and Emma unpacked their clothes and made up the beds.

Simon went outside with his uncle and they wandered down to the orchard at the end of the garden. The hedge separating it from a meadow where a herd of cows grazed, was thick with blackberry bushes.

"We're thinking of having some beehives in the orchard, Simon. How do you feel about helping me build them?"

"I'd like that very much."

"Right, we'll talk about it later. There are some other things I want to speak to you about too. You know that we've started a scout group for evacuees – and any local boys who might be interested. How would you like to help me run it?"

"I'm too young to be given a warrant as a Scoutmaster or even an Assistant but I can certainly help with general training and organising."

"In fact, Imperial HQ has started a 'Carry On' scheme where Patrol Leaders can step up and take over when their Scoutmasters are called up. I've spoken to the District Commissioner and he's happy for you to be given a certificate. We can make you 'Troop Leader'. How do you feel about that?"

"I'm very happy to help in any way that I can."

"I thought that would be your answer. Well, the first step will be to enrol you as a member of our troop. The next meeting is on Friday evening; oh, and there's a Church Parade on Sunday. Now, there is something else I want to raise with you. What are your plans for the future now your mother has sold the forge?"

"I want to do something with aircraft. Flying itself is probably out of the question but I was thinking of aircraft maintenance or repairs, perhaps ground crew with the RAF."

"Very admirable. How do you think you can achieve that?"

I'm not sure, Uncle. It's just been a dream until now. I expected to stay at the forge and develop the mechanical side of the business while Dad carried on with the smithy but that's no longer an option."

"Well, let's sit down with your mother sometime and see what ideas we can come up with. Now, I need to go and prepare my sermon for Sunday."

Chapter 7.   Elmdene

2nd July 1940

The following morning, Simon woke in the same room he'd used when staying at the rectory while his mother was ill. For a moment, he was disorientated, thinking it was 1933, his father was still alive and there was no war. But that hiatus passed as he realised where he was and why. Glancing out of the window, he could see it was another sunny spring day.

He swung his legs out of the bed, stood up and walked over to the chest of drawers, he poured water from the jug standing there into a bowl and washed his face before dressing. Downstairs, his mother was in the large kitchen with Aunt Ida.

"Come and have some breakfast, Simon. There's some bacon and eggs, and some lovely fresh baked bread," Aunt Ida told him. Ida turned to Emma "The eggs are from our chickens; the bacon comes from parishioners with their own farms or smallholdings. One of the first things we must do this morning, though, is to register all of you with the local shops for your rations."

As Simon was wiping the last of the yolk off his plate with a piece of bread, his uncle came into the kitchen. Ida who had been pouring cups of tea for Emma and herself, made one for him and he sat down opposite Simon. He added half a teaspoon of sugar and stirred the dark brew.

"Emma, I think we need to discuss what Simon is going to do while you're here."

Emma wiped her hands on her apron and she and Ida joined Simon and her brother-in-law at the table.

"I spoke to Simon before agreeing to sell the forge to Samuel. I know his real interest is in aeroplanes and he'd like to work on them. That's right, isn't it son?" Emma said.

"Yes, mum. If I can't fly them myself, and I know that's not likely, then I want to work on them. They are going to be the future once this war is over. Thousands of passengers already fly every year from Croydon Airport to Paris and other cities in Europe," Simon enthused "It's twenty-one years since Alcock and Brown flew across the Atlantic, Amy Johnson has flown to South

Africa and Australia. I just know that it won't be long before airlines fly those routes too."

"Well, let's not get carried away, Simon. Flights to the continent may be possible but everyone seems to believe airships are the only way to get the range for longer flights – and look what happened to the Hindenburg and the R101. I can't see much of a future for them." His uncle interjected.

"Even airships will need mechanics, Uncle," Simon pointed out.

"That's true," his uncle conceded.

"You're not planning to fly on one of those death traps are you, Simon?" his horrified mother asked.

"Not really, I think my best chance of working with aircraft is with the maintenance crew on the ground," Simon said.

"I'm relieved to hear it, son," His mum replied.

"The Royal Air Force did have a scheme for what they called Boy Entrants to study engineering – but they've stopped that training at the moment so I'd need to wait until I can join up as an adult at eighteen. They'll train me as a mechanic. When the war is over, I can either stay in the RAF or find a job with an airline."

"Which brings us to the question of how to allow you to achieve that," said his uncle. "You've already got some practical experience of working with motors but, having left school when you did, you don't have the academic qualifications."

Simon twisted his lip. He was well aware that this was his weakness.

"So, what I propose, Simon, is that you register with the Technical School in Westchester from September to study sciences and mathematics. You might also find it useful to study a foreign language, French perhaps, as there's bound to be travel involved after the war."

"How can I afford that, sir? I need to pay my way; I can't rely on your charity."

"I'm sure you'll more than pay your way around the place, Simon. Between now and September, you could find work on a local farm. After that, I'm sure there will be other jobs you can do – keeping my car running for a start, helping to build the bee hives, maintenance work around the rectory and the five churches I'm now responsible for," said his uncle.

"And we have money from the sale of the forge, Simon, some of that should be yours as you built up the mechanical side," added his mother. "I'm going to be helping your uncle with managing the two parishes in exchange for our keep; so altogether, I'm sure we can manage."

Simon was relieved to see that his dreams of working with aeroplanes might be feasible – then immediately felt guilty as he realised it was the death of his father that had made the difference and he didn't want to feel glad about that.

"So," his uncle said, "are you happy with those arrangements, Simon?"

"Absolutely, sir – and thank you and Aunt Ida for making it possible by taking us in."

"Don't worry, my lad, you'll earn everything you get, of that I'm sure – and you will have to work hard at the Technical School, make no mistake. Now, if you've finished breakfast, perhaps you and I can get started on building the beehives."

At lunchtime, Simon and his uncle returned to the house having assembled and positioned three hives around the orchard. Ida and Emma had been shopping in the village and had registered the family with the local grocers and butchers for their rations.

"What are your plans for this afternoon, Simon?" his mum asked.

"I'm going to cycle to the Technical School to see if I can register for September."

"Do you want your uncle or me to come with you?"

"I don't think so, I'm sure I'll be fine."

"I think so too, son. You've certainly grown up over the past few weeks. Not that you were immature before, but you seem to have more confidence to follow your dreams."

"There hasn't been much choice has there?"

With that, Simon picked up his plate and stacked it in the sink ready for the girls to wash with the other crockery and put away.

"See you all later," he called cheerily as he picked up the map his uncle had provided.

His ride to the Technical School took him over the railway line from Westchester to Prestham to the main road between the two towns then almost into the city centre itself. He parked his bike out of the way at the entrance to the building then found his way to the secretary's office.

"How can I help you, young man," asked a middle-aged lady in a twin set and sensible shoes, wearing horn-rimmed glasses and with her hair tied in a bun.

"I was after information on enrolling on a course in September, if that's possible?" he told her.

"I see, I can certainly give you relevant information and an application form but it will need to be signed by your parents if, as I suspect, you are under twenty-one years of age."

"My father is dead; he was killed at Dunkirk. My mother, sister and I have moved in with my aunt and uncle, he's the Rector at Elmdene."

"Ah, so you must be Simon. I know your aunt and uncle – I'm one of his parishioners. He did mention you to me and said you might be applying." She collated some leaflets and an application form and slid them into a foolscap envelope.

"Now, if you have any questions, please let me know. In fact, would it be helpful if I came around to the rectory to assist with the form? Your uncle was a tower of strength when my mother died last year so this is the least I can do."

Cycling home, Simon watched a biplane, he was reasonably certain it was a Tiger Moth, flying quite low overhead then apparently landing nearby. He wondered if there was an aerodrome or if the aeroplane had simply landed in a field. If there was an aerodrome perhaps he could find some work there for the summer rather than on a farm.

"How did you get on, Simon?" his mum asked as he entered the kitchen.

"Fine, I've got details of the courses and an application form. The secretary said Uncle Geoffrey had already spoken to her and she's offered to help me fill in the form."

"That's very kind of her," Emma said.

"Mildred's one of the parishioners, I think she's grateful for the support we were able to give her last year when her mother died – not that we wouldn't have done the same for anyone," Ida explained as she rolled out pastry to cover a pie for dinner. "I hope this pastry is going to be good, it doesn't feel right using margarine and cooking fat instead of butter."

Chapter 8.   Summer 1940

3rd July 1940

t's Scouts tonight, isn't it?" Emma asked as Simon removed his boots after working in the garden the next day.

"Yes, mum. I'm being enrolled in the troop then made assistant leader."

"Does your uniform need ironing after being packed in the case?"

"Probably, but I can do it. I need to polish my shoes, too."

"Well, go and get it now while I put the irons to warm on the range. Then it'll have time to air before you get changed."

As he'd been taught, Simon spread a blanket on the end of the table then laid his uniform out; he dipped his fingers into a mug of water and flicked it over the material then smoothed it with the iron.

After dinner, Simon and his uncle changed into their uniforms and walked down to the village hall where a number of the other scouts were waiting for them to open up.

There was a general mêlée as the lads prepared for the meeting opening ceremony. Eventually, they assembled into a horse-shoe with Rev Bartlett, in his role as Scoutmaster, and Simon in the open end.

When everyone was in position, Rev Bartlett nodded at Harry Brown, Patrol Leader of Bulldog patrol.

"Troop Alert," Harry instructed. Everyone brought their feet together, stamping their right foot down in unison and bringing their arms to their sides. Harry then marched to the front of the hall where a furled Union Flag hung from a pulley. He took hold of the cord and pulled smartly to release the flag. He tied the end of the cord to a cleat, took two steps backwards and saluted before returning to his place in the horseshoe.

"Troop stand easy," he instructed.

"Thank you, Harry. Troop, tonight we welcome Simon as a member. As you may know, he is my nephew but more importantly, he is a First Class scout so will be a valuable addition to our group. He will officially be Troop Leader and act as Assistant Scoutmaster." They turned to face each other.

"Simon, do you wish to become a member of First Elmdene Scout Troop?"

"I do."

"Then make the Scout sign and recite the Scout Promise. Troop salute."

Simon brought his right hand level with his shoulder, palm to the front, thumb resting on the nail of the little finger and the other three fingers pointing upwards.

"On my honour, I promise that I will do my duty to God and the King, to help other people at all times and to obey the scout law."

He snapped his right hand back down at his side.

His uncle draped the troop scarf around his neck and slid a woggle up the ends to hold it in place. He then handed Simon the troop name tape, and the county badge to replace those of his old troop and a third stripe for him to sew onto the left-hand shirt pocket to indicate his rank of Troop Leader. He held out his left hand for Simon to shake and saluted him.

"Welcome to First Elmdene Scouts, Simon."

Chapter 9.   Lucy Calls

5th July 1940

"What are your plans for this afternoon, Simon?" asked Daphne as they sat and ate breakfast two days later.

"Some jobs around the house then plan some activities for the scouts for next week. Why?"

"It's just that Lucy is coming over this afternoon and she was asking if you'd be around."

Hearing Lucy's name reminded Simon of having to dress up for a play when he was eight. He remembered her as a nuisance with ponytails and a way of teasing him.

"Fine, it will be nice to see her again – but I'm sure we've all changed an awful lot since I was here before."

Daphne and Grace were playing hopscotch with Mary at the side of the rectory when Lucy arrived. They stopped playing and hugged her.

Lucy then joined in their game but made several mistakes when throwing her stone into one of the numbered squares.

"You seem distracted, Lucy. I wonder why?" said Grace.

"I don't know what you mean," retorted Lucy.

"No? Are you sure? Are you not wondering where a certain cousin might be?"

"Not at all. It's of no interest to me. Well, maybe just a bit. I'm curious to see what he's grown up like."

"Well, you don't want to give him the impression that you're interested in him – that would be a very bad move. Mind you, if you want to see him, he might be thirsty by now, he's been digging the vegetable garden for an hour or so. We could get a jug of orange squash and some glasses and take it to him."

Simon was planting some runner beans when the girls arrived with the refreshments.

"We thought you might be ready for a drink, Simon."

Simon stood up and took the glass Lucy was holding out to him.

"Thanks, it's very welcome."

"You do remember Lucy, don't you Simon?" asked Daphne.

"Of course. How are you, Lucy?"

The young woman who stood before him was far from the ponytailed brat that had teased him when he was eight. He realised he'd been staring, so dropped his eyes.

"I'm very well, Simon. I was very sorry to hear about your father." She rested her hand on his arm and looked him in the eyes as she expressed her condolences.

"Thank you. We were fortunate that Uncle Geoffrey and Aunt Ida have offered to let us stay."

"We'd better let you get on with the gardening. I'd offer to help, but I don't want to get my dress dirty. Maybe another time, I'll wear something more appropriate," Lucy said.

Simon drained the last of the orange squash from his glass then watched as the girls walked back to the house, surprisingly pleased when Lucy turned around and gave him a wave before disappearing into the building.

At nine o'clock that evening, the family, except Mary who was in bed, sat around the radio and listened to the BBC news. The newsreader announced that there had been attacks on shipping and locations on the South Coast but they had been beaten off by aircraft of the Royal Air Force. The details were scant to avoid giving away useful information.

Chapter 10. Village Fete

13th July 1940

Simon got up early on the morning of the Village Fete. He was responsible for the scouts setting up various stalls on the sports field behind the village hall. The weather looked unsettled with most of the sky covered in clouds but the sun was trying to break through.

Unfortunately, due to rationing, the traditional baking competitions and cake stall couldn't be held but there would still be a beer tent run by the pub and tea provided by the Women's Institute. Between the two refreshment tents, in another marquee, there was a display of chutneys and bottled fruit made from locally grown produce and a vegetable contest; the flower competition also having been cancelled as being frivolous when the nation was being encouraged to grow as much food as possible.

The scouts set out the games including Skittles, Hoopla, Pin the Tail on the Donkey and Horseshoe Throwing and erected trestle tables for Name the Doll, Tombola, Hook the Duck and a second-hand book stall in an oval — leaving space in the centre for an afternoon programme of Morris Dancing, Fancy Dress, Tug of War, Sack and Three-legged races and a dog show. They also erected one of their ridge tents as a first-aid post for the St John's Ambulance.

The fete officially opened at two o'clock and within half an hour most of the village seemed to be gathered on the field. Satisfied that all the setting up work had been completed, Simon split the scouts into three groups led by the Patrol Leaders and himself to act as messengers for the fete committee.

Simon reminded the others of their times concluding with "Don't be late for the handovers. Everyone clear on that?" Simon instructed.

The two Patrol Leaders signalled their agreement.

"Fine, then dismiss and enjoy the fete."

The scouts were kept busy running around, passing messages from the organisers to participants in the various competitions to keep the programme on schedule.

Five minutes before the take-over time of 15.30, Harry Brown returned to their base with his Bulldog Patrol.

"Ready to relieve you, Simon," he said as he saluted.

"Thank you, Harry. I'll see you later."

Simon then dismissed his section with instructions to return at five minutes to five.

For the first time that day, he was free to do what he wanted. His priority was a drink and he walked over to the WI tent. As he joined the queue, he realised Lucy was serving.

"Hello, Simon, what can I get you?"

"Some lemon squash please."

"That's a penny, please. Are you off duty now?"

"Yes, I'm off until five o'clock."

"So am I. You're my last customer. I'm going to have a look around the stalls. What about you?"

"Probably the same." He hesitated. "Would you like to look around together? Or are you meeting up with Daphne and Grace?"

"No, I'm not meeting them until later. They're helping with the local produce stand with your aunt."

Simon drained his glass of squash as Lucy told the lady running the stand that she was going.

"You look very smart in your uniform. Grace tells me you are the Assistant Scoutmaster, what does that involve?"

Simon drew his shoulders back and held himself erect.

"I'm Troop Leader as I can't be an official leader until I'm eighteen. It's like in the army – the adult leaders are the equivalent of officers. As Troop Leader, I'm like the Sergeant Major."

"Oh, I see, it still sounds a responsible role. You've certainly grown up a lot since you were here while your mum was ill."

"I should hope so. You've changed too."

"I suppose you saw me as an irritating brat, didn't you? I know I used to tease you."

Lucy rested her hand on Simon's arm and looked into his eyes. "I'm sorry about that. Will you forgive me?"

"Nothing to forgive, Lucy. I dare say you girls were annoyed to be stuck with a boy."

"True, apart from that one afternoon when we did the play."

"Yes, well, the less said about that the better."

They arrived at the Hoopla stand.

"Come on, Simon, I challenge you."

The operator exchanged their pennies for three coloured rings each and they tried to get them to land on the hooks set in a board. Each of their first two attempts bounced off the backboard. When Lucy cast her third ring, it bounced back but, instead of jumping over the hook, was caught and settled there. Simon held his last ring and tossed it towards the board. It hit, bounced off, touched the hook, wobbled then fell to the floor.

"Ha! I won!" Lucy exulted.

Simon pretended to sulk then asked, "How are you at knocking the tins off the shelf?"

"Let's find out."

He managed to knock five of the pyramid of six tins off the shelf with his three bean bags; Lucy only managed four. They gradually made their way around the stalls occasionally stopping to watch the Tug of War, Morris Dancing and Welly Throwing.

"Is anyone else interested in the juveniles' three-legged race? If so, and you are ten to sixteen years old, come to the start line now. The adult's race will follow the juveniles," blared over the loudspeakers.

Lucy took hold of Simon's arm. "Come on, it'll be a laugh."

Simon was shorter than average for a boy and only an inch taller than Lucy, so they were well-balanced in the race. They slipped their arms around each other's back and held tight. Simon hoped Lucy found the sensation as pleasant as he did. They were pipped at the post into second place but didn't mind.

After untying the ribbon from around their ankles, they watched the egg and spoon and sack races followed by a fancy dress competition, standing close together.

Lucy let her hand brush against Simon's, wishing he'd put it around her waist but not wanting to be too obvious by taking the lead. Simon wondered if the touch had been accidental or if she wanted him to take hold of it. The moment passed while he dithered and they wandered further around the displays.

As the arena events finished, Simon looked at his watch.

"It's time I was meeting up with the other scouts ready to pack up. I've really enjoyed myself this afternoon."

"Me too."

Simon paused. *'Nothing ventured, nothing gained,'* he thought.

"Are you going to the dance in the village hall next Saturday?"

"Yes," she said, looking him in the eyes, willing him to say more.

"I don't suppose you'd go as my partner, would you?"

'Yes!' Lucy's inner voice shouted. "I'd like to," her demure voice answered.

Chapter 11. Finding Work

w/c 15th July 1940

The next day, Simon, his mother and sister, joined his Aunt Ida and her two girls for the morning family service at All Saints church. His uncle had left much earlier to officiate at Holy Communion at St Margaret's in the neighbouring village of Little Woodend – and would be going on to St Philip's at Beckhall for a third morning service after All Saints. After lunch, he would be out again for two evensongs at Holy Trinity and St James. It was a busy schedule ministering to five churches due to the vicar of an adjoining parish enlisting in the army.

Fortunately, the Rev Bartlett could rely on Churchwardens or Sidesmen at each church to open up and prepare for the services – then tidy and lock up afterwards. The schedule had to rotate the services so each church had Communion, Family Services and Evensongs on a regular basis.

In church, after kneeling and saying a prayer, Simon looked around for Lucy but couldn't see her among the congregation.

Daphne, realising what he was doing, whispered "Lucy doesn't attend All Saints, she and her mother are Roman Catholics. They go to Holy Cross in Westchester. You were looking for her, weren't you? She told Grace and me that you'd asked her to partner you at the dance next weekend."

Simon hadn't expected the news to be kept secret but was still embarrassed by Daphne's comments. "Alright, yes, I was looking for her. Satisfied?" he protested.

"Touched a nerve, have I? And are you blushing?" She jabbed Simon in the side with her elbow.

Her mother leant forward over Grace, who sat between them, and gave Daphne a stern look. Daphne picked up her hymnal, sat back in the pew, looked up at the board behind the pulpit and found the first number in her Hymns Ancient and Modern.

After the service, Rev Bartlett remained briefly to speak to his parishioners before making his apologies and leaving for St Philip's. Daphne and Grace helped to tidy the prayer books and hymnals, collecting the occasional one left in the pews, before catching up with some of their friends – while their mother introduced their aunt to other members of the congregation. Simon led Mary outside to sit in the sunshine while they waited for the others.

"So, you will be staying with us for a while, then, Mrs Ferguson?" asked one of the ladies. "If so, you must join the WI, I'm the chair – Mrs Bartlett is our treasurer."

"Yes, Ida had mentioned it and I'd be delighted to join you, Mrs …."

"Oh, how remiss of me, Emma, I should have introduced you," apologised Ida. "This is Mrs Forbes-Harrison."

"I look forward to seeing you at the next meeting. Now, I really must dash," Mrs Forbes-Harrison said as she pulled on her leather gloves then turned away from Ida and Emma and strode towards the door.

"She's a bit of a stuffy old thing and a stickler for etiquette. But her husband chairs the Parochial Church Council, so we have to humour her," Ida remarked to her sister.

Their business concluded, the two women rounded up their offspring and walked home. Ida changed out of her 'Sunday Best' and wrapped her apron around her waist. From habit, she checked the time, although she knew exactly what it would be. The mutton was already roasting slowly in the range; the vegetables had been prepared the night before and just needed cooking. She had the process off to a fine art to ensure the Sunday lunch would be on the table ready for her husband to return from St Philip's – and allow him ample time to eat the meal in a civilised fashion before leaving an hour and a half later for his next service.

Monday morning, Simon cycled to the aerodrome he'd noticed the previous week. He rode in through a gate off the main road and found his way to a row of hangars on the edge of the aerodrome itself.

The main doors of one of the hangars were wide open and some ground crew were bringing a Fairey Battle out. Simon stood and watched as the aircraft was positioned on the tarmac apron and a petrol bowser was driven up to refuel it.

"Oy, YOU! What are you doing here?" Simon was roused from his daydream about flying by a brown-coated middle-aged man carrying a clipboard.

"I'm looking for work, sir. I wondered if you had any jobs going."

"Depends what you can do, lad. What experience do you have?"

"I've worked on vehicle engines. My father and I ran a blacksmith's and I did the mechanical side working on tractors, cars, lorries and the like."

"Why aren't you still doing that?"

"My father was killed at Dunkirk and we've moved to Elmdene to stay with my aunt and uncle," Simon muttered, his eyes cast to the floor.

"Sorry to hear about your father. Come into the office and tell me more about the work you've done with engines."

Simon followed him through the gaping hangar main doors into a timber-framed office attached to the interior side wall.

"Take a seat. My name is Mr Robertson. What's yours?"

"Simon Ferguson, sir."

"Right, Simon, do you have any qualifications?"

"Not yet. I'm going to Technical School in September to study mechanics. I want to work with aircraft."

"So, are you just looking for work until then?"

"Well, sir, I was hoping I might be able to work full time during the summer – then at weekends."

"So, what do you know about aircraft? Can you identify the one outside?"

"It's a Fairey Battle light bomber, sir. Single engine and crew of three."

Robertson stroked his moustache while he thought. Simon reminded him of himself at 16, keen as mustard. He'd joined the army in 1899 where he'd first learned to drive, then service, motor vehicles. He'd transferred to the Royal Flying Corps when it was formed in 1912.

"Quite right. We're part of the Civilian Repair Organisation. We do work that can't be done by the RAF squadrons including overhauling engines and airframes. I tell you what I can do for you. I'll take you on as a general hand. Most of the work won't be on the aircraft; you'll be a dogsbody. You'll run errands, collect parts from the stores, keep things tidy and maybe, occasionally, help the engineers working on the aeroplanes. Would that suit you?"

"Yes, sir, thank you, sir, I won't let you down."

"Don't you want to know how much your pay will be, or your hours?"

"Oh, yes sir."

"Your hours will be 8am 'til 6pm Monday to Friday. You'll have half an hour for lunch and your pay will be nine pence an hour – that's two pounds eleven shillings and seven pence ha'penny a week before deductions. If you do overtime, it will be at the same rate. You can start tomorrow. If you want to, you can work Saturday to make a full week."

"Thank you, sir, that's wizard, sir."

"Right, well, first I need you to fill in this form," Robertson said, passing Simon a paper asking for name, address, date of birth and other details. "I need to mention that you'll be working a week in hand – so you won't be paid this Friday."

Simon flew home on his bike, buoyed by the fact that he'd not only found work but that it was with aircraft. Even the news that he'd have to wait for his wages didn't worry him. He had enough for the dance – and, in future, he'd be able to contribute to the family's finances.

The next morning, Simon woke even earlier than normal to ride the three miles to the aerodrome by eight o'clock. As he entered the kitchen, his uncle was already eating his breakfast before celebrating an early Holy Communion for the more devout of his parishioners.

"Your breakfast is on the table, love," his mother told him. "I've done you egg with a rasher of bacon and slice of fried bread as it's a special day for you. There's also some sandwiches for your lunch."

While he savoured the treat, Simon and his uncle discussed plans for the weekly scout meeting and how the troop might help with the war effort.

"Other groups have done newspaper and scrap metal collections. Maybe we could try that?" his uncle suggested.

"Or what about acting as messengers for the ARP? Isn't that how Baden-Powell used boys in the Siege of Mafeking?" asked Simon as he speared the last piece of fried bread and bacon on his fork.

"We'll organise a council with the two Patrol Leaders and see what they think. Now I must be going."

"Yes, me too. Don't want to be late on my first morning."

Chapter 12. Aero Engineer

w/c 15th July

The mist was clearing from the fields as Simon mounted his bicycle and rode out of the drive. As he left the outskirts of the village, he passed the post lady in her dark blue uniform, carrying her sack of mail as she delivered the last few letters of her round.

'How did he know it was the end of her round, rather than the start?' Simon pondered as he rode on. Then he realised, *'her bag had been quite flat so must have been empty.'* He felt pleased with himself that he'd been so observant without any effort.

As he approached the aerodrome, he saw an Avro Anson taking off. A few minutes later, the Fairey Battle he'd seen being pulled out of the hangar roared down the runway and passed less than fifty feet above his head.

Simon was about to leave his bicycle at the side of the hangar when Mr Robertson called to him.

"Bring your bike into the hangar Simon – don't want to leave it where any enemy parachutist can steal it, do you?"

Robertson pointed to a space by the wall. "Stick it over there, lad. Glad to see you're punctual. I'll get one of the engineers to show you around then you can make a pot of tea for everyone," he told Simon then turned to one of the engineers. "Percy, have you got a minute?"

The engineer, Percival Mason, put down the spanner he'd been using and walked over to Robertson and Simon; nodding at the youngster. "How do?" he said.

"This is Simon, he's starting today as a general hand. He says he has experience working with vehicle engines so he might be able to lend a hand with some of the mechanical work. Show him around will you please? I'd do it myself but we've got two more repairs coming in this morning and I need to sort out the scheduling."

He turned to Simon. "Mr Mason is one of our best engineers – you'll do well to follow his example."

"Right Simon, first things first. Over here is the canteen area. No doubt the guvnor has told you to make a pot of tea when we're finished with the tour. That's probably the most important job on the site. If the engineers don't have their char, they can't work," he remarked with a twinkle.

"The stores are at the back of the hangar. That's Rhys Williamson's province. He's from Cardiff so is generally known as Taff. The other facilities you might need are over there." Mason added, pointing out the toilets.

Simon's morning passed in a whirlwind of making the tea, sweeping the floor and fetching and carrying for the engineers. When an Airspeed Oxford, the first of the repairs they were expecting, landed and taxied to the hangar, he was surprised to see a woman climb out of the cockpit. She wore a dark blue uniform and carried a parachute over her arms. He expected to see a man follow her out of the aircraft but no one else emerged.

Mr Robertson had come and stood next to him as he watched from the hangar door.

"Surprised to see a woman pilot, Simon?" he asked.

"Well, yes sir."

"The Air Transport Auxiliary has both men and women pilots. They collect damaged aircraft and bring them to places like this where they can be repaired and deliver new and repaired aircraft to the squadrons. The male pilots tend to be those who are considered too old or medically unfit for front-line operations. The women only fly trainers and communications aircraft like the Oxford and Anson. Mark my words though, they'll be used on other types before long."

"What, even fighters and bombers?"

"Why not? Right, come on everyone, let's get the Oxford into the hangar."

By the time the Oxford had been pushed into the hangar, the second repair, a Fairey Battle like the one Simon had seen the previous day, landed. This time a male pilot appeared from the aircraft. He walked over to the control tower where his colleague was waiting.

Cycling home that evening, Simon was weary but buoyed by a feeling that he was contributing to the war effort – even if only in a small way. And, he was working with aircraft. True he hadn't physically worked on the Oxford or the Battle apart from helping to position them in the hangar. But, he'd been close enough to smell that mixture of oil, exhaust, glycol, metal and rubber and other aromas that he would find permeated all aircraft of the period.

The next few days followed a similar routine – aircraft flying in for repair and being collected for delivery to squadrons around the country. On his second day, Simon was asked, by one of the engineers, to go to the stores for a long weight.

"I'm not sure where it is, might take me a while to find it," the storeman told him, then disappeared into the rows of shelves.

After ten minutes, Simon wondered how much longer he'd be waiting for the long weight when the penny dropped. *'Long weight, long wait. Very funny.'*

The engineers ribbed him good-naturedly when he returned to the bay where the Oxford stood with the cowling removed from the port engine.

"Simon, can you come and help here, lad? Your hands are smaller than mine and you might be able to reach inside this bolt for me," the engineer called. "You'll need a five-sixteenth spanner."

Simon climbed up next to the engineer.

"See that bolt there holding the manifold in place? It's awkward to reach but might be easier for you to get your hand in there. See if you can undo it for me, will you?"

Simon's smaller hand slipped past the obstruction preventing the engineer from reaching the bolt and he soon had it undone.

"Well done lad. Have a go at the others for me, will you?"

As he undid the final bolt, Simon realised that Mr Robertson was watching him. Robertson said nothing but turned away and walked back to his office.

Other engineers also called on Simon to reach into tight spaces over the next few days and he was aware that on several occasions Mr Robertson had seen him doing so. As he hadn't been rebuked for this work, Simon took it as tacit approval so long as he kept up with his other official tasks.

At the end of the shift on Saturday, Mr Robertson called Simon into the office.

"So, Simon, how do you think your trial week has gone?"

"It's been very interesting, Mr Robertson. I hope what I've done has been satisfactory."

"Yes, lad, very satisfactory. I've been watching you and you seem prepared to get stuck into whatever you're asked to do and the other engineers have said you've been very helpful."

"Thank you, sir. Does that mean I've passed the week's trial?"

"Yes, Simon. With flying colours. Now go and enjoy the rest of the weekend and I'll see you on Monday."

Simon cycled home as quickly as he could – he needed to get ready for the dance. Lucy had insisted that she'd meet him at the village hall at seven-thirty.

Chapter 13. At the Dance

20th July 1940

Simon quickly washed and dressed in his Sunday Best – thankful, for once, that he still didn't need to shave, his face remaining stubbornly free of even the lightest fluff. At school, his slight build and lack of facial and body hair had made him the butt of his contemporaries' teasing. At least Lucy didn't seem to care that he was short. This evening, however, the few minutes he'd have spent shaving would have been the difference between arriving at the village hall by seven thirty and being late.

Lucy had told him that she would be helping her mother to set up the refreshments so he paid his entrance fee, left his coat in the cloakroom and went into the main hall. The four-piece band, made up of local musicians, was tuning their instruments on the stage at the far end. The left-hand wall had doors opening into a kitchen – which also had a hatch serving the main hall; a committee room, used tonight as a bar, and the cloakroom and toilets. Simon's stomach fluttered when he spotted Lucy through the servery hatch. She had her back to him and was talking to an older woman, presumably her mother. As he watched them, Lucy turned and saw him; a smile lit up her face, quickly turning to a blush.

As Simon walked over to the serving hatch, the kitchen door opened and Lucy stood there. She wore a knee-length swing dress; the skirt was a plain burgundy contrasting with the lilac, short-sleeved blouse; the waistline was high in the centre and curved away towards the back. Her shoulder-length auburn hair had been styled to add body at the sides framing her face. She wore a hint of burgundy lipstick to match her skirt.

"Hello, Simon,"

"H H Hello Lucy," Simon stammered. "You look lovely."

"Well, thank you, sir. You're looking very smart yourself. Now, come and meet my mother."

Concerned about the reaction he was about to receive, he, nevertheless, followed Lucy into the kitchen.

« Maman, ici est Simon, le cousin de Grace et Daphne, » Lucy turned to Simon, "My mother is French and has always insisted that we speak French – mainly to ensure that I can converse with our relatives in France when we visit but also to make sure she doesn't forget the language." « C'est vrais n'est ce pas, maman? » "She does speak perfect English though."

"I am very pleased to meet you, Simon. Lucy has told me much about you. I am sorry for the loss of your father. It is very sad that the boche have, again, despoiled the soil of France and men, like your father, have died," Lucy's mother said, her accent clearly betraying her origins.

"Thank you, Mrs Hall, I am sorry that your country has been invaded."

"Now, you two young people – go and enjoy the dance. « Vas-tu, Lucy. Ton jeune homme est gentil. »

Lucy kissed her mother on the cheeks then took Simon's hand.

In the hall, the band had finished tuning up and had started playing.

"How are you at dancing, Simon?"

"Err, I can just about manage a Waltz, Foxtrot and Gay Gordons."

"Well, I think this is a Foxtrot so come on."

They joined a few other couples on the dance floor. Simon took Lucy's hand in his and put his right arm around her back while Lucy rested her left hand on his shoulder. They circled the room without colliding with any other dancers and, when the music stopped, broke their hold and clapped each other.

"You were being modest about your dancing, you're very good, Simon, where did you learn?"

"My mother and father used to love dancing and mum taught me when I was young."

The Foxtrot was followed by a Quickstep, a Waltz then several circle dances, including the Gay Gordons before a progressive dance where the partners moved on after each sequence. Finding each other again after the progressive dance, they decided to take a break for some refreshments.

"How did your mother come to live in England, Lucy?"

"Maman met my father towards the end of the Great War when she was helping at a hospital where he was receiving treatment. He promised he would return after the war and find her – and he did. Maman and I spent most summers with my grandparents so she taught me French and it just became a 'thing' for us to only speak French to keep up our practice."

"I see, that's a lovely story. I'd love to be able to speak French. If I get a job in aviation, there's likely to be a lot of travelling – once this war is over. I already speak a little German. My grandad on my dad's side was a prisoner of war during the Great War"

"I'll teach you French, if you want."

"That would be great – so long as it's not too much trouble."

"No trouble at all, it'll be fun," Lucy added with a smile. "Come on, let's dance again."

The band took a break halfway through the evening, the members heading to the bar for much-needed and well-deserved refreshments.

"I need to help Maman for a few minutes, there's always a rush at the start of the breaks."

"Can I help?" Simon asked.

"Maman and I usually do the teas and coffees between us – you could do the orange squash, if you like."

They stepped into the kitchen.

« Ah, tu es arrivé. » "Simon, you are enjoying the dance?"

"Yes, Mrs Hall, very much."

At the end of the dance, Simon walked Lucy home, holding her hand.

At her front door, they stood slightly apart, still holding hands.

"I really enjoyed this evening, Lucy."

"So did I, Simon and don't forget I'm going to teach you French."

"Are you sure it's not too much trouble?"

"Not at all, Simon."

An awkward pause followed – neither of them sure what they should do or say.

Lucy was hoping Simon would ask her out again; Simon was scared that she'd say no – *'though the fact that she was going to help him learn French did suggest that she liked him and she WAS still holding his hand! But maybe it was safer to leave it at meeting up again for French lessons,'* he thought.

Sensing his hesitation, but not wanting to seem too forward, Lucy realised she'd have to take the initiative. "When do you want to start your French Lessons, Simon? I can't do it tomorrow, but maybe one evening next week?"

"How about Monday then?"

"That's fine. Well, goodnight, Simon." Lucy released his hand and turned to open the door.

"Goodnight, Lucy, thanks again for a lovely evening." Simon turned away as Lucy stepped inside and he seemed to float above the road as he walked home.

Chapter 14. French Lessons

22nd July 1940

When Simon reported for duty at the airfield on the Monday morning, he felt more confident than he had for as long as he could remember. He had a job working with aircraft; he'd registered with the college for an engineering course starting in a little over a month. To cap it all, he'd taken a girl out on a date AND she seemed interested in him – they were meeting again that evening for his first French Lesson.

Two more Fairey Battles and an Airspeed Oxford landed during the morning. Simon wasn't surprised this time to see a woman pilot climb out of the Oxford. She and one of her male colleagues were collected later by an Avro Anson the ATA used as a ferry while the other flew a refurbished Battle to its squadron 'somewhere in the South of England' as the news broadcasts would say.

That evening, Simon walked around to Lucy's for his first French lesson. The house was built of local Cotswold stone with a slate tile roof. The solid oak front door was set into an open porch with an old bell pull as well as a large brass knocker in the shape of a lion's head. Lucy's father was the manager of the branch of a major bank in Westchester and their home reflected his standing. The door opened so quickly to his tentative knock that he wondered if Lucy had been waiting for him. She led him into a large hall with stairs to the left.

"Maman and my father are in the drawing room listening to the wireless, come and say hello, then we'll go into the garden for your lesson," Lucy told him as she opened the door to their right.

As they entered the room, Mr Hall rested the pipe he was smoking in an ashtray, turned down the volume of the wireless and looked at this young man who had caught the eye of his daughter. Mrs Hall put down the piece of embroidery she was working on.

"Good evening, Simon," greeted Mrs Hall.

"Good evening, Mrs Hall, Mr Hall."

"So, Simon, I gather you are an aeronautical engineer?"

"Hardly, sir. But that's what I'd like to be. I'm working at the aerodrome until I go to Technical School in September."

"Good for you, my boy. Good for you. Well, perhaps we'll see you later before you leave." With that, he turned back to the wireless and picked up his pipe again.

Simon, looked at Mrs Hall who'd also returned to her embroidery, then at Lucy unsure if anything else was expected of him at this stage.

"Come on," said Lucy, "we can get into the garden through the French Windows."

They sat together on the bench in an arbour at the end of the lawn.

"Now, the question is where do we start? Perhaps by introducing yourself. So, I would say « Je m'appelle Lucy. » That's my name is Lucy. You try it. Repeat after me, je."

« Je »

« m'appelle »

« m'appelle »

« Simon. »

« Simon. Je m'appelle Simon. »

"Very good, très bien. Now, to say hello, we say bonjour and goodbye is au revoir."

They spent the next hour with Lucy pointing out items around the garden, their clothes and parts of the body such as arms, legs and hands and teaching Simon their French names.

"I think that's probably enough for now," she told him. "We don't want to confuse you with too many new words."

"Just one more phrase, Lucy. How do you say you are very pretty?"

"Why do you want to know that?" she asked, casting her eyes to the ground. « C'est tu es très jolie. »

Simon took hold of Lucy's hand and looked straight into her eyes. « Tu es très jolie, » he recited.

« Et tu es très beau, Simon, » "you are very handsome. Oh la la!"

« Ah, vous voila. » "Here you are," Mrs Hall's voice startled them as she appeared with a tray of drinks.

Mrs Hall was smiling to herself as she walked back to the house leaving the two youngsters flustered.

Simon and Lucy met again on the Thursday evening for another lesson. This time they walked along the river bank while Lucy continued to tell Simon the French names of whatever they saw. After about a mile, another watercourse joined the river. A smaller path followed this stream up the side of the hill through some woods. Simon offered Lucy his hand to steady her as she crossed a plank leading to the opposite bank. She didn't object when he continued to hold it as they made their way along the side of the brook as it rippled down the slope.

The path emerged from the woods onto a grassy knoll.

"Let's sit down for a while," Simon suggested.

"I want some water from the spring over there, first – it's where the brook starts. It's always so cool and refreshing. Try it."

They cupped their hands and caught some of the clear liquid.

"You're right, Lucy, it is refreshing. This really is a lovely place."

Simon lay back and closed his eyes as Lucy knelt beside him.

She picked a long stalk of ryegrass and tickled Simon's nose.

"Hey, you are meant to be learning French, not sleeping."

"Pardon Mademoiselle. What are you going to teach me now."

"How about bise?"

« Quesque c'est bise? »

Lucy leant over and kissed his lips quickly then sat up again.

« Ca c'est une bise. »

Simon was stunned. Amazed that Lucy had just kissed him.

He put his arm around her back and pulled her down again. She rested her hands on his shoulders as their lips met again and stayed locked together for several seconds.

She then rolled onto her side next to Simon; his arm under her shoulders and his hand resting on her waist while Lucy's rested on his chest.

Some of the lads in the final year at his old school had boasted of how far they'd got with girls; some even claiming to have gone 'all the way'. He hadn't taken part in those discussions. It went against the Scout Law that 'A scout is clean in thought and word and deed'. Not that he believed all of their claims – he was sure most had been idle boasts. But, if the claims had been true, they'd also have gone against what he'd been taught that lovemaking should only be between married couples.

What he wasn't sure of was how far was acceptable? Lucy had kissed him – so that was obviously fine. She was lying next to him and resting her hand on his chest. But would it be acceptable for him to put his hands on her breasts?

'How did Lucy now expect him to behave?' he wondered. The last thing he wanted to do was offend her. But would she be offended if he tried to do more – or if he didn't try to go further?

He decided the safest option was to kiss her again and see what her reaction was. When she responded and rubbed his chest, he caressed her waist and rested his other hand on the arm she had draped over him.

Despite his commitment to the Scout Law, he was tempted to let his hand drift down onto her bottom or rest his other hand on her breasts and see if she objected. But he resisted the temptation and, after a few minutes kissing, Lucy rolled away from him.

"It's going to start getting dark soon so we'd better head back," Lucy said as she got to her feet.

Concern that he'd somehow failed a test Lucy had set him was dispelled when she put her arms around his neck and kissed him again.

"Simon, can I say something without you getting upset?"

Simon wondered what she was about to say but, in spite of his fears, mumbled, "Of course."

"Well, I think I've shown you that I like you a lot – and you seem to like me. But you don't seem to want to take the lead and it would be nice if you did. Or, perhaps you don't really like me."

"Oh, I'm sorry. I do like you. A lot. It's just that I'm not sure what is acceptable and what isn't. You're the first girl I've been out with. I know it's pathetic."

"It's not pathetic, I think it's sweet."

She took his hand.

"Look, if you try to do something I don't want you to do, I'll let you know. I probably won't get upset for you trying but I will expect you to stop doing it. Is that fair enough?"

"Absolutely," Simon replied. He then put his hands around her waist pulled her to him and kissed her. She slid her arms around his neck and responded.

"Oooh la la, monsieur, you are a quick learner." She hooked her arm in his as they walked back down the footpath.

Chapter 15. Dark Clouds

July-August 1940

Over the next four weeks Simon continued to work at the aerodrome, help his uncle with the scout group on Wednesday evenings and met Lucy several times on weekday evenings as well as Saturday nights when they'd go to the cinema or a dance if one was on. Despite any pretence that their meetings were solely for French lessons having been dropped, Simon could now hold simple conversations with Mrs Hall who was impressed with his progress.

At work, the pressure was building as the Luftwaffe intensified its attacks on convoys, RDF Chain Home Stations and RAF airfields in the South East. Having demonstrated his mechanical aptitude, Mr Robertson asked Simon to prepare some Merlin engines by removing ancillary components ready for the engineers to work on.

"You've got a real talent for this work, Simon," Robertson said as they ate their sandwiches in the canteen. "Do you still plan to go to Technical School next month?"

"Yes sir."

"I'll be sad to lose you, lad. But I appreciate that you want to learn the theoretical side and get your qualifications. We didn't have the same opportunity."

"So, how did you get into engineering, Mr Robertson?"

Robertson packed his pipe with tobacco as he studied Simon.

"Well, in some ways, it wasn't so different to you at the beginning. I was in the army in South Africa when they started to look at making armoured vehicles to fight the Boers. I was one of those assigned to work with the engineer. Things were often breaking down so I watched how they were repaired then started to help. The war ended before the work led anywhere but as the army started to get more vehicles, it needed more mechanics to keep them running. Then when they started to use flying machines, I volunteered to work on them and joined the Royal Flying Corps."

"So, you've seen some huge changes in your time. Did you stay in the RAF after the war?" Simon remarked, engrossed in Mr Robertson's tale.

"Aye, lad. I have seen big changes and, yes I stayed in the RAF after the war. I served in Aboukir in Egypt from '27 to '30, and Khormaksar in Aden until 35 before a final posting in England. I retired from the RAF as a Warrant Officer and joined Imperial Airways at Lake Habbaniya in Iraq to service their Empire flying boats. That wasn't a bad place to be – sailing most afternoons on the lake and there was RAF Habbaniya not far away where there'd always be a welcome in the mess."

Robertson took a sip from his enamel mug of tea and drew on his pipe.

"Mind you it was known as Dhibban when I was there. It nestled next to the Euphrates about 50 miles west of Baghdad. I could also wangle flights further east with Imperial. I even got out to Singapore on one trip. I came back to Blighty in 1938."

Simon could see a faraway look in Mr Robertson's eyes as he related his story.

"Fascinating, sir."

"Well after the last unpleasantness, I had hoped we wouldn't see another war but that man Hitler had other ideas." Robertson tapped out his pipe and blew through the stem.

"Right Simon, those engines aren't going to sort themselves out and the lads in the squadrons are depending on us."

They had started work at their benches when the air raid warning started to wail its mournful sound and they put down their tools and ran to take cover in the slit trenches across the apron. High overhead, they could see vapour trails from specks that were being chased by other smudges against the blue sky.

"I think they're Heinkel 111s," Simon remarked. "Can't really tell if the chasing fighters are Hurricanes or Spitfires. I think they're heading for the Gloster factory. They must be two or three miles southwest of us anyway."

"Whatever they are, they're asking for trouble coming this far inland – it's too far for their own fighter escorts. Yes, look, one of the bombers is trailing smoke. Go get him boy!"

They watched as the stricken bomber fell out of formation and turned to attempt to escape the determined fighter on its tail. Its course brought it closer to them. The smoke from its port engine seemed to be getting thicker and they could now see occasional flickers of flame as well.

The fighter was still on the Heinkel's tail and it was now close enough for Simon to confirm it was a Hurricane.

"Your young eyes are sharper than mine," said Percy Mason, one of the engineers.

As they stared at the bomber trying to shake off the fighter, the group in the trenches saw the pinpricks of light on the wings as the Hurricane's eight machine guns strafed the Heinkel. They were then spellbound as four black blobs fell from the bomber before their descent was arrested by parachutes.

"Four of the crew have bailed out, should be one more. Probably the pilot who stayed at the controls until the others had got out. He'd better get a move on or it'll be too late for him," Percy added. Just as he finished speaking, a fifth body dropped from the bomber and fell for a few seconds before a parachute blossomed above him. The bailed-out crew appeared to be drifting away from the aerodrome – four of them quite close together and the fifth on his own.

"Wish I could get my hands on those bastards," said Vincent Green, one of the other engineers. "My brother was on a collier that was attacked in the Channel." Vince's words reminded Simon of his own father killed in France.

The stricken Heinkel's dive steepened as the engine fire spread to the wing and fuselage.

"Look out lads, it's heading this way," shouted Rhys Williamson, the storesman.

Simon and his workmates all crouched lower as the bomber screamed over the hangar and their slit trench and crashed into the middle of the airfield, missing the runway by less than fifty yards. Debris was scattered over a wide area and, as the ammunition for the defensive guns exploded, bullets shot out from the burning wreck.

The airfield's own fire tender headed across the grass towards the crash, its bell clanging as it went. In view of the exploding ammunition, the tender's crew, realising that there was no threat to life from the burning remains, pulled up short and watched as the fire burned itself out. After the explosions had stopped, they approached the tangled wreckage.

Once the 'All Clear' sounded, Mr Robertson addressed his team. "Back to work men. No doubt the RAF will be along sometime to collect the Heinkel for scrap."

Simon would have loved to get a closer look at the German aircraft but didn't want to appear childish so he took a final glance over his shoulder as they went back into the hangar.

The engineers seemed to take the attack as a personal affront and galvanise them to work even harder with the usual banter diminished as they focussed on repairing their charges and getting them ready to re-join the fray.

At the end of the day, Simon was about to ride off when Rhys and Vince wheeled their own bikes out of the hangar.

"You coming to look at the Heinkel, young Simon?" asked Rhys.

"Are we allowed to?"

"Why not? Damned thing nearly took off our heads. Don't worry the police are there to stop souvenir hunters. Probably be my brother-in-law, Joseph."

They rode over the grass to the downed bomber, guarded by a solitary police constable. The final fifty yards were close to the scars left by the Heinkel as it had struck the ground.

"Thought you'd be along, Rhys," said the constable.

"How's things Joe? You don't mind if we have a quick look around, do you? Young Simon here was particularly interested."

Simon was about to protest when Rhys winked at him.

"Look, but don't take nothing, any of you!" Joseph replied.

At that moment, an open-top Alvis bounced over the grass towards the crash site. As it approached, Simon could see that the occupants were all in RAF uniform. Four men jumped from the car, three of them slapping the fourth on his back.

"Well done, Douglas, your first Hun," the driver of the Alvis said. He then turned to Constable Anderson. "You don't mind if we take a bit of the tail, do you? It's Pilot Officer Carter's first kill."

Simon noticed that the speaker wore the two rings of a Flight Lieutenant while Carter and one of the others wore a thin braid and the fourth officer had the thicker braid of a Flying Officer. All wore pilot's brevets above their left breast pocket; the Flight Lieutenant had the Distinguished Flying Cross ribbon below his.

"I shouldn't let you, gentlemen. But, under the circumstances, I suppose it's all right." Anderson responded after a moment's consideration.

"Right Douglas, first things first though, stand over by the tail so we can get a snap of you with it."

They then removed a section of the rudder that was hanging by one hinge.

"This will do, put it in the boot of the Alvis. Right, where's the nearest pub for a jar or two?"

As the Alvis disappeared back towards the hangar, Simon took the opportunity to look inside the remains of the cockpit. There wasn't much to see as the fire had destroyed any flammable material. He was glad that the crew had bailed out – even if they were the enemy. He'd hate to imagine anyone being caught in a burning aircraft.

Chapter 16. Battle of Britain

August - September 1940

The sight of the Heinkel being shot down by the Hurricane had brought the battle in the skies much closer to home. The machines they worked on weren't just job numbers – they were tools to hit back at the Germans.

The wireless news each evening reported on the Luftwaffe's attacks on ports and convoys in the channel then on RAF airfields in the south-east. Names like Biggin Hill, Hawkinge, Kenley, Tangmere and Manston soon became familiar. Each day the announcers, such as Alvar Lidell, reported how many aircraft had been lost by each side.

"Wizard result for the RAF yesterday nearly two hundred Germans destroyed for thirty of ours," said Rhys over a mug of tea.

"If that's the real numbers," replied Vince. "Chances are, our lads will have overestimated their claims. That happened in the last war. You get two pilots taking a shot at an enemy aircraft and see it going down and both of them claim it. But, even if it was only half that number, you're right it was a good day."

Simon listened to the two engineers' discussion. He wondered how many aircraft the Germans had to throw at Britain? If they were losing even one hundred a day, surely they couldn't keep that up long enough for him to get into the war, could they? It would be another two and a half years before he was able to sign up and avenge his father's death. And what damage would Britain suffer in the meantime? Could the RAF survive the attacks on its airfields? How many aircraft did they have? What about pilots? He knew that even if the RAF lost an aircraft, the fighting was over British soil and many of the pilots would be able to bail out and be back in the battle later. The Germans from the Heinkel may also have bailed out but they were now prisoners of war.

He took a last swig of tea, careful not to get leaves in his mouth, then left his mug on the counter before returning to his workbench.

A few days later, the Prime Minister told the nation that 'Never in the field of human conflict was so much owed by so many to so few.'

The BBC news continued to report attacks on RAF airfields, usually with the comment that 'some damage was done to ground installations' or 'there were some casualties'. Simon could only wonder what that really meant. It would certainly involve more families, like his, receiving telegrams announcing that loved ones had been killed.

As August turned into September, the Luftwaffe turned its attention away from the airfields to attack London and other cities and Simon started at Technical School. The course combined practical skills with theory including mathematics, physics and technical drawing. He soon realised that much of the practical side covered work that he'd been doing for years.

The teaching staff also recognised that Simon was way ahead of his classmates when it came to dismantling and reassembling engines and diagnosing faults with mechanical components.

The principal telephoned Mr Robertson at the airfield and explained a scheme that he'd been considering.

When he was told the principal wanted to see him, Simon wondered if he'd done something wrong or if there had been a problem with his registration. He didn't think it was the former and, presumably, the school secretary would deal with registration problems.

Mildred Simpson looked up from the papers on her desk when he knocked on the door to her office through which all the principal's visitors had to pass.

"Ah, Simon. Yes, Mr Davies wants to speak to you."

She rose from her desk and walked across the room to the door to the principal's office, knocked then opened the door slightly and peered in.

"Simon Ferguson is here Mr Davies."

"Good, good. Send him in."

Mrs Simpson stood to one side and gestured to him to go through.

"Ah, come in. Sit down, please. I want to run something past you."

Being invited to sit down suggested to Simon that he wasn't in any sort of trouble; surely he'd have been left standing in front of the principal's desk if that had been the case.

"Your teachers tell me that you are already very experienced on the practical side and I can see why from your application form. We don't get many students who have run their own garage business or worked at an aircraft repair shop. They've suggested that the practical side of the course is unlikely to be teaching you anything most of the time. In fact, Mr Walker says you've been completing each task quicker than he can and you then give the other students a hand."

Simon was wondering where this was leading but it didn't seem appropriate to make any comment at this point.

"I've had a word with Mr Robertson, who was very complimentary about your work, by the by, and proposed that you should attend the theory classes here and any special practical sessions on areas you're not familiar with but spend the rest of your time at the airfield. I think that would make much better use of your time. What do you think? I should say that Mr Robertson supports the scheme."

"That would be very good, sir."

"Right, well, that's agreed then. You can sort out the airfield end with Mr Robertson and Mrs Simpson will deal with the school paperwork."

"Yes, sir, thank you so much sir, I won't let you down."

"I know you won't, Simon, you're a credit to your mother and father."

As he closed the door to the principal's office behind him, Simon hardly heard Mrs Simpson when she wished him good luck.

The new scheme worked well. Simon cycled into town each morning to attend the theory classes then rode the four miles out to the airfield and spent the afternoon servicing engines or repairing airframes and finally cycled the two miles home again. Despite working four hours a day and all day Saturday at the airfield, the technical school course had reduced his hours and cut his wages. Fortunately, Mr Robertson had increased his hourly rate by a penny ha'penny so he now earned one pound seven shillings and eight pence farthing a week. As he'd only been expecting to be able to work at weekends this was still more than the family had budgeted for.

The approaching autumn had reduced the risk of a German invasion and the Luftwaffe seemed to be less keen on undertaking large bomber raids in daylight. The ATA pilots collecting the repaired Ansons, Blenheims and Hurricanes said the RAF airfields in the southeast were also being spared daily attacks. They did report, however, that London, Coventry and Merseyside were being attacked at night and that the RAF didn't have any effective defence against such raids.

He felt, however, that he was in limbo. He knew he was doing valuable work at the airfield but desperately wanted to get up in the air and really take the battle to the Hun. He was even too young to join the Home Guard although he knew some lads his age had lied to join early. That wasn't really an option for him as his uncle was too well known.

He saw Lucy regularly and enjoyed her company and their French lessons, he could now converse with her mother, but, whilst other lads his age constantly boasted about their conquests, he didn't share their obsession with 'going all the way' with girls. Lucy and he kissed and cuddled but it seemed she was the one who instigated the moves most of the time. He almost convinced himself that he was just respecting her and that being 'clean in thought and word and deed' was a cornerstone of the Scout creed. There was also his uncle and his church teachings. But he suspected this wasn't the full story. He just didn't know what it was.

Chapter 17. Manoeuvres

September 1942

Simon had joined the Home Guard in January, as soon as he'd had his seventeenth birthday. Some of the other members were old enough to be his grandfather, if not great-grandfather. Most had served in the Great War and a couple had served on the Northwest Frontier of India and the Sudan – or, like Mr Robertson, had fought in the Boer War.

Their duties weren't particularly onerous now the immediate threat of invasion had been averted and America had joined the fight. They drilled weekly and mounted patrols to watch over the airfield where Simon and several of the other volunteers worked. There was now little prospect of having to fight off an assault by German parachutists but they continued to stand guard. Occasionally members would be asked to keep watch over unexploded bombs until the disposal teams could deal with them.

This weekend, however, they were leaving for a week's training in the Brecon Beacons. As well as shooting on the ranges and fieldcraft, they would be acting as 'hares' for the 'hounds' of the regular forces to track and capture on an exercise later in the week. They would be under canvas while at their base camp but need to build their own shelters for up to two nights while 'on the run'.

It was mid-afternoon by the time they arrived at their base camp and it was drizzling. Simon was well used to such conditions from his scout camps; he was also familiar with the bell tents his patrol was allocated and they soon had it erected and their kit stowed inside. Rhys Williamson, storeman from the airfield and corporal in the Home Guard, had gone off with his rifle soon after they'd arrived to see what he could bag for dinner. He returned soon after they'd erected the tent with two rabbits that he proceeded to skin and gut ready for the pot.

"If you trap rabbits with a snare, you can kill them by holding them by the back legs and giving a firm chop to the back of the neck," Rhys explained to Simon who was peeling potatoes and cutting them up with carrots and turnip before throwing them into the black dixie with the rabbit.

"It'll take a couple of hours to cook, but it'll be good eating. Better than compo rations anyhow."

That evening, the company commander, Captain Harrison called them together under a large awning they'd erected as a mess tent.

"This is Sergeant Hill who will brief you on how to evade capture over the next few days. Take heed of what he has to say. He has practical experience. He was trapped behind German lines at Dunkirk and managed to work his way back through northern France."

"Thank you, Captain Harrison. Right, your role is to try to avoid being captured by the regulars. They, on the other hand, won't want to be beaten by a group of kids and old men. Sorry if that sounds insulting – but it's how they're bound to see you."

There was a general murmur of resentment around the group.

"But you're going to surprise them," Hill continued. "The first thing to learn is what can give you away. It's the seven Ss."

Hill held up his right hand with just the thumb extended.

"One. Shape. The human body is a distinctive shape and if seen will immediately give you away. You need to camouflage that shape with leaves, twigs, grass or anything else you can find that will break up that outline."

He extended his index finger.

"Two. Shine. If something reflects the sun, it will draw attention. So, against all you've been taught so far, we don't want nice shiny brasses or badges."

He stretched out his middle finger.

"Three. Shadow. Don't let your shadow give you away – be aware of where the sun is – another S."

His ring finger joined the others.

"Four. Silhouette – if you stand out against a contrasting background, you'll be easy to see. And, that brings me to five: Skyline. Avoid crossing over ridge lines and being seen against the sky if at all possible. Six. Spacing. Even spacing is almost certainly man-made. Nature is far more random."

Hill looked around the room. His audience seemed to be paying attention but whether they'd remember anything was another matter, though the young lad might do.

"Seven. Sudden movement. You can be looking straight at something but if it doesn't move, it might blur into the background. Moving quickly will draw the attention."

"What about Sound, Sergeant? Isn't that one of the Ss?"

Hill looked at the questioner. Unsurprisingly, it was the young lad.

"It is, and there are a few others that we could add to the list as well. Just because the army only recognises the seven I've taught you, think about what you're doing. Smoke, for example, could be visible or the lingering smell from a fire or even a cigarette might give you away."

The following morning, they assembled for rifle practice. Simon had become proficient with .22 rifles at an indoor range but they'd be using far more powerful weapons on the external range.

First, they had to be shown the weapons they'd be using.

"Listen up," commanded the sergeant. "This is an American M1917 Enfield Rifle. It's your main weapon. It was developed from the standard army issue Lee Enfield 303. Some claim it's superior to the Lee Enfield. The Americans provided us with a supply of these after Dunkirk but because it uses a different cartridge, they were allocated to the Home Guard to avoid screw-ups with mismatched ammunition."

He proceeded to demonstrate how to strip it down and how to clean it. He then repeated the process with Bren and Lewis machine guns and a Thompson submachine gun.

"Right," he said at the end of the demonstrations. "Get some grub, then reassemble here at thirteen hundred hours prompt."

The range was a mile and a half away and they were to march there. At the range, one section was detailed to the butts at the other end of the ranges.

Simon was one of the first group allocated, in pairs, to each of the targets. The butts were open on just one side. Between them and the firing point and overhead the butts were protected by earth banks. In front to the open side were ten metal frames with white wooden panels, each about four feet square with circles painted on them, that could be raised or lowered. Beyond the targets was another, much larger, earth bank to absorb the bullets being shot. On top of one end of the bank was a flagpole with a red flag flying.

The regular army corporal with them explained their duties.

"You will raise and lower the targets as instructed. If your target is hit, you will raise the pointer to indicate where the bullet hit. When the target is lowered, you will stick paper over the holes. Is that understood?"

He was answered with a general, almost inaudible, mumble.

"I said, is that understood?" he shouted.

"Yes, Corporal," they answered in unison.

The corporal operated the field telephone at one end of the butts to advise the firing point that they were ready. A few minutes later, the first 'crack' made some of them jump as a bullet hit one of the targets. It was followed in quick succession by a barrage as others fired their rifles at the targets. As each hole appeared, Simon and the other markers, held up their pointers to indicate where the bullets had hit.

Simon still reacted as bullets flew over his head and he saw puffs as they hit the bank beyond the targets. The first few times it was, he had to admit, quite scary but he eventually got used to the whistle overhead and the sharp cracks as the bullets smashed through the wooden backing to the targets.

Then the shooting reduced and just one shooter was finishing his five rounds.

The field telephone rang and the corporal answered.

"OK, lower your targets and paper over the holes, ready for the next group."

The process was repeated twice more as different groups took their turn at the firing point.

"Right, when you've finished repairing the targets, pick up your kit ready to march back to the firing point."

As they marched back up the range, they passed another group heading towards the butts to replace them.

Simon was initially caught out by the loudness of the shot when he squeezed the trigger and by the recoil, as it punched his shoulder. The acrid smell of the cordite threatened to make his eyes water, but he blinked it away. As he operated the bolt to load the next round, he saw the marker signal that his first shot had been an outer at eight o'clock. He adjusted his aim.

The marker indicated an inner at two o'clock. He'd over-compensated and adjusted his aim again.

Bull. Simon smiled to himself. That was better.

He repeated his previous shot.

Another bull. Yes, he'd got the hang of it.

Taking his final shot, he knew he'd pulled the trigger instead of squeezing it. It was an outer at three o'clock. Disappointed with his final attempt, he lay down his rifle and indicated that he had completed his shots.

Unsurprisingly, Rhys who was often out with a rifle or shotgun supplementing his family's meat ration, usually at landowners' expense, had scored highest. Simon's was the fourth-highest score.

Chapter 18. Escape and Evasion

September 1942

Simon had been paired with Rhys Williamson for the escape and evasion exercise. Rhys may have been more than three times Simon's age, but his poaching practices had kept him fitter than most of the others in the platoon.

The elderly Bedford 3-ton truck had struggled to get them over the hills but picked up speed as it headed down into a valley. It stopped where a track from the left-hand side met the road they were on. The signpost indicating where the roads went had been removed to foil any attempted invasion. At least, that was the excuse. It probably caused more disruption to the home war effort with vehicles getting lost and petrol being wasted.

Beyond a hedge, Simon could see farm buildings with smoke curling from the chimney. Cattle were lying down in the field next to the farm, chewing the cud.

"Right, first two, out you get," instructed the sergeant, as he came around the back of the lorry.

He turned to the first two who had dismounted.

"Your present position is grid reference eight-four-five, one-four-five. You have until eighteen hundred hours on Friday to return to base. That gives you a little under fifty-four hours to cover about seventeen miles as the crow flies. Not that I expect you to make it that far – the hounds will probably pick you up later today and you'll be back in your tent this evening."

The sergeant then climbed back into the cab and the Bedford wheezed and juddered its way up the road.

After about a mile, they stopped again. Simon watched as the second pair dismounted and the sergeant gave them their current location. He waved as the truck drove away in a cloud of exhaust smoke leaving them at the side of the road.

"Right, out you get," the sergeant told Rhys and Simon who were the only ones left. "I don't expect the others to make it back to camp but you two just might have a chance. Your position is eight-four-seven, one-six-nine. The camp is zero-nine-three, zero-nine-one."

Simon and Rhys left their rucksacks on the ground while they studied their map, identified their current location and where they needed to get to.

"The hounds probably expect us to take this southern route," Rhys said, tracing a line on the map. "The question is, do we want to just go through the motions, get captured and be driven back to camp, or do you want to see if we can really beat the regulars and their 'boys and old men' comments?"

Simon looked up at the grey sky and wiped the rain off his face.

"Let's go for it," he responded, smiling.

Rhys winked.

"Right, well, if they're expecting us to take the shortest route and approach camp from the west, we'll do the opposite. We'll skirt around to the north then approach the camp from the east."

"So, that takes us near Pen-y-Fan?" Simon asked. It was the highest peak in the area.

"We'll keep clear to the north. Now, we should be safe for the first few hours as we'll be heading in the opposite direction to what they'll expect and they'll probably be busy rounding up the others. If we can get to this woodland here, we can lie up for the night then cross to the east of Pen-y-Fan tomorrow morning before the hunters get back up here from camp."

"Sounds like a plan," Simon replied.

The two of them hoisted their rucksacks on their backs and started hiking northeast along the road. After about a mile, they left the road and followed a stream uphill through a wooded valley which widened into a small wood.

"We'll keep inside the tree line, it'll give us more cover," Rhys said.

Simon was relieved to be with Rhys. He was experienced at map reading and no stranger to hiking with a full rucksack with the scouts but Rhys had years of experience of avoiding discovery by gamekeepers.

Leaving the wood, they cut across undulating open ground before they could take cover again. About three miles from their drop-off point, they were faced with a steep-sided valley.

"We want to head northeast but that takes us down into the valley and up the other side, young Simon and that's not a good idea. Always try and maintain height in hill country, don't go taking the shortest line. We'll keep this side of the stream and cut around the top. It's probably another half mile but a lot easier than climbing the slope over there."

Simon saw the sense in Rhys' reasoning, eased the rucksack straps on his shoulder and followed as Rhys strode off again.

At the head of the valley, they stopped and looked around. The tops of the mountains, several hundred feet higher than them, were covered in mist and the drizzle persisted. Simon wished he was wearing his hooded anorak. Made from water and wind-resistant canvas, it pulled over his head, had a zip that drew the collar tighter around the neck and a drawstring to snug the hood around his face. Instead, the army issue battledress and cape let water drip down their necks.

Looking at the map, Simon remarked "I reckon we've done about five miles."

"Sounds about right, we've been climbing quite a bit so far. Should be easier from here if we can maintain our height."

"Not much cover though for a while, mainly open moorland."

"True, but we're now quite a way from the roads and I doubt if they'll be looking for us around here. At least, not yet. We'll have to keep our eyes peeled."

Apart from diverting slightly and being careful not to be seen from isolated farmhouses, the pair made good time. They reached the edge of a wood on a steep slope leading down to a main road that they needed to cross. They carefully descended through the trees before stopping about five yards from the edge of the road.

"Stay here, Simon, while I check for traffic."

Rhys crept out from the trees and lay in a ditch. It gave him a clear view of the road for more than half a mile each way. Seeing that it was clear, he signalled for Simon to join him.

"When I say 'go', get across the road and hide in the ditch on the other side."

"Fine."

"Right, all clear, GO."

Simon sprinted across the road, reaching the other side as a lorry came around the distant corner. He ducked down as low as he could and pressed himself into the ground. He counted the seconds down. If the lorry was doing twenty miles per hour it could take at least a minute and a half to pass him. If it was much more than that, it might indicate that he'd been seen and the lorry was slowing to look for him.

As he reached seventy-five in his count, he heard the lorry approaching. The engine noise sounded normal and a few seconds later it passed him, belching smoke from the exhaust.

Simon let out his breath then inhaled, breathing in some of the noxious gases from the lorry.

A few moments later, Rhys joined him.

"Right lad, let's get away from the road, then we can make camp for the night."

They refilled their water bottles from a stream they crossed before entering the next wood. Rhys looked around him.

"This'll do fine. We can build a shelter next to that fallen sycamore. The wind's blowing away from the road so we should be fine using the Tommy Cooker to heat some rations, I can't see anyone smelling it."

They gathered branches and other materials and made a lean-to shelter against the fallen tree trunk. Covered in twigs and leaves, it blended in and, when Rhys checked, it was well camouflaged from more than fifty yards. They lay thin pine branches and needles on the ground inside the shelter and their capes on top to provide a reasonably comfortable 'bed' for the night.

The next day, they lit up the hexamine stove again for a cup of tea and porridge from the ration pack before scattering the shelter they'd built and striking out once more. To the south, they could see the imposing peaks of Pen-y-Fan and its escarpment. At one point, they stopped and took cover when they saw men on the ridge leading to the summit. At that range, it was impossible to make out any details but they eventually disappeared down the other side of the mountain.

"I think they're looking for us south of the peaks. It may not occur to them that we'd take a much longer route around to the north. At least, not 'til they've eliminated sensible alternatives," Rhys said.

"Let's hope that's true. I'd hate to think we'd come all this way and still get caught."

Chapter 18 Escape and Evasion

They didn't see anyone else for the rest of the day and reached their planned halt in another wood by mid-afternoon. A logging trail ran through the wood but they built their shelter out of sight on the other side of a slope.

There was a steep incline to negotiate at the start of their final day but, from then on, it was mainly downhill for the remainder of their journey. The disadvantage was that much of it would be in sight of roads and habitation. They had decided, therefore, to set off by six am. By seven, they'd passed the village that stood between them and their target. The camp lay three-quarters of a mile west of them, along a road they'd arrived at. The check-in point was at the entrance to the camp and its perimeter was likely to be patrolled. The chances were that the sentries would be tired from night duty and less than totally alert but it would be a pity to get caught so close to the finish.

"We'll cross the road and come up to the camp from the south," Rhys told Simon.

As they hid in a copse to observe the traffic, a milk lorry trundled past, the churns on the back clattering as the vehicle bumped over potholes. Once that was out of sight, the pair crossed the road and slid down the bank on the other side into a stream.

They crawled along the edge of the watercourse, keeping their heads down to avoid being seen from the road. Two hundred yards further on, their path took them past a cottage where a dog started barking. The pair of them froze until they heard the owner chastise the animal. The next barrier was a lane. Simon was about to dart across when Rhys grabbed his ankle and pulled him back just as a tractor came into view.

They only had another few hundred yards to go once they crossed the lane. Simon thought they might actually make it against all the odds.

Once more, they hugged the bank of the stream until they were opposite the entrance to the camp.

"Now!" Rhys yelled. They scrambled to their feet and ran over the road and through the camp entrance to the checkpoint.

Chapter 19. Per Ardua

February 1943

Simon attended the RAF recruitment office in the city centre on his 18th birthday.

"So, what role do you want to do?" asked the recruitment sergeant.

"I want to be a pilot, sir, if at all possible," Simon enthused.

The sergeant smiled and laid the pencil he'd been writing with down on the table.

"Yes, well, so do almost all the men who come in here, but there are other jobs that are just as important. And, I'm afraid we have more pilots than aircraft for them to fly now. You look like an intelligent bloke, have you thought about clerk or storesman? Aircrew can't fly without their work you know. Oh, and don't call me 'sir', I'm not an officer, I work for a living."

"I thought there was a shortage of pilots, Sergeant. That's what the ATA pilots told me."

The sergeant looked more closely at Simon at the mention of the ATA.

"Where was this?"

"I work at the aerodrome at Elmdene, it's part of the Civilian Repair Organisation."

"I see, and what do you do there?"

"Officially I'm a general hand but I help with overhauling the engines."

"Tell me more about overhauling engines."

"I dismantle engines and replace worn out or damaged parts then reassemble them. Sometimes I go on air tests in the Oxfords or Battles to make notes to diagnose problems or check out engines after repairs."

"Do you ever get to take the controls?" the sergeant asked as he studied Simon's application form.

Simon wasn't sure how to answer. He didn't want to get anyone into trouble for letting him fly the aircraft unofficially.

The sergeant picked up on his hesitation.

"Don't worry, I'm not going to report anyone. I can imagine any pilot letting a keen lad like you have a go."

"Yes, Sergeant. Once we'd done the tests, the pilots showed me the controls and let me fly the aircraft back to the aerodrome."

"Well Simon, I think we do have the perfect role for you as Flight Engineer. It's an important job. You'll act as the pilot's assistant, monitor the performance of the engines, fuel, oil and cooling systems, carry out emergency repairs in the air and liaise with the maintenance crew at the base. You'll also act as stand-by gunner. I see from your application that you did well on your shooting tests in the Home Guard."

It wasn't quite what he'd hoped for but, at least he'd be aircrew and, as Flight Engineer would effectively take on the role of co-pilot.

With an initial training course starting almost immediately, he reported for duty at the beginning of February. The first few weeks involved being issued uniforms, drill, physical training, map reading, shooting and field exercises; much of which he was familiar with from his time in the Home Guard and the scouts.

They also had lectures on the history and traditions of the RAF including talks about its formation under Hugh Trenchard, and of heroes such as Mannock, Ball, Bishop and, more recently, Douglas Bader who'd fought in the Battle of Britain in spite of having lost both legs in a flying accident.

Simon wondered how he'd live up to those men's examples as he lay in his bed after one such lecture.

Indeed, how would any of the dozen men in his barracks cope with what lay ahead? He looked down the row of six beds on his side of the room matched by six on the other. A coke stove glowed in the middle of the space between the rows of beds; the light reflected off the highly polished linoleum floor. A floor kept as shiny as possible with the efforts of everyone taking turns to swing the heavy 'bumper' from side to side, its felt covering buffing the floor with every swing. And heaven help anyone walking on it wearing boots—other than the Corporal, of course, or the Duty Officer and Sergeant when they made their inspections.

Further down the room, Simon could hear wheezing from one bed and snoring from a third – while there were squeaks and rattles from a third as the occupant tossed and turned trying to get comfortable.

It was very different to his life at the rectory where he'd had his own room. That thought took him to Lucy. Their relationship had faded, though they were still friends. He hadn't felt comfortable when she wanted to do more than kiss and cuddle. All his teachings had told him it was wrong before marriage. But that wasn't the only reason he'd not given in to her. He didn't actually *want* to make love to her. He'd convinced himself that he was respecting her but wondered if it went further. He did really like her; he liked the way she looked and the way she dressed; she always looked so pretty. So why didn't he want to 'go all the way' with her?

He hadn't seen her since Christmas. She'd been invited to an interview in London with the First Aid Nursing Yeomanry. Which was odd as she hated the sight of blood. At Christmas, when he called in to give her a present, he'd overheard her talking to her mother and telling her that the FANY interviewer had tested her on her French – then they'd stopped speaking as soon as he'd entered the room. He'd wondered about whether she was to support French refugees who'd escaped when the Boche invaded. He sighed, then rolled onto his side and turned his mind to tomorrow's training.

In preparation for a camp, they were having lectures on map reading, first aid and knots. Well, that wouldn't pose any problems for him.

The next morning, the class were given short lengths of rope by a giant of an RAF Regiment Sergeant.

"Watch carefully," he barked. "I'm going to demonstrate how to tie a reef knot. This is to join two pieces of rope of similar thickness. You will then do the knot yourselves."

Simon sighed. The reef knot was one of the first he'd learned in the Wolf Cubs ten years ago. He took his rope into his lap out of sight of the sergeant and tied it without looking. He finished before the instructor held his knotted rope above his head for the trainees to see.

"Right. You do the same."

He stared at Simon who sat in the front row, motionless.

"Come on lad, surely you can do that."

Simon held up his rope with the perfect knot tied.

The sergeant looked through hooded eyelids, then moved along the row to check the next recruit's attempt. Satisfied the class had managed the reef knot, he then demonstrated the sheet bend, figure of eight and fisherman's knots. Each time, Simon had completed the knot almost as soon as the sergeant had said its name. This really was too easy.

"Finally, I'm going to show you the bowline. This makes a non-slip loop which can be used to lower someone down a mountain. Make a loop in the rope, that's the 'hole' and the long part of the rope is the 'tree' and the shorter end is the 'snake' to help you remember how to do it. Now watch, the snake comes out of the hole, goes around the tree and back down the hole. Got it?"

Simon had learned to do the bowline one-handed with his eyes closed before he was ten years old. He'd completed his before the sergeant.

"Not so easy, eh lad?" the instructor challenged seeing Simon sitting still while others were tying their knots.

Once again, Simon held up his rope for inspection.

"Now, I'm going to demonstrate how to lower someone down a mountainside on a stretcher. We need a volunteer." The sergeant pointed at Simon. "You'll do."

His cockiness with the knots had come home to roost, but he lay down on the stretcher so he could be securely tied to it.

"Now, to demonstrate how effective this is, we'll turn the stretcher over. I'll take the head, you two take the feet," he said, pointing to two of the other recruits.

Within a few moments, Simon found himself facing the floor from a distance of about three inches, his nose even closer, his arms strapped to his sides and unable to move. He'd never felt so helpless before. Perhaps he shouldn't attract attention in future. When he was eventually turned back over and released, the instructor held out his hand and helped him get to his feet. As Simon looked at him, he saw the hint of a smile on his lips. He had a feeling that the message was 'Don't think you can get one over me,' but the twinkle in the sergeant's eyes suggested he wasn't in trouble. At least, not this time.

The exercise over the next few days reminded Simon of the 'Escape and Evasion' operation he'd done in the Home Guard with Rhys Williamson. This time, however, when the instructor told them they were 'aircrew who had bailed out over occupied Europe, trying to avoid capture,' it was almost certain that at least a few of those present would find themselves in that situation within a matter of months. Each of the men at the briefing knew, of course, that it wouldn't be them – but they'd still do the best they could.

Simon and his partner for the exercise, a Geordie lad called Jack Hodges, were captured on the second day, trying to cross a road. Simon had crossed first and was hiding in a ditch on the other side when Jack started across just as a lorry came around the corner. He'd immediately turned back to find cover but twisted his ankle and couldn't put any weight on it and was spotted hobbling the few yards back to the ditch.

Other trainees had been caught on the first day so they didn't feel too bad about their performance.

At the end of the initial training, those who had been successful took part in a passing out parade. Three others who had just missed making the grade were 're-treaded' and joined the following course to have a second attempt to pass. If they failed a second time they would remain as 'erks', the lowest form of life in the RAF instead of training as Flight Engineers.

With a few weeks before the next engineering course, the intake, including Simon, was sent on Junior NCO training as they would be promoted to Sergeant if they were eventually appointed as Flight Engineers – an attempt to ensure better treatment if they ever became prisoners of war. The group lost three more of its number at the end of this stage. Two were held back to join the next tranche; one was not considered suitable for promotion to Non-Commissioned Officer and was sent for training as a ground engineer instead.

"What do you think they'll do with us now, Simon?" asked Jack Hodges who had scraped through the course.

"Well, there's still a month before our engineering training at St Athan. Maybe they'll send us on a gunnery course. They might even give us a month's leave instead of just the usual week."

"Pigs might fly! No chance of them giving us a month off. Still, gunnery could be fun. Quite fancy blasting away with four Brownings."

"So long as we don't have to do it for real," Simon mused. "It'd mean we'd be in trouble if we were taking over from a gunner."

Simon's prediction came true. A notice appeared on the board that afternoon announcing they were to attend gunnery school at RAF Sutton Bridge.

"Where the heck is Sutton Bridge?" asked Jack as he and Simon studied the notice.

"The other side of the country, near Kings Lynn."

"I'm still none the wiser, Simon"

"Good job you're not training as a navigator then, isn't it?"

Chapter 20. Leave

April 1943

After completing the gunnery course, Simon and the other members of his cohort dispersed for a well-deserved leave. The journey across country from the flatlands of the Fens at Sutton Bridge, skirting the southern edge of the Midlands, to the gentle hills of the Cotswolds around Elmdene, took Simon nearly twelve hours. This included interminable waits for connections and other delays as they were held for priority trains to pass.

He took advantage of changing from the London Midland and Scottish Railway onto the Great Western at Royal Leamington Spa to leave his kitbag in the left luggage and wander into the town for some refreshments.

He found a pub not far from the station. The bar was half full and a smoke haze hung below the ceiling and shone in the sunlight through the windows. A group of three men stood at the bar while two others played darts.

"Make way for the RAF," called out one as Simon made his way to the bar.

"What can I get you?" asked the barmaid, a woman Simon estimated to be in her mid-thirties, wearing a low-cut blouse displaying an ample bosom.

"A pint of bitter and can you do a sandwich?"

"Yes, love. Spam or cheese?"

"Cheese please."

"Your sandwich will be a minute or two." the barmaid, said as she served him his pint. "Don't mind me saying, but you look young to be in the RAF."

"I'm old enough," he said before taking a draft of his beer. "I signed up on my eighteenth birthday."

"Good for you love. My old man was in the mob. Air gunner he was. Shot down last year."

"Sorry to hear that. I've just finished gunnery training myself."

"Well, best of luck to you. But, if you've finished your training where's your brevet and shouldn't you be a Sergeant?"

"I'm not a gunner, I'm training as a Flight Engineer." As he said it, he wondered if he should have revealed anything remembering the 'Be like Dad, Keep Mum.' posters.

"That explains it. Don't worry I won't tell old Adolf!"

The man standing next to Simon turned to him, took a puff on his pipe, adding to the smoke curling up to the yellowed ceiling.

"You give them hell lad when you get the chance. My old lady was killed in the Coventry blitz in 1940. The shelter took a direct hit. I was fire-watching when it happened. Bastards the lot of them, excuse my French."

It brought home the civilian cost of the war. He'd recognised that servicemen died but neither Andover nor Elmdene had been targeted – in fact, so far, the only enemy aircraft he'd seen had been the raid that led to the Heinkel crashing at the aerodrome. He knew the raids on Coventry had, however, been bad.

"Sorry to hear about your wife, sir." Simon seemed to be apologising to everyone today. "I'll certainly do what I can to hit back."

After eating his sandwich, he drained the last of his beer, put on his greatcoat, made his goodbyes and returned to the station.

His train had been due fifteen minutes after he reached the platform but, inevitably, was nearly an hour late. When it did arrive, it was packed and he had to stand until he changed again at Stratford-upon-Avon. Most of the compartments were busy but, as he looked into one, a woman picked up her young son, put him on her lap and offered him the seat the boy had been sitting on.

Simon hoisted his kitbag onto the luggage rack then sat down.

"Thanks very much, missus."

"That's all right. Are you going far?"

"Elmdene, on leave." It hardly gave any information away to reveal that much. "How about you?"

"Westchester."

The boy, Simon estimated him to be about four or five years old, looked at him and whispered something to his mother.

"I don't know darling, why don't you ask him?"

The boy buried his head in his mother's shoulder, too shy to look at Simon.

Simon looked at her and raised an eyebrow.

"Sorry, he asked if you were a pilot."

"No, I'm not a pilot. I look after the aeroplane's engines." Simon told him. "What's your name? Mine's Simon."

The boy looked up at his mother.

"Go on, answer him. You can tell him your name."

"Peter," he finally said.

"Nice to meet you, Peter."

Peter turned his head away and stared out of the window as the train chugged its way along an embankment, over a small bridge with a stream running through it. A herd of cows grazed in the next field, lifting their heads as the train passed. Houses ran parallel to the track with a meadow between their back gardens and the bottom of the embankment. In the middle of the field, a group of three lads and a girl sat on or stood next to the trunk of a tree that lay on the ground. The children waved to the train and Simon saw two of them writing something in notebooks – probably the engine number he thought. He'd never been a trainspotter himself, he preferred more modern forms of transport.

Once the train had left Prestham, Simon lifted his kitbag from the rack and made his way to the carriage door ready to dismount. He lowered the window and, ignoring the sign cautioning against the practice, stuck his head out as the train approached Elmdene station. He gripped the handle, twisted it and opened the door as the train slowed next to the platform. He then stepped out before the train came to a complete stop. As he passed the engine, he waved at the driver and fireman.

"Thanks for the safe trip," he shouted. His call was acknowledged by a nod from the driver.

Simon, kitbag on his shoulder, strode out of the station and turned towards the village. The sun was setting as he tramped up the hill but there was still sufficient light for him to see his way.

Chapter 20 Leave

"You should have phoned from the station. I could have picked you up," his uncle reproached him when he opened the door. "Your mother's in the kitchen."

"I'd been cooped up in trains for hours so needed to stretch my legs anyway, Uncle and I didn't want you wasting your petrol ration," he said, shaking hands.

He dropped his kitbag on the floor as the door to the kitchen opened and his mother stood there wiping her hands on her apron. He walked over to her and they hugged tightly.

"Good to see you, son. You've lost weight, don't they feed you? We ate earlier but there's some rabbit stew left for you."

"Good to see you too mum, the stew sounds fine. Is Mary not around?"

"She's at Guides but should be back soon with Grace and Daphne. Mary's very proud of her big brother."

Simon followed his mother into the large kitchen where his Aunt Ida was ladling a large helping of the stew into a dish for him. He washed his hands at the sink before sitting down at the table.

"There you are, love," Ida said, putting the bowl in front of him.

He inhaled the aroma and turned to his aunt, "Smells great."

He took a spoonful.

"That's delicious, much better than we get in the mess."

While he ate, Mary came bursting into the kitchen, ran over to Simon, threw her arms around him and planted a kiss on his cheek.

"Sally and I have been allowed to go up from Brownies to Guides a few months early," she told him. "That's because we'd already passed all of our badges. And there were other younger girls wanting to start Brownies so we made space for them."

"Well done, Mary. So, which patrol are you in?"

"I'm in Kingfisher patrol. Or, I will be when I'm enrolled." Mary broke a piece of bread off the slice resting on his plate, dipped it into the stew and popped it in her mouth.

"Hey, you little minx, that's my dinner," he scolded – his eyes giving away that he was teasing.

Daphne and Grace had followed Mary into the kitchen and greeted Simon then poured themselves a cup of tea before sitting at the table.

"Have you heard from Lucy recently?" Grace asked.

"Not since Christmas. Why? Isn't she in London with the FANYs?"

"That's where she said she was going but she hasn't kept in touch and her mother seems evasive if we ask about her."

"Maybe she's found someone else down there and thinks it might upset me if I found out."

"Wouldn't it? You seemed very close at one time."

"We were, but we're just friends these days. I don't think we wanted the same things."

"Well, if you do hear from her, tell her not to forget us."

The next morning, Simon asked his uncle if there were any jobs he needed doing around the rectory.

"Thank you, yes there's some logs that could be cut up and some of them made into kindling. You could also dig over the potato patch and fork in some manure ready for planting, if you've got time. I must admit, with five churches to look after, it's a struggle to do everything in the garden as well. Your mother and aunt do what they can but the potatoes are heavy work."

"Not a problem, Uncle. I'm going to cycle over to the aerodrome later to see Mr Robertson and the others and I want to look up my instructors at the Technical School. Maybe I can come along to the Scout meeting too, while I'm here."

"Sounds like you've got a busy schedule."

Chapter 21. Technical Training

April – September 1943

A week later, Simon stood in the hall of the rectory, his packed kitbag at his side.

"You look after yourself, son. Don't take unnecessary risks, do you hear?"

"Yes mum, I hear. Don't worry, I've still got months of training to do, almost all of it on the ground before being posted to a squadron."

Mary stood on tiptoes and wrapped her arms around her brother's neck and kissed him."

"You look after mum, now Mary," he told her.

"I will. But you look after yourself too," she replied, echoing their mother.

With a final kiss for his Aunt Ida and a shake of his uncle's hand, Simon hoisted his kitbag onto his shoulder, put on his side cap, or 'chip bag' as it was usually referred to, and, with a final wave, strode down the hill towards the station while his mother wiped tears from the corners of her eyes.

St Athan was very much larger than previous RAF stations he'd been posted to and was spread over two camps, East and West split by the cross runway.

Having reported in and been directed to his accommodation, Simon found the appropriate barracks and chose his bed from those that were still free. He already knew most of his roommates from their earlier training but there were a couple who were re-doing the course who were able to show the newcomers around.

He soon discovered that Flight Engineer training was in a state of flux with different groups following different programmes. Candidates had been taken originally from existing ground engineering staff but the role had been opened up to direct entry from outside the service when that route couldn't provide the numbers needed. Some of the new recruits, including Simon, had previously worked on aircraft, some on motor vehicles while others were starting from scratch.

The intake was assigned to particular aircraft types at random. The instructor had called out "Who has a seven in his service number?" "Who has a hole in his sock?" or other arbitrary question. If the numbers answering roughly matched the requirement for Lancasters, Halifaxes, Stirlings, Sunderlands or Flying Fortresses, the group would be allocated accordingly.

Having worked on Merlin engines, Simon hoped for Lancasters – but the 'nine' in his service number consigned him to Short Stirlings, the first of the four-engine heavy bombers to enter service. It wasn't a popular choice. It had a much lower operating ceiling than Lancasters and Halifaxes – and higher losses.

When they were dismissed from the parade, Simon turned to a friend from initial training.

"What have you got, Tony?"

"Sunderland flying boats, what about you?"

"Stirlings,"

"Oh, bad luck."

With his previous practical experience and his technical school training, Simon was assigned to an accelerated programme. For practical work, he was partnered with one of the other students. From his accent, he thought Henry Palmer was out of place; he'd have expected him to be an officer rather than an NCO. But Henry's choice was his concern and none of his business. He certainly didn't seem standoffish when they worked together.

As they were working on an engine, Simon's spanner slipped and he scraped his knuckles.

« Merde! » he exclaimed, using a word that Lucy's mother would not have approved of her daughter teaching him.

« Tu parles français? » Henry asked.

« My former girlfriend was half French and taught me so I could speak to her mother in her own language. How do you know French? » Simon asked continuing in the same language.

« I lived in Paris. My father was in the diplomatic service, we got out just before the Germans arrived. I used to help my father's chauffeur service our car and got interested in engines which is why I applied for Flight Engineer. »

« So, if you don't mind me asking, why haven't you gone for a commission? » As Henry had brought up his background, Simon didn't feel he was intruding with his question.

« I want to fly and engineering officers are nearly all ground based. »

« I see, that makes sense. Would you mind if I practised my French with you? » Simon asked.

« Pas du tout, » Henry replied.

After hundreds of hours of lectures, practical work and spending time at aero engine manufacturer's factories, Simon passed out in the top ten per cent of his course and was now entitled to wear the Flight Engineer's brevet of a single wing and the letter E above his left breast pocket and sergeant's stripes on his arms.

His next posting was to an Operational Conversion Unit where he would join a four-engine bomber crew, probably one that had just completed their training on Wellingtons which didn't carry Flight Engineers.

"Where are you posted, Simon?"

"Stradishall, wherever that is. How about you, Henry?"

"Pembroke Dock – deepest Wales. Isn't Stradishall somewhere in Suffolk?"

"God knows. Well, I'll soon find out. Where are you spending your leave, at home?"

"Yes, better go and see the parents. I might try to fit in a couple of nights in London before heading for Chester."

Simon collected his rail warrants for both his trip home for leave and from Elmdene to Haverhill, which, he was told, was the closest station to Stradishall.

The platform at St Athan was packed with dozens of men in RAF blue, many with their newly awarded sergeant's stripes and aircrew badges, when the train from Swansea pulled in. Almost all of them would be spreading out from Cardiff for London, the south coast, Birmingham and the Midlands, the north or even Scotland or Northern Ireland. Some were likely to be travelling for more than twenty-four hours. Simon's journey to Elmdene was relatively short.

Chapter 22. Ad Astra

September 1943

The skies opened as the train pulled out of Prestham on the first leg of Simon's cross-country journey to Haverhill.

"Looks like we made it just in time, Sarge," a corporal sharing his compartment remarked.

"Yes, thank goodness."

"You heading far?"

"Fair enough, what about you?"

"Brize Norton. It's the heavy glider conversion unit. I work in the stores. What are you on? Lancs or Halifaxes?"

"Stirlings."

"Oh, right. Done many ops?"

"No, just joining the operational conversion unit."

"Well, best of luck."

With that, the corporal closed his eyes and fell asleep.

Simon thought back to his leave. As usual, he'd done some odd jobs around the rectory, visited his old colleagues at the airfield and his tutors at the Technical School. Having completed his training, he no longer felt like a student or the odd job boy but as an adult ready to take his place among other fighting men.

There had been no sign of Lucy; she was apparently still in London as far as anyone knew.

Out of the window, Simon watched the gentle hills of the Cotswolds give way to lower ground as the railway followed the valley of a river which tumbled over outcrops causing bursts of white shoals. Trees, beginning to turn browns, reds and golds, crowded the banks of the river while hedgerows laden with red and black berries bordered the roads and the railway line.

The train passed occasional cottages and farmhouses built from the buff-coloured local stone topped with dark slate roofs. As the land flattened, pastures gave way to fields of oats, barley and wheat. Farm labourers and land girls worked in the fields to gather in the last of the harvest, encouraging horses pulling trailers or ploughs to greater effort. In other fields, and on the lanes between them, tractors, belching black smoke from their exhaust stacks had replaced the horses.

Simon sighed. The scene reminded him of the time spent with his father at the forge, his dad shoeing the horses while he worked on the tractors. Now he was about to start the last stage of his training to help get a twenty-five-ton aircraft a thousand miles or more into enemy territory and drop six tons of bombs from sixteen thousand feet. The contrast could hardly be starker.

At Oxford, he stretched his legs and freshened up in the gents then had a cup of tea while he waited for his connection on the 'Varsity Line' to Cambridge. The station canopies and other nearby buildings hid Oxford's dreaming spires described by Matthew Arnold. The platforms were busy as trains from London en route for the Midlands, the West Country and mid-Wales and those heading in the opposite direction pulled in; followed by others from the Midlands and the North going to south coast ports – or taking goods from Southampton that had survived an Atlantic convoy to factories around Birmingham as well as others, like Simon's, heading across country.

Men and women from all of the services gathered in the buffets and waiting rooms. There were uniforms of all colours: RAF blue-grey, the darker blues of the Royal and Merchant Navies and other shades of Empire and Allied forces and hues of greens and browns. Mixed with them were other uniforms – police, fire, nurses and railway staff.

By late-afternoon, Simon's train was approaching Bedford. Tall chimneys marked the brickworks to the south of the town.

"Largest brickworks in the world," remarked one of the other passengers. "I noticed you looking at the chimneys," he added to explain his uninvited comment.

"Is that right? They certainly look huge."

"It's all the clay that this area stands on and it's not far from London. With all the bombing, there's a big demand for bricks of course."

The stranger stood up to retrieve his bag from the luggage rack.

"Well, nice to meet you. This is my stop. Good luck."

As the train pulled out the other side of Bedford, Simon could see the enormous hangars he knew had been built for the R101 airship designed by the same man that had invented the mines used to attack the Ruhr dams four months earlier. Barnes Wallis' name had been whispered around St Athan because he'd also designed the Wellington bomber. The R101 no longer existed but Simon could see a scattering of barrage balloons now manufactured there near the giant hangar.

The country was now relatively flat as it followed the valley of the meandering River Ouse. The golden stones of the Cotswold village cottages earlier in the journey had been replaced by red bricks, presumably from the brickworks they'd passed. Then it was on to strange sounding stops: Sandy, Potton and Gamlingay before the colleges of Cambridge appeared alongside the track.

Relieved to be making his final change, Simon made use of the facilities before climbing into the second carriage behind an elderly tank engine. The sound of a whistle followed by a jerk as the engine took up the slack and the train pulled out in a cloud of smoke and steam, gradually picking up speed before slowing again after less than ten minutes to call at the next station.

Finally, as the train pulled into yet another stop, the stationmaster on the platform called out.

"Ayvrill, this is Haverhill. Change here for the Colne Valley and Halstead line."

Simon looked around as he came out into the car park, immediately spotting a five hundredweight RAF utility vehicle, affectionately known as a Tilly, parked outside. A WAAF, wearing the twin propellor insignia of a Leading Aircraftwoman, leant against the mudguard smoking a cigarette. Seeing the RAF roundel and B/3 that indicated it belonged to Bomber Command 3 Group, which included Stradishall, Simon guessed it was his transport.

Seeing him approach, the WAAF straightened up and pinched out her cigarette.

"You here for me?" Simon asked. "My name is Ferguson." He was still not used to claiming his rank.

"Yes, Sergeant. I'm LACW Walsh. Do you want to put your kitbag in the back?"

He did as she suggested then joined her in the front of the little vehicle. She pulled out of the station car park and drove back towards the west before turning right up a long hill that challenged the Tilly's ten horsepower engine.

"Have you been stationed at Stradishall long?" Simon enquired as they reached the top of the hill and the vehicle started to speed up, the canvas cover behind the cab flapping in the wind.

"Two years, Sarge. Since completing my training. Mind you, I'm from Haverhill. I was happy to leave when I joined up. There's not much to do. Joke was on me, though, wasn't it? I got posted to Strad instead of somewhere more interesting."

"So, what's the camp like?"

"It's not too bad, it was built before the war so the accommodation is mainly in permanent buildings rather than Nissan huts. It's remote, of course. Haverhill is the nearest town and that's little more than a village as you saw. There's a couple of pubs either end of Strad and another in Cowlinge. If you've got transport, Newmarket's about ten miles from the 'drome and, if you keep on this road, Bury St Edmunds is about twelve miles. Few more pubs in either Newmarket or Bury."

They drove in silence for the next few miles.

"We're just coming up on the camp now, you can't see it, but the main runway is just over there," she said pointing out of her window. "The officers' married quarters and mess are on the right around this next bend, then you'll have the sergeants' mess on the left and the station technical area on the right. Do you want to drop your kit at the mess before reporting in? Save you carrying it later."

"Good idea, thanks."

The driver waited until he came back out of the mess then drove him to the guardroom where he officially reported his arrival.

The Tilly had gone by the time he had finished and the Duty Sergeant had given him directions back to the sergeants' mess.

"Thanks, see you around, perhaps."

"More than likely."

As he walked towards SHQ, he heard the roar of aero engines approaching from behind him. He stopped and turned around in time to see a Stirling bomber fly overhead then continue over the airfield before it disappeared in the darkness. He heard it returning to line up with the runway and land.

Simon straightened his side cap and strode out, saluting an officer who came out of SHQ as he turned up the path as he'd been directed.

Chapter 23. Meet the Stirling

September 1943

After breakfast in the mess, Simon walked through the camp to the briefing room. The skipper, Pilot Officer Chapman, introduced the rest of the crew.

"We're quite a mixture. Like me, Alf Stewart is from Canada. Steve Murray is from the Australian outback. Eric Hunter, who's well-named as he's our rear gunner, is from South Africa. Donald Webb and Gordon Campbell are from Scotland. Don's the other newcomer to the crew as mid-upper gunner. The rest of us have been training together on Wellingtons. Guys, this is Simon Ferguson. For those who can't read the E on his brevet, Simon's our Flight Engineer."

Simon raised his hand to acknowledge the welcomes.

The other members of the crew all looked a year or so older than him. The skipper sported a David Niven moustache, possibly to make him seem a little older than he was. Or maybe it was the start of a full handlebar set, Simon mused. He brushed the top of his own lip – there was no chance of him growing a moustache. He hardly ever needed to shave though he went through the motions every morning. Chapman wasn't tall but was still a couple of inches taller than him. In fact, looking around it was apparent that he was the shortest member of the crew. He felt he was back at the first year of 'big school' amongst all the older and bigger pupils.

He hadn't taken in all of the others' names but he could identify their roles from the initials on their brevets. The wireless operator was probably the tallest member of the crew, not far short of six feet, Simon estimated. He was well built and, if he played sport, Simon guessed it would be rugby.

The two Scots, Campbell and Webb, were talking together, but which was which? Was Campbell the bomb aimer or the new mid-upper gunner?

Apart from P/O Bill Chapman and Alf Stewart, the crew were all sergeants and would be living in the same mess which would give him a chance to get to know them better.

"Do you want a coffee, Simon? I'm Eric, in case you missed the names when Bill introduced us all. We've got an unofficial percolator."

"Coffee would be great, thanks. Yes, it was a bit much to take in all at once. Where in South Africa are you from?"

"Do you know South Africa? I'm from near Cape Town."

"I know roughly where Cape Town is, but, no, I don't know South Africa at all. We don't get taught much about it apart from the Cape colonies and the Boer War and the relief of Mafeking."

"Well, that's probably more than the average person knows, but it's a beautiful country."

At that moment, a Squadron Leader and Flight Lieutenant entered the room. The skipper called them to attention.

"Sit down gentlemen, please. My name is Squadron Leader Cunningham. I'll be responsible for your training here at Stradishall. The first phase is two weeks ground training to get you all familiar with your positions on a Stirling, especially for the pilot, flight engineer and wireless operator. After that, you'll start flying the aircraft, initially with Flight Lieutenant Barrett and his crew. As a first step, we are going to have a look at a Stirling."

Simon's first impression of the aircraft was its huge size.

If he hadn't seen one overhead the previous day, he would have questioned whether something that big could really fly. It was twice as long and twice the height and width of the Fairey Battle aircraft he'd worked on. The main undercarriage wheels were taller than he was. The four Bristol Hercules engines he'd be responsible for each produced 1600 horsepower, clearly more than enough to haul this monster into the air.

The pilot stood looking up at the cockpit towering above him.

"Hell, we'll still be up in the clouds when the wheels hit the runway, Skipper," Campbell remarked.

"True, and from all accounts, they don't float at all, they just drop like a stone if you're not careful. Come on, let's see what it's like inside."

The crew followed the pilot through the fuselage door at the rear of the aircraft and Simon climbed the steep slope to the flight engineer's and wireless operator's panels just forward of the wings. Beyond them was the navigator's table and the pilot's cockpit forward of him. The main wing spar cut across the fuselage aft of the wireless operator's desk with various internal stores on top of the spar and a rest bunk under it. Simon suspected there wouldn't be much opportunity to use the bunk on operations.

At the nose of the aircraft, was the front gunner's turret with twin Browning machine guns and below was the bomb aimer's prone position. Behind Simon's station, was an upper gun turret, also with twin Brownings and, right at the back, the four-gun rear turret.

Simon turned his attention to the panel for which he was responsible with gauges indicating engine output, oil pressure, temperature and the stopcocks for the seven fuel tanks located in the wings. He'd seen mock-ups of the panel but the actual equipment brought home what he'd be faced with and the added complications of the noise from the four engines, the airflow and, almost certainly, explosions from flak and the Stirling's own guns if they were attacked by fighters plus being shaken around as the aircraft was buffeted by up and down drafts or nearby flak explosions – not to mention any evasive manoeuvres by the pilot.

'Oh well,' he thought, 'too late to back out now.'

After two weeks of intensive training on the ground, the crew was finally driven around the perimeter track to a dispersal point on the far side of the airfield. They alighted from the bus and gathered around the aircraft that had been allocated for their introduction to flying the Stirling. As they'd been told, for their first few flights, each member of the crew would be supervised by their opposite number from Flt Lt Barrett's crew. The instructors had recently finished a 'tour' of thirty missions and were being 'rested' before their next posting.

The Flight Sergeant in command of the ground crew reported to Barrett.

"Everything in order, Chiefy?" Barrett asked.

"Yes, sir. Top of the line."

Barrett, Chapman and Simon and his instructor walked around the aircraft to carry out their own pre-flight checks. Simon ensuring there were no leaks from the engines or hydraulic systems. Satisfied that all was well, they climbed aboard where more checks were carried out before the engines were started, then more before the signal to remove the chocks from the huge main wheels could be given.

The aircraft then followed the taxiway to the eastern end of runway 24 which pointed into the prevailing south-westerly winds. P/O Chapman applied the brakes and ran up the engines under Barrett's watchful eyes. Simon watched his gauges as the pilot gave more power to the starboard engines to counteract a tendency for the Stirling to swing in that direction. Then they were off, trundling down the mile-long runway, gradually building up speed until the wheels left the ground and Simon heard the undercarriage being retracted followed by the flaps. All of the gauges were within normal ranges as the aircraft climbed to cruising height.

"Captain to gunners, we shouldn't encounter any enemy fighters, but keep your eyes peeled in any case."

The nose, mid-upper and tail gunners all acknowledged the instruction.

The first flight was mainly to get the crew used to the Stirling – especially the pilot – and the instructors didn't throw any challenges at them. After about two hours, they landed back at Stradishall and taxied to their dispersal point where the aircraft was refuelled and the ground crew serviced it.

While waiting for the crew bus to pick them up, Simon looked around the horizon. Stradishall appeared to be the highest point as far as he could see.

One of the ground crew saw him looking.

"Nothing between us and the North Sea and when an easterly wind blows, we know about it. Freezes the whatsits off."

"I can well believe it," Simon replied. "Should think it's pretty isolated in winter."

"I've not been here that long, but I'm told it sometimes gets cut off by snow."

The bus drew up and the crew climbed aboard to be taken back to the flight office where they were debriefed.

Over the next three days, they undertook more training flights, carrying out 'circuit and bumps' – taking off, flying around the airfield then touching down on the runway before opening up the throttles and taking off again without stopping. Once the instructor was happy with P/O Chapman's performance, he climbed out of the Stirling and left him to go solo. The next phase was to repeat the 'circuit and bumps' at another airfield then at night. More complex flights were then added with cross-country trips to challenge the navigator, practice bombing runs first with dummy bombs then live explosives and mock attacks from RAF fighters.

After one trip, the crew returned to their flight office to be debriefed. They didn't notice an instructor from one of the other flights enter the office, casually light a cigarette then discard the match into the stove. It was only when he threw open a window and jumped out, followed by other crews from their flight, that they wondered what was going on. A few seconds later there was a hiss and crackle and a red glow from the stove followed by coloured smoke that filled the room. The visitor had dropped the powder from Very cartridges onto the burning coke with his used match.

In the mess that evening, Simon was drinking a beer watching a game of 'Are you there Moriarty?' which involved two blindfolded men lying head-to-head, their left arms extended and gripping the other's left hand. They held 'clubs' made from rolled up newspapers in their right hand. One would call out 'Are you there Moriarty?' and the other would have to reply – allowing the first to aim a blow at his head. The roles would then be reversed.

With the intense training, using old aircraft no longer fit for front-line service, and inexperienced crews, accidents were inevitable and Simon reflected that it was hardly surprising that the crews and instructors found ways to let off steam with occasional hi-jinks.

Chapter 24. Operational

Late September 1943

On completion of their training, the crew were posted to another station a few miles away from Stradishall. They hardly had time to unpack their kit and make their numbers with their squadron commander before they were listed for operations the following day.

After breakfast, the crew was driven out to their aircraft, P-Patsy, to carry out an air test to check that everything was working including oxygen supplies, heated flying suits, the eight Browning machine guns and, in Simon's case, the engines. They then dispersed to their messes for lunch before meeting again for the briefing in the afternoon.

Bill Chapman and Alf Stewart, as pilot and navigator, attended the navigation briefing. They took their places at trestle tables and waited apprehensively for news of their target. The gen picked up from the ground crew was that the aircraft was to be loaded with mines which if, pukka, meant a gardening mission – laying mines to attack German coastal shipping. The planned fuel load was relatively light – so it wasn't likely to be a long trip. It could, however, still involve some dicey targets.

A shuffling of chairs on the wooden floor, as those present stood up, indicated the arrival of the briefing team led by the Station and Squadron Commanding Officers, Flight Commanders, the Met and Intelligence Officers and other specialists. The door to the briefing room closed behind them to be guarded by RAF Police. They took their places on a raised platform at the end of the room. Behind them were curtains similar to those in front of cinema screens.

"Sit down, gentlemen, please," instructed the CO. "The target for tonight is…" He nodded at an aide who pulled back the curtains, revealing a map. "The estuary of the Elbe and Wesel rivers. The main bomber force will also be operating tonight so we hope to split the German defences." He used a billiard cue to point to the ribbons on the map.

"Your route is out over the coast at Cromer. You throw in a dogleg feinting towards the Ruhr before your final turn into the target area – keep clear of the flak batteries on the Frisian Islands. Navigators, get your exact locations for turning points from the Navigation Leader."

The Intelligence Officer took over from the CO. "We've provided details of known flak and night fighter bases in your notes. Nothing has changed, as far as we know, since our last trip to the area."

Finally, the Met Officer provided the latest weather forecasts for the route paying particular attention to anticipated winds and cloud cover.

Alf Stewart made copious notes on his charts during the navigation briefing including anticipated wind speeds and directions, course changes, the time the attack was due to start, and known flak and searchlight positions near their course.

The rest of the crew then joined the briefing for more general information about the operation.

Simon was relieved, when permitted to enter the room by the Snowdrop guarding the door, that their target wasn't 'the Big City' or 'Happy Valley'. The gen from the ground crew had, indeed, proved to be pukka. He knew that sooner or later he was likely to have to attack Berlin and the Ruhr Valley; both heavily defended by flak and demanding long trips facing the gauntlet of night fighters – but it would be good to avoid them for their first operation. He was well aware that inexperienced crews were at most risk of Going for a Burton.

After the briefing, Simon and the remainder of his crew were free to rest until it was time for their last supper before kitting up for the mission. He returned to his barracks and lay on his bed, his arms around the back of his head, eyes closed; trying to remember all he'd been taught; hoping he wouldn't let the rest of the crew down. He tried to put his concerns out of his mind by thinking about the forthcoming meal given to aircrew on operations of bacon and eggs – real eggs, not the powdered stuff. His family were quite fortunate in that respect, as local farmers belonging to his uncle's church sometimes gave them bacon and they had their own hens. But it was a while since his last leave when his mother had sent him on his way with a cooked breakfast.

Others in the barracks were writing letters in case they didn't come back, some were smoking, some reading.

Eventually, Simon looked at his watch and decided it was time to get moving. He swung his legs onto the floor, pulled on his boots and, with other members of his crew, left their hut. More crews appeared from other barrack blocks and joined the cluster of men walking towards the mess, jostling each other and exchanging banter.

After dinner, they headed to the parachute section to collect their Mae West life preservers and parachutes. Simon paid a last visit to the khazi before pulling on his flying suit; there was an Elsan toilet in the aircraft but using it was a major operation and it was a lot easier to do what needed to be done on the ground.

A bus, driven by a WAAF, waited outside the crew room to take the seven of them out to their aircraft. Chapman and Simon carried out a final check and ran up the engines before the pilot signed the Form 700 proffered to him by the Flight Sergeant in charge of the ground crew confirming he was now responsible for a fully serviceable aircraft.

"There you are, Chiefy. See you in a few hours."

"Thank you, sir, have a good trip."

The rest of the crew had gathered at the tail for the traditional wheel pissing for luck, each member taking their turn to urinate over the tailwheel. They then climbed aboard, stowed their parachutes in the racks and took up their positions.

P-Patsy took its turn to join the queue of aircraft taxiing along the perimeter track. Once the aircraft ahead of them had started its take-off run, Chapman manoeuvred onto the runway. At a signal from the control trailer parked nearby, Chapman released the brakes and the Stirling lumbered along the concrete runway, gradually building up speed before leaving the ground.

Once clear of the English coast at Cromer, Chapman flicked the transmit switch on his intercom.

"Gunners you can test your weapons now."

The rattle of eight machine guns quickly filled the aircraft, adding to the roar of the engines.

"Front gunner, weapons fine."

"Mid-upper, fine here too."

"Rear gunner, no problems."

As they flew on, Simon focused on his panel, carefully monitoring the engine temperatures and oil pressures and the fuel levels in the seven tanks. Next to Simon, Stephen Murray, the wireless operator, monitored messages from control. They wouldn't transmit themselves except in an emergency. Forward of him, Alf Stewart, the navigator, plotted their position on his charts and gave course corrections and changes to the pilot.

At the rear of the aircraft, Eric Hunter rotated his turret from side to side. He was in the most vulnerable position as any attack was likely to come from behind. If they were shot down it was by no means certain he'd be able to escape. The turret was so cramped, he had to man it without wearing a parachute. He'd have to swing the turret back in line with the fuselage so he could open the doors behind him, get out, pick up his parachute from the rack, clip it on then bail out – probably while the aircraft was diving to earth.

Forward and above him, Don Webb, the mid-upper gunner also swung his turret from side to side watching for the slightest sign of twin-engine Junkers 88 or Messerschmitt 110 night fighters.

"Enemy coast ahead," Stewart announced bringing everyone to an even higher state of alertness. "Course to target is zero-eight-zero."

Gordon Campbell left his turret and took up his position as bomb aimer. He plugged in his intercom system ready to convey course corrections to the pilot as they commenced their bombing run.

The skipper adjusted the throttles to allow the aircraft to descend to the six hundred feet needed to drop the mines.

Murray released a bundle of window – thin strips of aluminium foil designed to confuse any enemy radar.

Webb and Hunter continued to swing their turrets from side to side keeping a careful watch for night fighters.

"Bomb doors open," announced Campbell.

Simon countered the extra resistance caused by the bomb doors by adjusting the engine throttles as he stood next to the pilot.

"Left a little. Steady. Left a bit. Steady. Steady. Hold that! Steady. Steady. Bombs gone!" declared Campbell as the Stirling, relieved of tons of mines, leapt upwards. Chapman then banked the aircraft away from the target area, diving slightly to build up speed before climbing to sixteen thousand feet, Angels sixteen, for the trip home.

Alf Stewart turned the switch on the front of his oxygen mask to transmit. "Course two-six-five, Skipper."

"Roger. Pilot to crew. Well done everyone. I think our vegetables were bang on."

Simon turned to Murray at his post and gave him a thumbs up. Their gardening trip had been successful. Their vegetables had been planted where intended. Now they could hope that German shipping would be sunk by the mines.

At the debrief, the skipper reported the mission had been a piece of cake, the mines had been laid as briefed and there had been no issues with the aircraft.

"Wizard show," the intelligence officer acknowledged.

Chapter 25. Hit

Late September 1943

Two days later, Simon and the other sergeants from his crew walked over to the flight room after breakfast.

"We're on again tonight," Pilot Officer Chapman announced as they joined him at the notice board.

"Wonder what it'll be this time, Skip?" Gordon Campbell mused.

"We'll find out soon enough."

"I see we've got P-Patsy again," Simon said.

"Let's get out to her then, and do an air test if the ground crew have finished with her."

The test confirmed that the aircraft was serviceable – with only minimal issues for the ground crew to deal with.

As the crew bus drove around the perimeter track, they passed other aircraft at their dispersal pans. Armourers were already winching the bomb loads into some of the aircraft while others were being fuelled from bowsers drawn up to the wings.

"Looks like another gardening run," Simon remarked. "They're loading mines again."

His theory was confirmed at the afternoon briefing. Their target was the eastern end of the Keil Canal and the shipping lanes to Norway, Sweden and the Baltic. The route ribbons on the map showed feints towards the Ruhr before crossing the Jutland peninsular.

Still keen to avenge his father's death, Simon wanted to hit back as hard as he could. He accepted that there was a chance he'd be a casualty. He considered those who thought it could never happen to them had their heads in the sand. He hoped it wouldn't happen to him, but, if it did, well, that was the luck of the draw. He just prayed he'd do his duty and not let his mates down and not fail due to Lack of Moral Fibre.

"Enemy coast ahead," warned Alf Stewart. "Seventy-five miles to target. Course zero-eight-five. Twenty-four minutes at current speed." Stewart made another note on his chart. He didn't have time to think about anything other than where they were, where they needed to be and how to get there as he sat in his curtained-off position.

"Roger, Navigator," acknowledged Chapman, touching his lucky mascot teddy bear hanging from a switch. "Gunners, keep your eyes peeled."

In the upper turret, Don Webb shook his head. What did the skipper think they'd been doing for the last couple of hours? He continued to swing his turret from side to side. Eric Hunter in the rear turret did the same, wondering why he'd left South Africa where all he'd faced were lions, leopards and hippos. They were dangerous enough but he was in control of his actions. Stuck in the back of a Stirling, he was dependant on where the pilot flew them and he had to go where he'd been ordered to attack.

Gordon Campbell left his front guns and took his place at the bomb aimer's position. From there, he could advise the navigator as they passed over the checkpoints they'd planned.

Two minutes later, P-Patsy was over land. Searchlights off to their starboard side caught one of the other aircraft, a second searchlight also fastened onto it but it broke their hold leaving the beams of light flicking from side to side as they tried to find them again.

Lying in the nose, Campbell wiped sweat off his brow as he watched the searchlights probing the blackness.

Anti-aircraft guns fired at P-Patsy as it sped overhead, the shots close enough to buffet them but not cause any significant damage.

Stephen Murray keyed a message in Morse to advise HQ that they were crossing the coast – there was no need now for radio silence.

Simon monitored his engine instruments and adjusted the crossflow of fuel from one tank to another.

Once past the coastal defences, they weaved towards their target – ensuring their track wasn't predictable – and banked gently from side to side to give the gunners the chance to check blind spots below the wings for any fighters that might be trying to sneak up on them.

"Twenty miles to target, Skip. We cross the coast again in three minutes. We change course on to one-two-zero in five minutes."

"Roger, Navigator."

Chapman reduced power to the engines and pushed the nose down to descend to the attack height.

"Coast coming up now, crossing now," Gordon Campbell announced.

Stewart glanced at his watch and marked his chart. "Bang on schedule. Come on to one-two-zero in thirty seconds."

Chapman levelled the Stirling off at six hundred feet and held the aircraft on course until the bomb aimer announced that the mines had been dropped – not that he needed to be told, as the aircraft, now several tons lighter, leapt upwards. They then closed the bomb bay doors and turned onto a new course given by the navigator.

"The Boche will know we're here and have had chance to get ready for our return flight – so stay alert everyone," Chapman reminded the crew.

Simon compared fuel consumption with the anticipated rates and was satisfied the predictions had been reasonably accurate and there was sufficient to get them back to base with a reserve.

"Corkscrew starboard, Skipper," cried Hunter from the rear turret as he opened fire. "We've got a Junkers 88 behind us."

The aircraft dived down to the right then pulled up and to the left as it tried to throw the night fighter off their tail.

Webb in the upper turret joined in the firing as the Junkers passed them on the port side before veering away.

"He's coming back in for another run from port," Webb warned.

Simon couldn't see what was going on but continued to monitor his panel. He then heard a 'ping' and felt something tug at his right sleeve and realised a round had penetrated the fuselage and hit his jacket. Fortunately, it hadn't damaged any flesh or bone.

"Shit," cried Stewart from his navigator's position. "A round just missed me."

The aircraft then lurched before levelling off again.

"The Junkers flew over us. I think he hit the fuselage just forward of me and, maybe the port wing," Webb reported. "I may have hit him too."

"I think he may have winged me in the leg. Anyone else injured?" Chapman demanded.

Simon and Stewart reported their close calls; the others said they were fine.

"Murray, come and take a look at my leg. Ferguson, come and take the co-pilot seat while he sorts me out," Chapman ordered

Simon took the co-pilot's control, thankful that the Stirling had been designed with dual controls and was relatively spacious, unlike the Lancaster.

"It's only a flesh wound, skipper," Murray told Chapman. "Bleeding a bit but not much, hasn't damaged any arteries or bones. Probably hurt like hell though. I'll put a field dressing on it. Good job it wasn't a few inches to the right or you might have lost your tackle."

"We're clear of the coast now, Skipper," advised Stewart. "Course is two-four-zero."

Simon banked the aircraft onto the new course and continued to fly it while Murray bandaged the skipper's leg.

"Skipper, I think we may be losing fuel from one of the port wing tanks, there's a stream of vapour," Don Webb announced.

Chapman turned his head to check the wing.

"I can't see anything from here. I'll take the controls again, Ferguson," Chapman advised. "You go and check your instruments. Murray, have a look and see if you can spot anything from the astrodome."

"Skipper, there is a leak, just inboard of the inner engine," Webb reported from the mid-upper turret.

"Skipper, Flight Engineer here, we're losing fuel from one tank. I'm transferring as much as possible into the other tanks. I'll work out how much we've lost."

Simon took readings from his gauges and compared them with the planned status at this point in the mission.

"Skipper, we've lost about fifty gallons so far. At that rate, if it doesn't get any worse, we should have enough to get us home but without much of a reserve. Hopefully, transferring the fuel from the damaged tank should reduce the loss rate."

"Thank you, Engineer. Navigator, what alternative airfields are there for us if we can't make base?"

"So long as we make the coast with a few gallons, there are fields every four or five miles along our track. We should be able to divert to one of them."

Simon was relieved that he'd stayed calm when they'd been attacked. Even when the bullet had nicked his jacket, his reaction had been surprise, not fear. Then, when he'd been asked to fly the Stirling, his training had kicked in and he hadn't doubted that he'd at least be able to keep the aircraft on course. Whether he'd have been able to land it was a different matter.

"Navigator, how far to the coast now?"

"Thirty miles, Skipper. We're on course to cross just north of Hemsby."

"Engineer, how is our fuel looking?"

"Should be fine, Skipper, the damaged tank is now empty so we're not losing any more."

"Coast ahead, Skipper," called Campbell from the front turret.

"Roger. Murray, send a signal to base reporting we need medical attention when we land and would appreciate a straight-in approach."

Murray tapped out the signal on his wireless.

"Base has acknowledged," he told the pilot.

The Norfolk broads slipped by below them soon after they crossed the coast, then the spires of Norwich were left to starboard as they continued southwest.

"Fifteen miles to base."

"Roger, Navigator. Ferguson, come up to the cockpit to give me a hand."

Simon climbed into the second pilot's seat, strapped himself in and plugged in his helmet intercom.

"I'll fly the aircraft. I want you to handle the flaps, throttles and undercarriage for me and monitor our speed and height on the approach."

"Roger, Skipper."

As the Stirling flew over the abbey in Bury-St-Edmunds, Chapman adjusted his heading to line up with the runway. The touchdown wasn't one of his best. P-Patsy dropped the last twenty feet, hitting the runway hard.

The blood-wagon met the aircraft as it pulled into its dispersal point.

Chapman's head fell forward, the pressure of keeping the aircraft flying now ended.

"Christ, that hurts," he cried through gritted teeth.

Simon and Alf Stewart helped carry Chapman out of the aircraft and hand him over to the medics from Station Sick Quarters.

"You may want to look at this," said the ground crew Flight Sergeant, leading Simon around to the port wing.

"Looks like a shell caught the edge of the tank and damaged it. Good job it didn't go straight through the tank or it might have ignited the fuel."

"Yes, that might have been a bit dicey, Chiefy."

Chapter 26. The Waiting Game

11th October 1943

In a country house about sixty miles north of London, 'Lynx' and 'Alouette', sat in the library with their escorting officer, Lieutenant Denise Barrett. They were waiting for an aircraft to be available to drop them to join an existing Special Operations Executive team near Chartres, southwest of Paris – where they were to act as courier and wireless operator.

Their papers identified Lynx as Eloise Dubois and Alouette as Suzanne Baume. It was their first missions and both were apprehensive about their futures – not that they dared express their concerns. It had been difficult enough completing their training with no allowances made for them being women. They were expected to reach the same standards as the men – even in physical tasks. Giving any hint of trepidation was out of the question.

SOE had approached Lynx at Holy Cross church in Westchester where she was working with French refugees and invited her to join them as a coder. As cover for her secret work, she would officially be a member of the First Aid Nursing Yeomanry. The chance to escape Elmdene's conservative atmosphere enticed the unconventional attitudes she'd inherited from her mother. Her father had been reluctant to let her go but she'd appealed to his patriotism. Even so, she implied that her work would only be an extension of what she was doing at Holy Cross and she'd be based near Leighton Buzzard well away from the Luftwaffe's main targets.

Her initial fascination with the messages she was decoding developed into frustration that she was stuck behind a desk while others got more directly involved. The village, where the grandmother she'd stayed with before the war lived, was now occupied by the Germans. Cousins she'd played with had been conscripted to work in forced labour camps – news that had come via an aunt who had married a Spaniard and lived in Barcelona. When she expressed interest in working in the field, her section head had, reluctantly, supported her.

Alouette had been recruited directly from the Wrens where she'd been a wireless telegraphist. Like Lynx, she was bilingual, had a French mother, and had grown up in Beauvais, fifty miles from Paris.

Their initial field selection process had involved five days of psychological and personality tests; being woken brusquely in the middle of the night to see if they automatically responded in English when questioned and tests of their powers of observation. This had been followed by six weeks in Scotland to toughen them up – and train them in map reading, concealment, unarmed combat – including killing a man (or woman) with their bare hands or a knife; how to use explosives and where to plant them for maximum effect. They'd been given a test mission to destroy a railway bridge over the River Spean in the shadow of the Ben Nevis range.

There had been parachute training at Ringway airfield just outside Manchester – then finishing school at Beaulieu, SOE's centre in the New Forest, being taught the tradecraft they'd need to avoid capture and, in Alouette's case, how to set up and repair her wireless set, string aerials and other tasks that she'd not previously needed to do. They were also taught what to do if they were captured and subjected to realistic mock interrogations.

Parachute drops were, inevitably, dependent on weather conditions, the state of the moon – it needed to be within a few days either side of full – the reverse of normal bomber missions – and the availability of suitable aircraft.

Mid-afternoon, Lieutenant Barrett was called to the telephone. After receiving the news, she returned to the library.

"You're on for tonight. Collect your gear."

Lynx and Alouette exchanged glances.

"This is it then, Lynx. How do you feel?"

"Glad the waiting is over, Alouette. And that all the effort we put into the training is now going to be used. How about you?"

"The same. I have to admit to you that I am nervous but I wouldn't tell anyone else that."

"Me too. Well, come on, let's go and fetch our kit."

They collected their bags from their room then met Barrett at the car.

They drove out of the estate then through country lanes to the Great North Road where they turned south. Rain splattered the windscreen and the wipers struggled to keep it clear. Gusts hit the car from different directions as the road twisted and turned.

"I hope it's not this windy when we jump," Alouette remarked.

"Don't worry, you won't go if the weather is this bad at your drop zone. Last information I had was for a clear night and light breezes. We'll get an update at the barn."

The road took them through the village of Eaton Socon and an old coaching inn opposite a solidly built Renaissance period church with its square tower. It seemed the very essence of what the country was fighting for.

"It's not as old as it looks," Lieutenant Barrett said, seeing Lynx turning her head as they passed it.

"Really?"

"It was badly damaged in a fire in 1930, the roof was destroyed and one of the walls collapsed. I grew up in Eynesbury, the other side of the river from here," Barrett explained. "Not far now."

The road ran alongside the River Ouse for a while then turned sharp left to cross over a bridge. A mile further they slowed before turning onto a side road which wound next to a wood before crossing a railway line and emerging with the airfield on their right.

"That's the main line from London to Edinburgh," Barrett said. "Passengers have a clear view of the airfield as they pass. Fortunately, it's a fast part of the line so they don't have much chance to see anything. Gibraltar Farm is on the other side of the field anyway."

They pulled up outside the final staging point for agents before they boarded aircraft and entered the building.

"You'll get your final briefing in a few minutes. In the meantime, we'll need to check you for anything that might give you away: bus tickets, labels on clothes, British cigarettes or any other item that people casually stuff into pockets or purses. You'd be surprised how often someone picks something up on the way here without thinking," Barrett told them.

Lynx shrugged her shoulders, "Fine by me, better safe than sorry. I have permission to wear this brooch, though, it is French; my grandmother gave it to me the last time I saw her before the war, she lives near Paris."

"Yes, that's fine. Another thing, from now on, you speak only French."

« Bien sur. »

While they waited for their own briefing, another agent climbed into a car and was driven over to one of the Lysanders. He was a replacement radio operator being flown to a resistance réseau near Tours. The group's previous operator had been caught by transmitting an urgent message long enough for German detector vans to locate him. His Lysander would refuel at Tangmere near the coast before crossing the channel.

A second Lysander waited for its passenger who was to join a group near Angers as a courier. Several Halifaxes and a Wellington were also being refuelled and loaded with stores to be dropped to groups in the occupied territories.

Chapter 27. Special Operations

11th October 1943

P-Patsy and Pilot Officer Chapman were both declared unserviceable due to the damage inflicted by the Junkers 88 – and were likely to remain so for a week. The rest of the crew couldn't be left idle, however.

Simon reported to the Engineering Officer, Flight Lieutenant Bailey.

"Ferguson, S-Sugar needs a Flight Engineer, the captain is Flight Lieutenant Evans," Bailey instructed. "You did well on that last trip, by the way. That's why I'm sending you with S-Sugar. Keep up the good work."

"Thank you, sir."

Simon was gratified by the praise. It didn't happen that often. You were expected to be good at your job – so why should you be commended for doing it?

He found the crew of S-Sugar in B Flight office and recognised one of the NCOs, Sgt Johnson, from the mess. Evans introduced the rest of the crew to him.

"Flying Officer Wilson is our navigator, Flight Sergeant Thomas, wireless op, Lewis – upper gunner, Roberts, rear gunner, Johnson, front gunner and bomb aimer."

Simon nodded and repeated their names as they were introduced to try to implant them in his mind.

"Our previous Flight Engineer completed his tour and is now instructing down the road at Stradishall so you might meet him sometime if he pops back for a jar or two," Johnson told him.

"We're being sent over to Tempsford for a few days, so pack what you need and report back here at thirteen hundred hours," Evans instructed.

The NCOs walked back to their mess, packed their kit, had lunch then met back at the flight office. A bus was already waiting to take them out to their aircraft.

After taking off, they set course to the west, passing south of Cambridge, before turning onto the approach to Tempsford, reputed to be the boggiest and foggiest of the RAF's airfields. The flight itself took less than fifteen minutes. Climbing out of the aircraft, Simon looked around the airfield and at the mixture of aircraft he could see.

Sgt Johnson stood next to him, pulled out his cigarettes and offered the packet to Simon.

"Do you use these filthy things?" he invited.

"Not for me, thanks."

"They fly SOE agents into Norway, Holland, Belgium and France from here," Johnson explained. "The larger aircraft drop the Joes, as they're known, or equipment by parachute," he continued, taking a drag from his cigarette.

Simon had recognised the Halifaxes, Wimpeys, and another Stirling. There were other stubby, black, single-engine aircraft with high wings and fixed undercarriages that he hadn't seen before.

"Are those Lysanders?" he asked.

"Yes, they were originally designed for Army cooperation but their short take-off run makes them ideal to get into small fields to drop off and pick up agents. Now that's not a job I'd fancy," Johnson told him.

"Flying them in or being an agent?"

"I meant flying them in – but being an agent would be even worse."

"Each to their own, I suppose. I'm not sure our job is much safer. We nearly bought it on our second trip."

"Well, chum, you shouldn't have joined up if you can't take a joke. At least we get treated as POWs if we have to bail out. Joes are lucky if they're simply shot."

"True enough," Simon said as he watched as the ground crew loaded stores in a Halifax's bomb bay.

"Come on you two," called Flight Sergeant Thomas.

They joined the others and made their way towards a Nissan hut that served as the flight office where they were to be briefed.

"Your mission tonight is to drop two agents and six canisters of stores near Chartres," the Squadron Leader informed them. "Your route crosses the coast between Hastings and Eastbourne then appears to be heading for

Rouen, crossing the French coast west of Dieppe. You then feint towards Poissy – hopefully, if the Germans spot you, they'll think you're heading for the vehicle factories. You then make your final run to the drop zone near Chartres. You return, crossing the French coast again between Le Havre and Caen. Keep as low as possible over the Channel then, as usual, after you've climbed to 1500 feet to get a fix, drop down again to 800 feet. Navigator, check the latest bumph for information about flak posts, fighter zones and balloons. Any questions? No? Well, good luck."

Simon turned to the wireless operator sitting next to him.

"What do you think, Flight?" he asked.

"Piece of cake. The Germans know we'll probably be over tonight but don't know where we're likely to go, unlike main bomber attacks. By flying low, we avoid most of their radar and don't give their fighters chance to see us."

"I hope you're right."

"Oh, believe me, I'd rather do one of these trips than Happy Valley or Berlin. If we do get shot down, we're usually over occupied territory with a chance of help, not over Germany where they see us as terror fliers."

It was dark by the time the aircraft had been loaded with the containers they'd drop later and the crew had boarded again – having observed the traditional good luck gesture on the tail wheel.

Simon stowed his parachute in its rack and prepared for the engine start procedure.

He wondered about the Joe or Joes they'd be carrying tonight. What made them volunteer for such a hazardous job? But, then, what had made him volunteer? He couldn't wait until he was old enough to join up. Perhaps it was the same with the agents. Perhaps they needed the thrill that danger created. Or, maybe they just didn't have nerves. He shook his head and focussed on his dials.

When Flight Lieutenant Evans saw the car approaching them, he gave the order to start the engines. Three figures climbed out of the vehicle. Two wore overalls and parachute harnesses, the other a female officer's uniform. The two agents climbed the steps into the fuselage while the uniformed officer stood by the car for a moment then got back into the driver's seat and drove off again.

Once the engines had warmed up, and pre-flight checks had been completed, Evans signalled the ground crew to remove the chocks from the wheels.

"Pilot to crew. Ready for take-off?"

The crew all confirmed they were ready.

"Despatcher, how are our passengers?"

The despatcher gave a thumbs up to each of them and received a thumbs up in reply.

"They're ready, Skipper."

Evans taxied the aircraft to the end of the runway then waited for the signal for them to proceed.

"Ready, engineer?"

Simon placed his hands behind the pilot's ready to assist. He edged the starboard engine throttles forward to increase power on that side to counteract the tendency of the Stirling to swing to the right during take-off.

"Ready, Skipper."

"Right. Here we go."

He released the brakes and the Stirling rolled down the runway, gradually building up speed.

The tailwheel lifted from the ground as the aircraft accelerated. Evans kept the nose down as they accelerated. Finally, he eased back on the control column.

"Gear up."

Simon moved the undercarriage lever.

"Coming up."

There was a clunk as the huge wheels were enclosed in the housing and the doors closed behind them.

They climbed to a thousand feet for the flight down to the channel coast keeping well clear of London as they crossed the Thames estuary – the capital's anti-aircraft batteries didn't always identify friendly aircraft.

"Enemy coast ahead," called the front gunner half an hour later. He checked his weapons were ready to fire in case they were spotted.

Evans eased the control column back and increased power to the engines to climb.

Flying Officer Wilson, the navigator, lay in the bomb aiming compartment to get a fix as they crossed the coast. Satisfied he'd identified the headland he'd marked on his charts; he returned to his curtained-off compartment and recalculated the drift due to the wind. He plotted the revised track and worked out a new heading to take them to their next turning point.

Evans reduced height again to eight hundred feet. High enough to clear obstructions such as power cables but low enough to give German radar little chance to pick them up.

Simon listened to the calm exchange between the navigator and the pilot and turned to his instruments. Fuel consumption was as planned and oil pressures and engine temperatures were within acceptable ranges. It was a regular milk run.

The Drop Zone was just to the west of Chartres. As they approached, Johnson watched for the expected signal from the ground and guided the pilot over the reception committee.

As the aircraft approached the DZ, the despatcher opened the parachute exit door, attached the agents' static lines to hardpoints in the aircraft and instructed them to sit on opposite sides of the opening in the floor. The navigator switched on a red light near the exit to prepare the agents. As the aircraft passed over the aiming point, Wilson changed the light to green. The despatcher watched the two agents drop out of the Stirling, the static lines pulling their parachutes out of their packs.

"Two Joes dropped, chutes opened cleanly," he advised. He then retrieved the static lines and closed the hatch.

Evans flew a circuit around the drop zone while Lynx and Alouette drifted down to the ground, opening the bomb bay doors as they circled. He then flew back to drop the supply canisters from the bomb bay.

"Right crew, passengers and supplies have been dropped. Time to go home," Evans announced.

Having checked his instruments for how many times he didn't know, Simon listened to the drone of the four engines relentlessly. Each engine producing fourteen hundred horsepower – a hundred times a family car might produce. He wondered about the agents they'd just dropped. What did the future hold for them? What would they be doing? Presumably, by now, they'd have collected the equipment that had been dropped with them and the local resistance would have spirited them away. Or had there been a trap waiting for them?

The shadow of the huge Stirling, cast by the light of the full moon, flitted across the French countryside as they headed northwest away from the drop zone keeping clear of Luftwaffe bases in the valley of the Seine and east of Caen before recrossing the coast between Deauville and Ouistreham.

The chances of being intercepted diminished the further they flew from the French coast but the gunners still remained vigilant. Over the channel, Navigator, Flying Officer Wilson, used his Gee system, now clear of German jamming, to calculate the course back to Tempsford.

Simon was relieved to have ticked off another sortie and that this trip had been without incidents. He realised, however, that not all his operations would be as straightforward.

Chapter 28. Goodwood to Mannheim

October/ November 1943

After two more sorties from Tempsford, and with the waning moon preventing further flights, S-Sugar returned to Chedburgh. As P-Patsy had been repaired and Pilot Officer Chapman had recovered from his injury, Simon re-joined his original crew.

They were briefed to undertake a further gardening mission the following night. It seemed that Simon's luck was holding as P-Patsy made it to their target area off Denmark and planted their six mines without encountering any opposition. The flight home over the North Sea was equally uneventful and they landed back at base, tired but relieved to have completed yet another sortie.

Fog curtailed any missions over Germany for the next few weeks and the squadron was limited to training and more small-scale minelaying missions bringing Simon's total to eleven.

On 18th November, the teleprinter chattered out a Goodwood order from Bomber Command – demanding maximum effort for the night's mission.

The crews gathered in the briefing room.

"Your target tonight is Mannheim Ludwigshafen as part of a force of Halifaxes and Stirlings. Main bomber force Lancasters led by Mosquitos of Pathfinder Force will be attacking Berlin at the same time so German night fighters will be divided."

This would be Simon's longest mission and likely to be the most hazardous he'd undertaken.

His crew was no longer considered sprogs; they'd 'got some in' and the 'ink was dry on their twelve-fifties' as the banter went; twelve-fifty being the reference number for RAF identity cards. They'd nearly survived the critical first twelve sorties when many inexperienced crews bought it. Basic tasks had now become automatic leaving them to concentrate on everything else that was going on around them. And they'd need to focus tonight as they faced night fighters and flak.

After the briefing, the crew carried out an air test to be absolutely certain P-Patsy was top of the line for the night's mission. As they pulled back into their dispersal, the petrol bowser pulled up to fuel the seven tanks in each wing while a tractor towed a train of bomb carriers ready to load a single 2000 lb high capacity and six 250 lb general purpose munitions into the bomb bay. Several of the bombs had messages chalked onto their casing including 'a present for Herr Meyer' – a reference to Herman Goering's claim that no enemy bombers would reach the Ruhr and, if any did, they could call him Meyer.

P-Patsy took off at 18:09 and climbed to ten thousand feet, rendezvousing with the other Stirlings from their own airfield and others within 3 Group en route. Halifaxes, flying higher and faster than the Stirlings, would join them near the target for the combined attack.

Searchlights and heavy flak greeted them as they crossed the Dutch coast between Rotterdam and Antwerp. The fingers of light probed the darkness, seeking out individual targets amongst the bomber stream. When they latched onto an aircraft, other searchlights would pick out the same target enabling the anti-aircraft guns to calculate the height and direction of their prey.

Off to P-Patsy's port beam, a Stirling was coned by the searchlights; within seconds, it was in the centre of a maelstrom of bursting flak. Its torment terminated in a massive explosion.

"Some poor buggers have just bought it," reported the upper gunner.

Cocooned in the Flight Engineer's station, Simon couldn't see what was going on.

"Did anyone bail out?" he asked.

"No chance. They just blew up. Direct hit."

"Cut the chatter, leave the intercom free and focus on your jobs or we'll be the next ones to go," Chapman warned the crew.

Moments later, a searchlight found P-Patsy.

Chapman threw the aircraft down and to the left then up and to the right to try to break the beam's hold. Shells exploded near their original path but didn't achieve a direct hit though there was the sound of several bits of shrapnel hitting the fuselage.

Simon checked his instruments automatically. As far as he could tell, the four Hercules engines were operating normally. He hoped that none of the fuel tanks in the wings had been damaged. They were, apart from one tank on each side, in theory, self-sealing. And, in accordance with standard procedure, they'd used fuel from the unprotected tank first.

"Crew, report damage," commanded Chapman.

One by one, the crew reported minimal damage– some additional ventilation in the side of the fuselage was the worst that they could see.

Once through the coastal flak belt, the bombers were harassed by Junkers 88 night fighters as they initially feinted towards Cologne which had already been attacked more than fifty times including the first thousand bomber raid fifteen months earlier.

The three gunners kept their eyes peeled, swinging their turrets from side to side, while Chapman weaved the aircraft – never flying straight and level long enough for fighters or flak to draw a bead on them.

"Dive starboard, Skipper," Don Webb, the upper gunner, yelled.

Chapman immediately sent the aircraft down to the right as another Stirling slid over them from left to right – through the airspace they would have occupied if they hadn't taken avoiding action. The other aircraft flew on, apparently ignorant of the close call unless their rear gunner had seen them.

"Everyone all right?" Chapman asked as he brought P-Patsy back to its designated height.

"Apart from needing a change of underwear, Skip," Webb answered. "He was flying off our port beam then suddenly swung towards us."

"It's bad enough being attacked by Jerries, but when our own try to take us out…." Gordon Campbell the front gunner and bomb aimer let his sentence drift.

"Right, excitement over. Focus on your jobs," Chapman ordered.

"Course change coming up, Skipper. One six zero in one minute."

"Roger, Navigator."

The stream of bombers, twenty-five miles long, two miles wide and half a mile deep, flew south-south-east at two hundred miles per hour, keeping well to the west of Dusseldorf, Cologne and Koblenz. At its final turning point, it headed for Mannheim.

Campbell climbed down into his bomb-aiming compartment and prepared to drop their load on the factories below – and ensure the camera was ready to photograph their aiming point. Without that corroboration, their mission would not count towards their tour.

Murray, the wireless operator, released bundles of window, thin strips of aluminium, to confuse any local German radar.

Simon checked his gauges and ensured that the fuel transfer cocks were feeding petrol from the right tanks and recalculated their consumption, how much they needed to get back to base and the reserve that should remain.

Stewart, at his curtained-off navigation table, revised his wind speed data and recalculated their route home once the bomb load had been dropped.

Hunter, in the rear turret, shivered in the cold but stayed vigilant, staring out into the darkness for any sign of enemy fighters.

Webb, in the upper gun turret, reflected on the earlier near miss and considered firing a burst across the nose of any other friendly aircraft that got too close.

Chapman scanned his instruments. Everything seemed fine. They caught buffeting from other aircraft in the concentrated stream which he needed to correct. But that was better than being isolated targets. P-Patsy was behaving herself. The crew seemed to have gelled together well and he was confident that they were all on top of their game.

"Coming up to target now, Skipper," warned Campbell. "Bomb doors open. I'm struggling to pick out the actual target, there are fires and marker flares all over, Skipper."

"Do the best you can."

"Right Skipper, left a bit, steady, that's fine, right a touch, steady. Bombs gone."

P-Patsy leapt upwards as two tons of bombs fell from her bay.

"Hold us on that heading for thirty seconds for the aiming point photograph."

It was the longest thirty seconds any of them could remember.

Just as Chapman was about to turn away, a massive canister fell in front of their port wing followed by several smaller projectiles.

The last one hit the wing outboard of the outer engine – smashing through the structure and leaving a hole through it.

"Shit, we've been hit. Must have been from a Halifax above us. The cookie missed us thank God, but I think one of the smaller bombs went through the port wing," exclaimed Chapman.

"Skip, it's gone through the number six fuel tank, the tank has pretty much drained out – thankfully it only had about twenty gallons left in it," Simon reported. "I've isolated the tank anyway."

"Thank you, Engineer, how does that leave us for fuel?"

"Depends whether the damage causes extra drag and higher consumption. I'll have some indication in a few minutes."

"Keep me advised, Engineer. Upper gunner, keep your eyes on the damage, let me know if it gets any worse."

"Roger, Skipper."

Simon noted that Chapman had increased power on the port engines to compensate for the extra resistance. That was bound to increase consumption but the question was, by how much? They were fortunate that the bomb hadn't exploded on contact but it probably hadn't dropped far enough for the fuse to activate.

Chapman regained the height that P-Patsy had lost when hit. With luck, the damage wouldn't get any worse.

Simon noticed that the port outer engine temperature was higher than the other three engines. It wasn't significant at the moment and was probably because they were running it harder to compensate for the extra drag.

"Skipper, Number one engine is running hotter than normal. If it gets much higher, we might have to reduce power on it and compensate with more on number two."

"Right Engineer, watch it and let me know."

The temperature continued to rise.

"Skipper, the temperature is still rising. It's also using more oil than normal. Maybe it was damaged by the flak earlier?"

"Do what you can, Engineer. Try and nurse it as far as the coast anyway."

"Roger, Skipper."

"Upper gunner here, Engineer, Number one engine is kicking out a lot of black smoke. Scratch that, there are flames from the engine."

Simon cut the fuel supply, activated the fire extinguisher and feathered the propellor to minimise the drag as it windmilled in the airflow.

Chapman increased power to the other engines and countered the asymmetrical power with the rudder to keep the aircraft flying straight.

The reduced power and extra drag from the rudder slowed them and they fell back through the bomber stream leaving them prey to the marauding night fighters.

Chapter 29. Attacked

November 1943

Corkscrew starboard, Skipper," cried Hunter from the rear turret. He fired his four 303 Browning machine guns at the Messerschmitt 110 that had appeared out of the darkness behind P-Patsy.

Chapman twisted the yoke to the right and pushed it forward – then pulled back and wrenched it to the left. The Stirling was often loved by its pilots for its manoeuvrability, likened to a fighter's. The damaged wing and loss of an engine, however, limited P-Patsy's response and the corkscrew was sluggish.

The tracer from Hunter's bursts did nothing to deter the 110's pilot as he closed in on P-Patsy. He was still out of range of the 303s and the cannons in the nose of his aircraft would be in killing reach long before the Stirling's guns could inflict serious damage. When he opened fire, the shells struck the rear turret, sending shards of Perspex flying before hitting Hunter as he fired back.

Webb aimed the two machine guns in his upper turret at the 110 when it appeared to one side of the rudder as Chapman continued to try to avoid the Messerschmitt by throwing the Stirling around as much as he could.

"He's pulled away, Skipper," reported Webb, deliberately keeping his tone as matter-of-fact as he could to conceal the adrenaline flowing through his veins.

"Keep your eyes peeled, he'll probably be back."

"Roger, Skipper."

"Rear gunner, are you all right?" Chapman asked.

No reply.

"Wireless operator, go and check on Hunter."

"OK, Skipper."

Murray unplugged his intercom and scrambled to the rear of the aircraft. The turret doors were hanging off and he pulled the rear gunner into the fuselage to examine him.

"Skipper, Hunter's dead. The rear turret is U/S. Looks like it took several direct hits."

"Right Murray, have a look for any other damage as you return to your position."

"Roger, Skipper."

"Upper gunner, keep your eyes peeled – you're our only defence from the rear now."

"OK, Skipper."

"Navigator, work out our position and ETA base at current speed. Wireless Operator, when you get back to your station, send out a signal giving our position and ETA and that we've been attacked and lost our rear gunner."

"Fighter attacking from port," Webb called over the intercom.

Chapman threw the Stirling into a corkscrew to the left, hoping that the attacking 110 would expect him to turn away rather than towards him. Murray was thrown against the side of the aircraft by the sudden change of direction.

The manoeuvre almost worked. Most of the Messerschmitt 110 Destroyer's cannon shells missed, but one hit the starboard aileron. The Destroyer then flew over the Stirling as Chapman dived away to the left. Webb took advantage of the opportunity to pour twenty rounds into the 110 in the half-second it took to pass in front of his guns. The bullets stitched a row from the nose, through the cockpit and into the Messerschmitt's wing, killing the pilot.

"I think I got him, Skipper."

"Good show."

"I think my arm is broken, Skipper," Murray reported.

"Navigator, check Murray's arm."

Stewart acknowledged the pilot's order and clambered to where Murray was sitting on the floor.

"Good job it wasn't your right arm, at least you can still operate the wireless. You'll get some sympathy from the nurses at the hospital when we get back," Stewart japed as he strapped Murray's arm across his chest – tucking his wrist inside his parachute harness to immobilise it.

"Just give me a hand back to my radios. I still need to send off that signal."

Simon had been watching his gauges.

"Skipper, we're using slightly more fuel than normal but we should make it back to base providing we don't encounter any more problems."

"Thank you, Engineer."

At that moment shells burst through the floor.

A second night fighter had sought out P-Patsy's vulnerable underbelly. Concealed by the wings and fuselage, it had crept into position underneath the Stirling before firing up into it.

Simon's instruments went wild as the starboard inner engine and fuel lines from the inboard tanks were hit. His training kicked in and he isolated damaged tanks and cut the engine which was vibrating wildly and threatening to tear the wing apart – or so it felt to Simon.

"Crew, report damage," instructed Chapman as he fought the controls to keep P-Patsy in the air.

"We've lost number three engine and fuel from the inboard tanks," Simon responded.

"No damage here," reported Campbell from the front turret.

"I can't see any sign of fire on the wings, thank God, the shells hit forward of me, about where Murray and Stewart were," said Webb.

"Navigator and Wireless Op, are you all right?" Chapman asked.

There was no response.

Chapman contemplated his options. He needed to know if Stewart and Murray required help. He didn't dare have Webb leave the upper turret as any further attacks were likely to come from astern, underneath or the side rather than ahead. The engineer needed to deal with the damage – which only left Campbell.

"Front gunner, go and check on Murray and Stewart."

Campbell gave Chapman an ironic salute as he passed the pilot.

He found the navigator and wireless operator lying near the door leading to the rear fuselage. Their bodies had been ravaged by the 110s canons. He felt bile rising in his throat but fought it down and plugged his intercom into the nearest socket.

"Skipper, Murray and Stewart have both bought it. There are plenty of holes in the floor too," he shouted over the noise of the engines, the vibration and the airstream rushing through the aircraft from the damaged floor and sides of P-Patsy.

Chapman considered their position. They were losing height and wouldn't make it back to the coast. They'd fallen behind the main bomber stream and were increasingly vulnerable to more night fighters. As they lost height they'd also come within range of more and more flak. Much lower and there may not be enough time for everyone to jump.

"Crew, bail out. Good luck," he ordered.

Simon grabbed his parachute from its rack and clipped it onto his chest. As he passed the pilot, he handed Chapman a parachute. It would save the pilot a few seconds once he left the controls to bail out himself. He then opened the nose parachute door and dropped into the void.

Campbell decided it was quicker to make for the rear exit than the cockpit hatch. The aircraft was filling with smoke drawn in through the damaged panels but he could see that Webb had already climbed down from his turret and was opening the rear exit trap door.

They quickly shook hands, shouted "Good luck" to each other then dropped through the hatch.

Satisfied that the crew had jumped, Chapman engaged the autopilot, more in hope than expectation, and, thanking the designers for the Stirling's relatively spacious cockpit, dropped down to the escape hatch, sat down then slipped out into the freezing airflow.

Simon waited until he was well clear of the doomed aircraft before pulling the ripcord. The harness dug into him especially between the legs, making his eyes water, as he was slowed by the parachute from more than a hundred miles an hour to about eleven. He looked up at the canopy that had bloomed above him and breathed a sigh of relief. He could hear distant aero engines but whether they were from Stirlings or night fighters, he couldn't tell. Nor could he make out much detail on the ground as he drifted down until he was at about a hundred feet. He was over a wooded area but, thankfully, seemed to be heading for an open space. He held his legs together, bent his knees and rolled to the side as he landed.

After catching his breath, he twisted the harness fastener and hit it with the heel of his hand to release the lock. The straps fell loose and he shrugged the harness off as he got to his knees.

He looked around him. Everything was quiet. There was no sign of the other members of the crew and he wondered if they'd made it safely out of the aircraft.

He bundled up his parachute then sought cover in the woods while he worked out what to do. Discovering a fox's den, he buried the evidence of his escape from the Stirling.

Simon knew that the navigator had given a heading of 285 degrees after leaving Mannheim. That was before all the evasive manoeuvres during their battles with the night fighters but still placed him roughly east-northeast of the target. He estimated that they'd covered about 140 miles.

But where were the other members of the crew? Should he spend time trying to locate them or strike off on his own?

Chapman would have jumped after him, but how much later? If it had been five seconds, P-Patsy could have covered another quarter of a mile. At least it was heading in the direction Simon wanted to go. He might catch him up. But, what about Campbell and Webb? They could have jumped before him or after him and be anywhere.

How far would P-Patsy have flown on before hitting the ground? He hadn't seen any sign of it crashing while he was drifting to earth. How long had that taken? It had seemed a long time but was probably between one and two minutes. If P-Patsy had continued at 150 knots, it must be at least three and probably more than five miles away.

Simon was sure the Germans or the local police would be looking for survivors from P-Patsy and he needed to avoid the crash site – wherever it was. That meant he couldn't keep heading in the same direction as P-Patsy. He'd be better off heading directly west for a few miles then swinging around to the west-northwest. Hopefully, the others would come to the same conclusion and their tracks might converge.

He took out his escape pack. As well as a waterproof map printed on silk, there were amphetamine pills to combat fatigue, a slab of chocolate, Horlicks tablets, fishing line and matches and a wallet containing some French and Belgian Francs and what appeared to be a spare tunic button which concealed a compass.

He stowed the various items then replaced the side of the box to make a water bottle that he would fill from one of the myriads of streams running down the valleys.

As far as he could tell, he was in the Ardennes region, near the Belgian/Luxembourg border probably about a hundred miles from the channel coast.

It was just after one in the morning and had now started to drizzle. Thankful for his flying suit, sheepskin jacket and helmet, he identified a vaguely visible peak on the horizon in the direction he wanted to head and struck out towards it. Entering wooded areas, the trees blocked the view of his landmark and he was forced to identify other objects, a particularly tall tree or a rocky outcrop, to keep him on track.

As dawn approached, he built himself a bivouac, as he'd learned on the escape and evasion exercise with the Home Guard. In spite of his protective clothing, he was cold and tempted to light a fire. He resisted and sucked a Horlicks tablet instead. He planned to rest up during the day and try to get his bearings.

He'd been lying in his den for just over an hour when he heard someone walking along a trail that passed about fifty yards from him.

Chapter 30. On the Run

November 1943

As the figure came into view, Simon recognised Pilot Officer Chapman. He'd made a crutch from a branch and was dragging his right leg with each step. Two hundred yards from Simon, he stopped and sat on a fallen tree trunk at the side of the track and looked around him.

Simon wondered if he should reveal himself to his skipper but hesitated. He decided to wait until Chapman was closer to him. It would be a useful test of how well concealed his burrow was – and give him chance to see if anyone was following the pilot.

Chapman stood up and started to trudge along the track towards Simon's hide.

Watching the skipper's sluggish progress, Simon wondered if he should go and help him or continue on his own. If they travelled together, it would slow him down. He chided himself for his selfish thoughts. The skipper might have only twisted an ankle and resting for a day might ease the injury.

Step by step, Chapman came closer and closer to Simon's hide. He willed the pilot to hurry but every few yards he stopped and rested on his crutch.

When Chapman was as close as the track would be to his den, Simon crept out and warily moved to the edge of the tree line. He couldn't see anyone else on the track and there were no engine sounds so he thought it was relatively safe. In spite of this, he wasn't prepared to just call out. He picked up a stone and threw it to land next to Chapman. The pilot took no notice.

'Perhaps he thought he'd kicked it himself,' Simon thought. He threw another stone.

This time, Chapman stopped and looked around.

Simon waved and ran over to him.

"Ferguson, thank the Lord, where did you spring from?"

"I've made a bivouac just over there, Skipper," he hissed, pointing towards his hide. "I planned to rest up today and get my bearings then move on again tonight. What happened to your ankle?"

"Twisted it badly when I landed. At least, I hope it's just strained and not broken."

Simon helped Chapman to his hide.

"You've done a good job with this, Ferguson. Where did you learn to do it? Were you a Boy Scout?"

"I was, Skipper. But we also did an Escape and Evasion exercise with the Home Guard."

"I'm impressed, but is it big enough for both of us?"

"Plenty of room – it goes back quite a bit."

"Well, look, Ferguson, while I outrank you, you clearly have more experience in this area so I'm going to defer to you while we are on the run."

Simon was surprised by Chapman's admission but it did make sense.

"Right, Skipper, in that case, let's have a look at that ankle of yours."

"First aider as well are you, Ferguson?"

"All part of my Boy Scout training."

Simon carefully removed Chapman's flying boot and gently felt around the ankle, testing its movements.

"It's not broken, Skipper. Hopefully, resting it for a few hours will relieve the problem," Simon said.

"I'll strap it up as well as I can using our ties. You'll need to sign a chit for me to get a replacement from stores when we get back."

"That's all very well for you, Ferguson, but officers have to pay for our own uniforms."

Once Simon had dealt with Chapman's ankle, they compared notes about their estimated location which were roughly the same. There were no obvious landmarks or features to help them refine their approximations. They'd crossed ridgelines and valleys with streams during their hikes from their landing points but they could be any of a dozen in the Ardennes Forest. They'd both avoided roads that might have been patrolled so hadn't seen any signposts that might help.

"Right, Ferguson, I agree, that the best option is to continue west-northwest tonight until we have a better idea of where we are or we encounter someone who might help us. Now, I suggest we take it in turns to keep watch. I'll take the first stint. I'll wake you in two hours."

Simon laughed to himself. The skipper had said he would defer to him at this stage but here he was taking control. *'Oh well, it goes with the commission,'* Simon mused.

That night, they estimated that they covered another ten miles. Chapman's ankle was much better than it had been but still slowed them down. Combined with skirting villages they doubted if they were covering more than one mile per hour. They'd also been delayed when they came across a burned-out French army lorry in a ravine.

"Looks like it was travelling along that road up there," Chapman said, indicating a track hugging the side of the hill. "Probably shot up by a Stuka."

"Let's see if there's anything we can use."

They found a haversack containing a mess kit and a water bottle that had been thrown clear when the lorry crashed.

By dawn, they judged that they were now at least twenty to twenty-five miles from the Stirling's crash site and that the Germans would struggle to cover hundreds of square miles of forest so felt relatively safe making camp for another day.

"This will do," Simon told Chapman. "We can build a shelter under that fallen trunk. That's our first priority."

"Not sorting out food or a fire?"

"No, Skipper. The priorities are shelter, water, fire and food in that order. You can survive three hours without shelter in a harsh environment, three days without water – so long as you have shelter and three weeks without food provided you have shelter and water. Judging by those clouds and the temperature, I wouldn't be surprised if it snowed later. There's plenty of Silver Birch around which doesn't produce much smoke, we can use that for a fire."

Once the shelter was erected, and they'd refilled their water bottles from the river running down the valley, Chapman collected wood to make a fire while Simon used the fishing line from his escape kit to catch some trout. They'd dug up some potatoes growing in a field on the edge of a village they'd passed. After washing them in the stream, they put them to boil in one of the sections of the mess kit they'd found and grilled the trout on sticks over the fire.

"That was excellent, Ferguson. All we now need is a snifter of brandy and a cigar."

"I'd settle for a cup of tea, Skipper."

He threw some birch twigs and leaves into the water used to boil the potatoes and, after steeping it for a few minutes over the fire, strained it into the other sections of the mess tins.

"Try that."

"Not bad, Ferguson. Not exactly Earl Grey but bit of a smoky minty flavour."

They took turns again to keep watch and stoke the fire while the other slept during the day.

The next night, they approached the edge of a village to identify where they were. The commune wasn't marked on their map but the signpost at the crossroads pointed to Brussels 130 kilometres to the north and to Cambrai 55 kilometres to the west.

"I reckon that places us about here," Simon said placing his finger on a crossroads.

"Looks about right. So still, what, a hundred miles to the coast?"

"There or thereabouts, Skipper."

"So, do we keep walking and avoid contact with anyone or try to find someone who might help us?"

"I think we're far enough away from the crash site and I can't think the Jerries would be actively looking for us around here. Mind you, it's possible another kite bought it near here and the Germans might be after that crew. But I didn't hear any sound of raids passing overhead so that's probably unlikely. I reckon we're as safe as we're going to be to look for help."

"I agree. I suggest we find an isolated farm and keep watch tomorrow then make contact in the evening."

The pair continued to keep within woodland while it allowed them to head in the direction they wanted. About five in the morning, the woods abruptly changed to open fields as far as they could see. The moonlight was sufficient for them to make out a farmhouse about two hundred yards from their position.

"I had hoped we'd get a bit further before stopping but it's too much of a risk. I think we should back up into the trees to make a shelter," Simon suggested.

"Fine, I'll start collecting material for a bivouac. I guess a fire's going to be out of the question today."

Rain that had started soon after they'd begun walking the previous evening, intensified. The bare branches of the trees did little to protect them and even their sheepskin flying jackets, leather helmets and sheepskin-lined boots couldn't stop the inexorable penetration of drips down the neck and through the upper legs of their flying overalls and uniform trousers. They shivered in their hide and kept watch on the homestead.

They hadn't been there long when a light flickered in an upstairs window. A few minutes later, it disappeared then reappeared on the ground floor. They watched as a door opened and a figure appeared carrying a lantern and made its way across to a barn.

The appearance of the farmer stirred other beasts into life. Chickens and ducks squawked in their coops, pigs grunted in the stye and several cattle stood up in the field then ambled towards a gate leading to the farmyard. The lowing of the cattle reached Simon and Chapman as they watched.

"Looks like they're waiting to be milked," Simon remarked.

After milking, the farmer let the cattle back into the field then went back into the house. By then, smoke had started to rise from the chimney.

"Looks like there's someone else in the building. Possibly his wife. I guess she's lit the fire and made his breakfast. Probably having croissant or bread and cheese and coffee."

Simon's mouth watered at the thought, all he'd had since the fish and potatoes had been some energy tablets from his escape kit.

The farmer reappeared and harnessed a horse between the shafts of a cart. He then loaded milk churns and other produce that Simon and Chapman couldn't identify at that distance onto the trailer. A woman appeared from the house, well-wrapped up in a heavy coat and a black shawl around her neck. She climbed up onto the trailer, took the reins in her hands and drove the cart out of the farmyard as the farmer led another horse into the yard.

"Looks like she's going to market, or maybe delivering to customers."

"Who knows, Skipper?"

The farmer walked the second horse into the field next to where the cattle were grazing and attached its harness to a plough.

The two evaders watched as he turned over the soil with almost straight furrows. At the end of each draw, he paused to put a flame to his pipe and take a sip from a wine bottle.

About midday, he let the horse loose with the cattle and went back into the house. He re-emerged forty-five minutes later, collected the horse and reharnessed it to the plough.

"Such a peaceful scene, you'd hardly think there was a war on, would you?"

"I was thinking exactly the same, Skipper."

As the sun set, the farmer unharnessed the horse, took a final swig from his wine bottle and returned to the farmyard where the cattle were already waiting at the gate for the evening milking. The woman returned, the cart apparently relieved of the produce she'd taken earlier. The milk churns look far easier to handle so were, Simon assumed, now empty.

"Maybe the best time to approach the farmer is when he's finished milking and letting the cows back into their field. We can get to the hedge by the gate and attract his attention. If it's a washout, we'll have the night to get out of the area. I can't imagine the farm having a telephone and it would take them a while to get anywhere to report us."

"I agree, Ferguson. Let's do it."

Simon and Chapman crept along the side of a hedge between the pasture the cows had been in and the field the farmer had been ploughing until they reached the gate. They waited there until the farmer emerged from the milking parlour driving the cows before him, tapping their rumps to urge them on.

Simon whistled 'La Marseillaise' to attract his attention.

« Qui est là ? » the farmer demanded.

« Nous sommes aviateurs Anglais. L'armée de l'air royale, » Chapman responded as they stepped into view. « Pouvez-vous nous aider ? »

Chapter 30 On the Run

The farmer stared at the two men facing him. They could be as they claimed. Their sheepskin jackets and overalls certainly looked genuine and they had RAF uniform tunics with apparently appropriate insignia. The accent of the one who had spoken was certainly excruciating enough for him to be an Englishman. But was it safe to help them?

« Comment puis-je savoir que vous êtes comme vous le prétendez ? Vos uniformes n'ont aucun sens. Les Allemands pourraient facilement les prendre aux prisonniers ou aux morts. »

The response was too quick for Chapman to understand.

« Parlez plus lentement, s'il vous plait. »

"He said how do I know you are as you claim? Your uniforms are meaningless. The Germans could easily take them from prisoners or those who have died," Simon told Chapman.

"I hadn't realised you spoke French."

"I had a girlfriend whose mother was French and I learned the language to impress her," Simon responded.

He turned to the farmer. « Can you put us in touch with someone who can check our identities? »

« Perhaps it would be safer for me to report you to the authorities, » the farmer replied, surprised to find an Englishman who could speak French without mangling the language – even if it was an Iles de France accent.

« You could do that and I wouldn't blame you, » Simon answered.

« Venez avec moi, » the farmer instructed seemingly having made up his mind. He led them into the farmhouse.

His wife stared with wide-open eyes as he brought them into the kitchen.

« We can do nothing tonight. It will be curfew soon and there is no time to contact anyone. Tomorrow, I will speak to someone who may be able to help. No doubt you are hungry and thirsty now. My wife can make you a meal. »

« Thank you, we don't wish to impose but a meal would be very welcome, » replied Simon.

« It is nothing. We have chickens that lay eggs, cows for milk, butter and cheese and grow our own vegetables and grain for flour. The Boche take what they can find but we keep enough for ourselves. Please sit at the table. A glass of wine perhaps while my wife prepares something for you. »

He poured four glasses of wine, handed one each to Simon and Chapman, another to his wife – who took a sip before setting it down next to the cooker. The farmer raised his glass.

« Vive la France, Vive L'Angleterre. »

"God, that's rough," remarked Chapman as he took a sip.

« Ç'est Bon? »

« Oui monsieur, ç'est très bon, merci, » Simon confirmed. Chapman raised his eyebrows.

The farmer's wife gave them a plate each with a folded omelette filled with potato and seasoned with herbs then placed a loaf of bread and dish of butter on the table.

« Mangez! » she instructed.

« That was superb, madame, » Simon announced as he wiped the last of the egg from his plate with a piece of bread.

« Tonight, you must sleep in the barn in case the Boche search the area. We can then deny that we knew you were there. Ça va? »

« Ça va bien, » Simon assured him.

« Tomorrow, it would be safer if you hide in the woods during the day. I will try to get a message to someone who might be able to help you. »

« That's fine, we don't want to put you at risk. »

The next morning, the farmer's wife brought them a bottle of wine, some boiled eggs and bread and cheese to sustain them during the day. They watched the farmer drive off in his cart after the morning milking and settled down to wait for the evening, shielding as well as they could from the persistent drizzle. The cows took refuge from the rain by lying down next to a hedge and even the birds seemed to be sheltering with just the occasional call of a pigeon.

"I wonder what happened to Campbell and Webb, Skipper. Do you reckon they got down OK?"

"They should have. I held the kite steady as long as I could to give them time to jump but didn't see any sign of them once I was coming down."

Late in the afternoon, just as the cows began to stir and make their way to the gate for milking, the farmer returned on his cart. He signalled for the two airmen to join him.

« Someone will come soon to collect you. They will take you to a safe location while they check your identities. »

An hour later, an ancient Citroën van pulled into the farmyard. The driver, who introduced himself as Maurice, instructed the two airmen to get in the back where they were hidden behind sacks of potatoes.

"I hope we're doing the right thing trusting these guys," Chapman remarked.

"Was there any real option, Skipper? I reckon it would have been more and more difficult the closer we got to the coast, hopefully these chaps will have connections to get us across the Channel."

The old Citroën rattled its way along the country lanes for twenty minutes, shaking Chapman and Simon as it hit potholes and ruts that hadn't been repaired since the war began, then turned off onto a farm track that was even rougher than the country lanes.

"Hell's bells, my bum is sore from bouncing up and down," Simon complained.

"Surely it can't be much further, can it?" As Chapman finished his sentence, the vehicle juddered to a stop.

« Venez avec moi, » the driver instructed, leading them towards a windmill.

« You stay here tonight and, perhaps, tomorrow night. We must first check with London that you are who you say. There is food and water. Keep away from the windows and do not leave the windmill. »

« Whatever you say, Maurice, » Simon agreed.

« I need information that London can use to verify your identities – we don't expect you to give us military or operational details; perhaps the school you attended, the name of a pet dog or something like that. »

Maurice returned two nights later with a bundle of clothes.

« London has confirmed your identities. Early tomorrow morning, you will be taken to the railway station for the train to Paris. You need to wear these clothes. I must take photographs for identity cards so please change into the top items now. We will provide travel papers as well. Someone will bring them with them tomorrow when they collect you. Be ready to leave at half past five. Your papers will say that you are engineers being transferred to work on the Atlantic Wall in Brittany. Are your flying boots the type that can be converted to shoes? »

« Yes, Maurice, we can cut off the calf section to leave lace-up shoes. » Simon replied as he stripped off his RAF tunic and shirt.

After they'd been photographed, the two airmen took the sheath knives from the calf of their boots and cut through the leather lower sections – leaving ordinary-looking shoes that wouldn't attract any attention.

That night, while they lay on their palliasses, the straw sticking through the flimsy fabric in places, they heard the drone of aircraft overhead.

"They're flying from west to east, wonder where they're heading this time? Sounds like Lancasters to me, definitely not Hercules engines," Simon commented.

"Wherever it is, sounds like they're in for a pounding from the numbers."

"Yes and, no doubt some of the crews will be in our position before too long."

The next morning, Simon and Chapman dressed in their civilian clothes. A young woman came up to the floor they were on.

« Bon jour, je m'appelle Nicole. I am your guide for this morning. » She shook hands with her charges.

Simon thought she must be in her early twenties; her brown hair, which matched her eyes, brushed her shoulders as she moved her head. She wore a grey pin-stripe skirt suit over a white blouse; overall she wore a khaki gabardine trench coat with a felt hat with a downturned brim and a shoulder bag.

« It is about two kilometres to the railway station. I will go first. You follow me at a distance. At the station, present your papers and ask for a single ticket to Paris. Your papers will be checked before you enter the platform and, very likely, on the train itself. Sit where you can see me but do not make contact. If I am detained, go to the Café Monet on the Place des Artistes near the Gare du Nord. Do you understand? »

« Yes, Nicole. »

« If you're caught, I regret that we will not be able to help you further. You understand, you will be treated as prisoners of war but if we try to intervene, we will be shot if we are lucky and more likely questioned by the Gestapo and their methods are not pleasant. »

« We understand completely, Nicole and you are very brave for the work you do and for helping us at all, » Simon assured her.

« We do what we need to do to free France again. »

With that, the three of them descended to the ground floor and stood by the door. Nicole slipped out and walked down the track to the main road. Simon and Chapman followed a hundred metres behind her.

At the station, Nicole had bought her ticket by the time Simon and Chapman reached the window. She was stopped at the barrier to the platform where an inspector examined her ticket and a gendarme checked her papers. After a brief pause, she was allowed to pass.

Simon asked for two second-class single tickets to Paris.

« How much is it? And what time does the train leave? »

« One hundred and eighty francs each, the train leaves at six twenty-six. It is due at Paris Gare de Nord at nine fifty-six, if it is not delayed. »

Simon passed over the cash and their papers.

The clerk studied the documents for what seemed like an age before passing them back to Simon with the two tickets.

« Merci, » Simon said, relieved, as he picked them up.

Chapman let out the breath he'd been holding while Simon had been carrying out the transaction.

The two of them then went over to the platform barrier.

The inspector gave their tickets a cursory glance while he clipped them. The gendarme took his time examining the identity cards and travel permits, his look switching from the photographs to each of the men's faces. Finally, he passed the papers back without a word.

They stood about thirty yards away from Nicole while they waited for the train to arrive. Eventually, they saw puffs of smoke above the trees hiding the single track as it curved around a bend about a mile away. Then the sound of the engine reached them on the wind. As it pulled along the platform, it discharged clouds of steam at the dozen or so people waiting.

Chapman and Simon climbed into the opposite end of the same carriage as Nicole. They found seats from which they could watch their guide but were disconcerted to see a group of German soldiers in several of the intervening seats.

The soldiers had noticed Nicole and were nudging each other. Simon recognised the signs of men making suggestive comments about attractive young women.

On the platform, the guard waved his flag; the driver responded with a hoot on the engine's whistle then opened the regulator to feed steam to the pistons. The wheels span on the tracks then gripped and the train started moving. As it left the village, it passed a few hundred yards from the windmill where Simon and Chapman had spent the last two nights.

Apart from the soldiers, the carriage contained several other men dressed in business suits, most apparently on their own but two other pairs who were having a conversation and a man and woman sitting next to each other.

One of the soldiers stood up and approached Nicole. The train swayed from side to side and the soldier held on to the backs of the seats to steady himself.

« Bonjour, mademoiselle, are you travelling on your own? »

Nicole pretended she hadn't heard him and stared out of the window at the passing countryside. He wasn't to be put off so easily and touched her on the shoulder.

She turned to look at him.

« I asked if you are travelling on your own? If so, my comrades and I would be delighted if you would join us. »

« Thank you, no. I prefer to be on my own. »

« Are we not good enough for you? I'd have thought by now that you French would have learned to be friendlier to your conquerors. »

The officer and gentleman in Chapman could see what was happening and he instinctively half rose out of his seat to intervene. Simon put his hand on his arm and pressed him down.

« We can't get involved, » he whispered in French, in case someone overheard.

Chapman nodded his head, reluctantly accepting the sense of Simon warning him off.

At that moment, the door to the next carriage opened and a German captain entered. He took one look at the soldier.

„What are you doing?" he demanded.

„Nichts, Herr Hauptmann."

„Then return to your seat."

The captain turned to Nicole.

« My apologies, Fraulein, » he said, clicking his heels together and saluting before he walked on through the carriage.

Chapman and Simon relaxed as the German officer moved on.

The train followed the single rail track through wooded areas, alongside rivers and roads with little traffic and past pastures with cattle grazing. It stopped at small country stations and halts where a few passengers left and others embarked to take their place. At the rear of the train, produce from local farms, destined for garrisons in the larger towns, was loaded into a goods wagon under the watchful gaze of soldiers.

At some of the stations, the line split into two tracks and they would wait for a train heading in the opposite direction to pull onto the passing loop before proceeding. At other places, the other train was waiting for them.

Eventually, houses and other buildings crowded the railway and it merged with a main line with twin tracks before arriving at a larger station. The train rattled over points leading to sidings – some ending alongside platforms, others at a goods yard.

As they sat waiting for the train to move off again, a convoy of German army lorries pulled up outside the ticket hall. Soldiers jumped out and formed up and were then marched into the station and spread out along the length of the platform.

Simon and Chapman looked at each other, wondering what was happening. Were the soldiers looking for them? Or for other aircrew that may have bailed out locally? Surely they wouldn't use this many soldiers to recapture them, would they?

Then, with a jerk and a deal of clanging, the train started to move again – but it was reversing back the way it had come.

Chapman looked over at Nicole but she simply gave a barely perceptible shrug of her shoulders to say she had no more idea about what was going on than Simon and Chapman.

She'd never known this to happen before. She was certain it had nothing to do with her or her charges but it was worrying. Nicole had a valid excuse for her journey, her papers showed she was a nurse returning from visiting her sick grandmother in Cambrai to Paris where she worked in one of the hospitals. It wasn't entirely fictional. She was a trained nurse. She'd started helping refugees when her fiancé had been killed trying to hold back the German invasion in 1940 and a colleague asked for her help.

A hundred yards out of the station, the train stopped once more for a couple of minutes then after a blast on the whistle it moved forward again, over the points and alongside one of the other platforms. Some of the passengers tried to get off the train to find out what was happening but they were roughly forced back into carriages.

A few minutes later, a fast train sped through the station. Hauled by a powerful black engine, wagon after wagon raced past. The first after the engine was a flat car with an anti-aircraft gun, then several box cars, followed by more flat cars, each carrying a tank or other vehicle, then more box cars, finally another flat car with a second anti-aircraft gun.

As it disappeared around a bend with woods on each side of the track, belching smoke and steam behind it, there was a roar as two aircraft flew about a hundred feet above their heads following the train.

"RAF Mustangs, on a Rhubarb mission probably." Simon's whispered comment to Chapman was inaudible to anyone else with the sound of the aero engines.

The two RAF fighter bombers, on their search and destroy mission, swept up into the sky then dived down again at right angles to the railway tracks. A salvo of rockets left the leading aircraft's wings, their flight ending in a series of explosions as the two aircraft climbed before they circled and attacked again with cannon fire. Then they climbed once more, and disappeared into the distance. It was over in a couple of minutes. Clouds of smoke billowed above the trees. There were more explosions as the box cars carrying ammunition caught fire.

The Germans at the station had taken shelter and had tried shooting at the RAF fighters but without success. Once the Mustangs had flown off, their officers instructed them to follow the rail tracks to the train that had been attacked to see if they could help.

The passengers on the evaders' train were confused. They got down to the platform and milled around. No one had any idea what would happen. Would their train continue on its way – or had the attack blocked the line?

Simon and Chapman tried to remain as inconspicuous as possible, leaning against a wall in a corner.

Nicole walked along the platform heading for the ladies' toilets, her path took her close to Simon and Chapman and, as she passed them, she dropped a piece of paper that had been folded several times. Simon put his foot over the note then bent down to tie his shoelaces.

"What does it say?" Chapman asked in a whisper.

"That if the line has been blocked, we'll need to go via Reims and follow her at a distance as before. In the meantime, we wait here."

Some passengers climbed back onto their original train to sit down, others found spaces on luggage trolleys, still others left the station in search of refreshments or alternative means of transport. Chapman and Simon sat on some crates and resigned themselves to an interminable delay.

News gradually filtered through from the station staff that the track had been blocked and was likely to remain impassable for at least twenty-four hours. There would be trains to Reims with possible connections to Paris from there – though that couldn't be guaranteed.

« When is the next train to Reims due? » Simon asked.

« Who knows? » the elderly stationmaster replied with a Gallic shrug of the shoulders. « It's all very well the RAF blowing up German trains, but it also stops Frenchmen going about their business. » He then shuffled off to give the news to other passengers.

Nicole walked past Simon and gave a slight tilt of the head to indicate that they should follow her to the ticket office. She changed her tickets to route via Reims instead of Soissons. Simon followed suit with his and Chapman's.

The Reims train arrived an hour later and they boarded an already crowded carriage and were forced to stand. When they disembarked at

Reims, they were obliged to show their papers when changing platforms. The gendarmes examined their travel permits and ID cards carefully – though it seemed that women and couples were not subjected to the same scrutiny.

It was eight o'clock by the time the train from Reims pulled into Paris' Gare de l'Est station, nearly an hour late and only an hour before curfew was due to start. The fact that they'd had to divert their journey might have been an acceptable excuse for law-abiding citizens but Simon and Chapman couldn't afford the closer questioning that it might involve. The original plan would have seen them arrive in Paris by early afternoon and even with several hours delay, well before curfew. Once they had been forced to divert via Reims, every hold-up had added to Simon's concerns; he was very relieved when they pulled into the platform.

Nicole allowed the crowds surging through the ticket barrier to carry her close to Simon.

« We need to get to the safe house as quickly as possible. It is about a twenty-minute walk from here, » she whispered.

They walked quickly through the almost deserted dark streets. Just a few others rushing home, their heads down, or police or German Army patrols shared the pavements. The only traffic was the occasional military vehicle or the ubiquitous black Citroën Traction Avant cars favoured by the Gestapo.

As they turned into a side road, Nicole signalled Simon and Chapman to hold back. She knocked on a door that looked as though it hadn't been maintained in years; the remaining paint was peeling off to reveal rotten areas. When the door opened, Nicole stepped inside for a few minutes then reappeared to gesture for the men to join her.

They slipped through the door and followed Nicole and another woman down a hall, past stairs to upper floors, to a kitchen at the rear of the building.

« This is Louise, you can stay here for now. I must get home before curfew starts. Bon Chance! "

« Thank you, Nicole and good luck to you too. Thanks for all your help. » Simon replied.

Nicole kissed Louise on both cheeks.

« À bientôt, » she said with a wave as she left.

The men looked around the kitchen. A window above two sinks looked out to a backyard. A pan was simmering on a range set against another wall, and a solid table and chairs sat in the middle of the tiled floor.

« Would you like some soup? I know you have had a long journey today, » Louise asked.

« Thank you, that would be most welcome, » Simon replied.

Louise ladled helpings from the pan on the range into earthenware bowls and sat them on the table. She added a loaf of bread.

« Please help yourselves, I am sorry this is all I can offer but rationing is very difficult. »

« This is fine, thank you, Louise. We are grateful for anything. »

Louise filled a bowl for herself and joined the men at the table.

« I think your plans were to try to get back to England over the Channel. Is that right? »

« That was our plan, yes. »

« I am afraid that won't work. It is too difficult to get close to the Channel coast. The German defences are too strong and even if you did manage to get to the beaches or steal a yacht, their E-Boat patrols would catch you before you got two or three kilometres from the coast. »

Simon and Chapman looked at each other. The news wasn't really surprising but they'd maintained some hope of getting through.

« So, what do we do? And can you help us? »

« Yes, we can help. But you will need to travel south to get to Spain. »

When they'd finished their meal, Louise removed the empty bowls and spread an old Michelin motoring map on the table.

« Tomorrow, we will take you to Versailles. You may have to stay there for a day or two while we prepare new travel documents then we will have couriers escort you in stages probably via Chartres, Tours, Poitiers and Toulouse. Some of the time you will travel by train, sometimes by bus, sometimes we will have to organise other transport and sometimes you will walk. »

« Thank you, Louise. That sounds perfect. We don't have much money left from our escape kit, though. How can we pay for tickets? »

« That is no problem. London provides us with funds to help get fliers home. Now, there are sleeping quarters in the cellar. There is a toilet in the yard and you can wash at the sink. It is not the Georges Cinq but it is all we can offer. »

« I'm sure we'll be fine; it's better than sleeping in the woods. »

The beds in the cellar were basic but far better than they'd enjoyed while hiking from the crash site or even in the windmill.

"I didn't imagine I'd see Paris like this," remarked Chapman. "I'd planned to see the Eiffel Tower, Notre Dame, the Louvre and the Moulin Rouge! And here we are, in a cellar in a house but where exactly in Paris, I have no idea. Did you ever plan to visit Paris, Ferguson?"

"I never gave it any thought, Skipper. If I'd still been going out with Lucy, I imagine we'd have visited her family over here. Pity we never got to see them, they might have been useful contacts. Mind you, one of the trips I did with S-Sugar was dropping a couple of Joes near Chartres. Maybe they'll be involved in moving us on if we're going that way."

"Were they SOE agents or MI9 evasion line bods? I don't think SOE get involved in the escape lines – they leave that to MI9."

"No idea, Skip. We didn't see them, let alone speak to them. Don't even know if they were men or women."

At five the following morning, Louise brought Chapman and Simon up from the cellar and offered them breakfast of bread and coffee substitute.

« We need to leave early. The Metro only works for a few hours. We will walk to the nearest station. Try to keep close enough to me to follow but not too close. If we get separated take Line 11 to the Republique station. There you take the Line 8 to Les Invalides. I will wait for you at the exit to the Metro. From Les Invalides we take the RER to Versailles Rive Gauche. Is that clear? »

« Perfectly clear, Louise. »

« At Versailles, turn right out of the station. This takes you along the side of the Hotel de Ville to the Avenue de Paris – it's a very wide boulevard, you can't mistake it. It leads to the Palace of Versailles to your left – but you turn right, along the front of the Hotel de Ville until you get to the Post Office. If we have lost contact, I will wait for you on the small road at the side of the

Post Office. Be very careful around the Hotel de Ville. The Germans are using it as the Kommandantur."

« Isn't it asking for trouble being so close to them? »

« Not really, the last place the Germans are likely to expect British evaders is under their own noses! But, Pilot Officer Chapman, I think you should avoid speaking at all as your accent wouldn't pass. Sergeant Ferguson's is fine. Your current papers should be sufficient as far as Chartres. If you are questioned by Gendarmes, they will probably be satisfied with you saying you wanted to see the palace while passing through Paris. »

The Metro was, as expected, very busy and Simon and Chapman lost sight of Louise as they changed lines at Republique. They caught up with her again on the platform for Line 8 – but the crowd carried her onto the train and the doors closed before they could squeeze into the carriage.

« Not to worry, we can meet her again at Les Invalides as she said, » Simon said to Chapman, hoping that he would understand his French. Chapman nodded his head.

« Bien sûr. »

The men saw Louise apparently looking at a map of the rail network as they emerged from the Metro. They followed her to the RER ticket office and bought their tickets to Versailles. The train was already crowded when it pulled into the platform, but they joined the scrum of bodies pushing their way into the carriages. Simon was trapped next to the door while Chapman managed to get further into the carriage and hold onto a strap.

Hemmed in by the crush, Simon wondered if his body odour was as unpleasant as some of those around him. They hadn't had a chance to bathe or shower since the morning of their mission to Mannheim. They had been able to sponge themselves down at the sink of the safe house the previous night but he doubted if that had done very much.

As the train emerged from underground Simon could see the upper parts of the Eiffel Tower emerging above buildings and trees lining the boulevard running alongside the rail tracks. A few minutes later, the train pulled into Javel station. Past Issy, the passengers thinned out and Simon was able to move away from the door and stand next to Chapman. By then, Louise had managed to get a seat.

More passengers left at Viroflay, leaving seats free but, as they were opposite two German soldiers, Simon and Chapman remained standing with their backs to them. Five minutes later, the train pulled into Versailles Rive Gauche.

The airmen followed Louise out of the station and turned right. After a hundred yards, they were alongside the Hotel de Ville. The building reminded Simon of pictures he'd seen at Lucy's of chateaux in the Loire valley. Sentries stood at the foot of the steps leading up to the side entrance. Simon and Chapman averted their eyes but they couldn't avoid looking at the impressive architecture.

Fifty more yards brought them to the junction with the Avenue de Paris. A cobbled road separated the buildings from twin paved footways with grass between them and trees on either side before the main roadway of the Avenue de Paris. The arrangement appeared to be repeated on the other side so it was about a hundred yards from one side to the other.

They stood and looked towards the palace but much of it was hidden behind the trees and, as Louise hadn't stopped, Simon and Chapman turned to follow her along the footway.

In front of the Hotel de Ville, a semicircle drive enclosing flower beds and lawns led to the bottom of steps leading up to the main entrance where soldiers stood on sentry duty. As the men passed, cars drove in one end, dropped their passengers then drove out the other. Even if the sentries at the door hadn't been busy saluting visitors, Simon was relieved to see that they were at least a hundred yards away so weren't likely to take interest in him.

Fifty yards past the appropriated Kommandantur, there was a junction with the main Post Office on the corner. Louise was walking slowly down the narrow, cobbled road at the side of the building. Simon and Chapman followed. Near the bottom, she turned left immediately before double gates set into a twelve-foot-high wall. Four-storey houses crowded each side of the narrow street. The road turned right again after a few yards and the men saw Louise waiting for them near the end of the cul-de-sac.

She knocked on a door then, when it opened, urged the men to go inside.

Chapter 31. Versailles

November 1943

The door led to a corridor with crude slab flooring, coats hung on hooks on the plain walls with boots and other outdoor shoes on the floor below. They were shown into a kitchen off the corridor.

« This is Isabelle, she will look after you while you stay here. "

Isabelle gave the men a welcoming smile. Like Louise, Isabelle was in her mid-twenties. Her auburn hair was cut short, barely collar length, and straight. She wore a white blouse and calf-length plain grey skirt.

« We will hide you in the loft of the old coach house and stables, which is now used as a garage. Not that we can get petrol for the cars these days. Come with me. »

They kept next to the twelve-foot-high wall which concealed them from view from the houses on the other side of the narrow road. Tall horse chestnut trees hid them from dwellings on the other side of the garden. They entered the coach house through a side entrance. Inside they encountered a black limousine facing double doors; its wheel hubs supported on wooden blocks. Squeezing around the back of the car, they stopped for a moment to admire an open vintage buckboard style vehicle with large spoked wheels and solid tyres that stood next to it. Beyond that were stalls for horses that drew the original carriages and a ladder leading to the old hay loft. A door at the end led back into the garden.

« You will be safe enough up there for tonight. There is bread and cheese and a bottle of wine in the loft. There's a tap for water in the corner down here and privy outside the far door. Please stay inside the building other than to use the toilet. You will move on the day after tomorrow to Chartres where you will stay while they prepare new documents for you. The train leaves from the Versailles Chantiers station. It is about half a mile from here. »

« Will you be taking us? » asked Chapman.

« No, it will be another guide. We divide the journey into sections so that if someone is arrested, there is a limit to what they can reveal under interrogation. »

Simon shook his head at the casual way Isabelle spoke about the possibility of arrest and torture.

« You're all incredibly brave doing what you do, » he told her.

« If we don't fight back, France will never again be free, » she answered.

When Isabelle had left, Simon examined the vintage car.

"I think this is an early Peugeot, eighteen ninety-six or thereabouts. What an incredible machine," he remarked.

"Isabelle said something about having left some food and wine in the loft. I don't know about you but I'm hungry."

"OK skipper, be with you in a minute."

The next morning, Isabelle brought more food and another bottle of wine for the men and assured them that all was in place for them to move on the next morning. With nothing to do, Simon and Chapman did their best to have a full body wash at the tap in the stable.

Isabelle returned, as promised, the following day with another member of the resistance.

« This is Yvette, she will take you to Chartres. There she will pass you on to another courier. »

The men shook her hand when it was offered to them. She was smartly presented with a navy coat over a fitted dress in a lighter shade; she wore a brimmed hat tilted to one side and matching gloves, shoes and handbag. Her make-up was flawless.

« After I leave, wait thirty minutes then follow. I will be sitting having a drink at the bar opposite the post office at the end of the road. When I see you approach, I will walk down the Rue des États Généraux. Follow me at a distance. At the station, purchase second-class tickets to Chartres. I will be in first class. At Chartres, get off the train and follow me. There will be a delivery van nearby that will take you to the safe house. Is that clear? »

« Yes, perfectly, Yvette »

The men did as instructed and left the coach house half an hour after Yvette. They followed the cobbled street back to the post office on the junction with the Avenue de Paris and Rue des États Généraux. As they approached, Yvette stood up from the table where she had been drinking a coffee. She walked along the pavement on the left-hand side of the road while Simon and Chapman stayed on the right-hand side.

They passed a boulangerie with queues stretching out of the door, customers hoping that there would be sufficient bread to last until it was their turn to be served. On the other side of a junction, more locals queued outside a general store. Then a petrol station with signs warning that they had no fuel to sell. Further along, a cycle shop was doing good business servicing, selling and hiring out bicycles instead of the taxi service listed on the sign above the windows. A second-hand furniture shop had a few items on the pavement and others inside.

After fifteen minutes, they walked up the approach to the SNCF station. Simon and Chapman let two other customers join the queue between Yvette and themselves then bought their tickets. Their papers were, as usual, examined at the barrier.

The train was due at ten-fifteen but was fifteen minutes late. The airmen found seats in a second-class carriage and stared out of the window. To the right of the train, houses bordered the tracks while a tree-covered slope climbed away from the railway on the left. As the houses were left behind, there was a glimpse on the right, between the trees, of a man-made lake and the side of the Palace of Versailles on a hill in the distance.

The train picked up speed and rattled over points to goods yards and local stations. Then it was through forests, possibly part of the hunting territory the various Louis had exploited when living at Versailles, thought Simon.

The men didn't converse. They'd agreed that Chapman's accent would put them in danger if they did, so each was left to his own thoughts.

Simon thought back to Elmdene and his family. What would they be doing now? He wasn't even sure what day of the week it was. He then realised it was Monday. His mother and aunt would be doing the laundry, his uncle visiting his flock, perhaps comforting someone who had received a telegraph about a husband or son missing in action. His cousins were probably at work in the factory in Westchester, his sister would be at school. No doubt they'd be worried about him as he'd have been posted as Missing in Action. Would they think he was dead? What about Lucy? Was she still working near London? No doubt she'd found a new boyfriend by now. His former colleagues would probably be busy repairing aircraft for the ATA to ferry back to operational stations. It was now eleven days since they had set off to bomb

Mannheim. How much longer would it take to get back to Blighty, Simon wondered. He closed his eyes and followed the service maxim to always take advantage of any opportunity to rest – or relieve yourself.

He was woken from his nap by Chapman elbowing him in the ribs. The skipper gestured to the window as the train pulled into Chartres station.

Yvette was striding along the platform as the men stepped down from the train. They followed a few yards behind her before they were funnelled into the line at the barrier. The inspector took their tickets and a Gendarme demanded their papers. He seemed to take an age examining them and Simon began to wonder if there was a problem. But the policeman handed them back and took the next set being offered to him as Simon reached the concourse. Yvette had stopped to light a cigarette, giving the men a chance to catch up.

She left the station and they emerged into a square. Beyond some houses on the other side of the forecourt, they could see the twin spires of Chartres Cathedral above the buildings facing them. There was no time to admire the view before Yvette crossed over then took a side street. Fifty yards down the road was the van they'd been promised.

« I now leave you. Marcel, here, will take you to the safe house. Good luck. »

« Thank you for your help, » Chapman said.

They were hustled into the back of the vehicle and hidden behind sacks of potatoes.

« Are you comfortable in the back? » Marcel asked.

« Fine, thank you, » they assured him.

« It isn't far to the house; just outside the city. »

Marcel started the engine which spluttered and coughed as he pulled away. They drove over a bridge spanning the railway then along a road through the outskirts of the town. As they left the built-up area, they were forced to stop at a police checkpoint.

« Merde! » swore Marcel, as he slowed to a stop. « Be absolutely silent in the back. »

« Papers, » demanded the Gendarme.

Marcel handed over his documents.

« What are you carrying? »

« Vegetables, I'm delivering to the Luftwaffe base at Nogent-le-Roi. It's a regular delivery. »

« Open the back for me. »

Marcel slowly climbed out of his seat and feigned a limp to take his time getting to the back of the van to the back of the van. He opened the doors and saw Simon and Chapman sitting there.

« What's the problem, cousin? » Simon asked.

Marcel realised Simon's ploy and went along with it.

« Nothing, just a routine check. »

« Who are you? » the gendarme demanded.

« I'm Marcel's cousin, Jules Calvet. This is my colleague, Phillipe Pascal. We are being transferred to work on the Atlantic Wall so I thought we could visit my Aunt Helene while in the area. I haven't seen her since the war began and my mother would never forgive me if I'd been this close and not visited her sister. »

« Papers! »

The gendarme examined the documents which tallied with the names Simon had given and confirmed the transfer to work on the coastal defences.

« And you are Phillipe Pascal? » he asked Chapman.

« Oui, » Chapman answered hoping that his accent would be good enough for such a monosyllabic answer.

« Would you like some vegetables, perhaps? » Marcel asked. « Maybe a cauliflower, some turnips and some potatoes? The Luftwaffe won't miss the odd one or two. »

The gendarme looked incredulous, and Simon wondered if he would investigate further or, perhaps, decide not to bother; maybe he recognised that the war had turned against the Germans and there was little point doing more than he needed to. He was relieved when the policeman accepted the offer and sent them on their way.

Marcel parked outside the safe house to drop the airmen off to meet their next courier before completing the vegetable delivery to the Luftwaffe base.

« Walk down the side of the café and knock on the door like this, » Marcel tapped out the code they were to use.

« Your next contact will be waiting for you, » he told them.

Simon and Chapman were totally unprepared for what was waiting for them.

Chapter 32. Capture

November 1943

Simon and Chapman did as they had been instructed and the door opened wide to reveal a rotund, middle-aged male of average height, wearing a black waistcoat over a white shirt and tie and a long grey apron over his trousers. He looked nervous as Chapman entered first. The moment that Simon stepped past the door, it slammed shut behind them to reveal another man in a leather greatcoat and carrying a Luger pistol.

„Hände hoch!" « Lèvez les mains! » he commanded.

Three other men wearing SS uniforms and carrying submachine guns stepped into the room and aimed their weapons at the airmen. Chapman and Simon looked at each other and recognised that they had no option but to comply and raised their hands.

"We are RAF and entitled to be treated as prisoners of war," Chapman declared. "I am Pilot Officer William Chapman; this is Sergeant Simon Ferguson."

"So. You say you are RAF terror fliers. And the patron here, is he also RAF? Is he also to be treated as a prisoner of war? I think not." The German officer turned to two of the soldiers. „Take him and the two waitresses to the Kommandatur, I will question them later."

He turned to the other soldier and gestured towards Simon and Chapman. „Put these two in my car. I will deal with them first."

At military headquarters, Simon and Chapman were separated. Simon was hustled into a cell while Chapman was taken to be interviewed.

"You claim to be an officer in the Royal Air Force, but where is your uniform? You are wearing civilian clothes. Do you have anything to prove who you say you are? At the moment, I think you are members of the resistance. You only pretend to be British. But, if you are British, then I am certain you are members of your Special Operations Executive. As saboteurs or spies, you are not entitled to be treated as prisoners of war. Unless you convince me otherwise you will be shot."

"I am Pilot Officer William Chapman; my serial number is –" His answer was cut short by the interrogator leaning forward until he was only inches away from Chapman's face.

"I don't care what your serial number is. That tells me nothing. What I need from you is your squadron number? Where it was based? What aircraft did you fly? What was your mission when you were shot down? Who helped you to evade capture? Where were the safe houses you stopped in? Perhaps that information might convince me that you really are RAF."

"You must know that I cannot provide that information and you are contravening the Geneva Convention by asking for it."

The German slapped his hand on the table.

"Do not dare to tell me what I can and cannot ask. You forget your position. You and your companion have been found with forged documents and without any evidence of being members of the RAF as you claim. At the moment, you are facing a firing squad unless you satisfy me that you are RAF officers."

Chapman considered his position.

Could he reveal sufficient information to convince the interrogator that he and his Flight Engineer were who they claimed to be without adding to what the German war machine already knew? They would obviously be aware of the attack on Mannheim and had probably found the wreck of the Stirling by now.

But even that would reveal that there would have been seven men on board. What if some of them were still at large? Would it help the Germans to know that?

Chapman thought about it for a moment. He realised that the Germans were bound to know that a Stirling carried seven crew. The same as the other British four-engine bombers.

It was possible, however, that the wreck might have been mistaken for an American-built Flying Fortress which carried a crew of ten. Both had four engines, were of a similar size and both had a single fin and rudder. There were significant differences but if the Stirling had been burned out after crashing it might have been difficult to be certain of its identity.

Did that help him and Ferguson though?

Would it help to spread doubt in the German's minds about how many crew were still at large by claiming they'd been flying a Fortress? Or did it risk casting more doubt about their own identity and increasing the chance of ending up in front of a firing squad?

Chapman decided it wasn't worth the risk. Where possible he would give the vaguest possible answers hoping that it would be of little help.

"We were flying a Stirling on a mission to Mannheim. We were attacked by two night fighters on our way home and came down somewhere in the Ardennes. We walked for several days before being helped," he admitted.

"Now we are getting somewhere. Where were you when you were helped?"

"I don't know. We've been so many places, it's all blurred. We found a farm and hid in a barn."

"Where? Where was this farm?"

"I'm not sure. We'd been walking for days – trying to get to the coast. We just knew if we kept walking north of west, we were bound to hit the channel coast. I'd injured myself landing so wasn't focussing on how far we walked. I just knew that every step hurt for the first day or so."

The interrogator lit a cigarette.

"I am sorry, would you like one?" He proffered the pack to Chapman who took one, confused at the sudden change of approach.

"It must have been a very difficult time for you. But this farm, was it on a hill or in a valley? How many buildings were there? Describe the main house."

"It was on the side of a valley, I think. It was just a typical French farmhouse there were two or three other buildings."

"Did the farm have cattle or other livestock? What crops did it grow?"

"It had a few cows and some pigs and chickens. I don't know what crops it grew, I couldn't tell one crop from another. It was dark when we got there in any event."

"Where were you taken after the farm? How long did that journey take?"

"I don't know where we were taken, I suppose the journey took half to three-quarters of an hour, I really didn't notice." Chapman hoped his answers were sufficiently vague to be of no help.

"What did you travel in? Who took you?"

"It was just a delivery van, driven by a Frenchman. They didn't say what their names were."

"You say 'they' was there more than one? How many?"

"It was just the driver. When I said 'they', I meant none of the people we met gave us their names."

"After that, where were you taken? How did you get to Chartres?"

"We were collected two days later in the same van and driven for several hours to Reims. Then we took the train to Paris." Chapman hoped changing how they had travelled would make it more difficult for the Germans to identify where they'd been.

"How do you know it was the same van? Was it the same driver?"

"I recognised the interior, there were areas where paint had been spilt."

"That will do for now. I will see how your comrade's answers match yours. If you are telling the truth there should be no problem and, maybe, you will avoid the firing squad."

„Take him to a cell and bring the other British prisoner," he commanded the SS soldiers who had been standing each side of the door.

Simon was hustled into the interrogation room and pushed down into a hard wooden chair behind the table. The German officer stared at him for what seemed like an age but was probably no more than a minute. He then looked at some papers in a folder in front of him, pretending to study them and turning over a page or two. He closed the folder then looked at Simon once more.

"So, you claim to be an RAF officer?" the interrogator said to Simon.

"No, I am not an officer, I am Sergeant Simon Ferguson."

"And what was your role in the aircraft? A Stirling, I believe."

"I cannot answer that question, sir."

"Come now, Sergeant, if you were in uniform, I would be able to see from your brevet what your role was. What harm can it do to tell me?"

"I am only required to give my name, rank and serial number."

"You don't seem to recognise your position. We have arrested you carrying false documents and in civilian clothes. The Geneva Convention only covers military personnel. You have no proof that you are a member of the RAF. Perhaps your reluctance to say what your role was in the aircraft is because you were never a member of the crew. Oh, I don't doubt that you flew into France and it may have been in a Stirling, or, perhaps, a Halifax or maybe a Lysander. The SOE use all of them to deliver agents. Is that not so?"

"I wouldn't know, sir."

"I think you do. Well, we will leave the matter of your position in the aircraft for now. Pilot Officer Chapman says your mission when you were shot down was to bomb Mannheim and you were hit by flak. Is that correct?"

Simon was surprised that Chapman had revealed even that, but came to the same conclusion as his skipper that it would add nothing to what the Germans already knew.

"Yes, our mission was to bomb Mannheim."

"And you were shot down by flak?"

"All I know is that we were hit and had to bail out."

"So, I can conclude that you were not a gunner or the pilot or you would have been aware of how you were hit."

Simon cursed himself for that slip.

"That means you were Wireless Operator, Flight Engineer or Navigator. It doesn't really matter which in any case. So, where were you when you were ordered to bail out?"

"I have no idea."

"If you had been Navigator, you would have known your position and would have given it to the Wireless Operator to send out a message. So, you must have been the Flight Engineer. Now why couldn't you have admitted that in the first place, Sergeant? Unless, of course, you were a passenger. A spy or a member of your SOE."

"My name is –"

The interrogator slapped his hand hard onto the table.

"You are a saboteur or a spy. You will be shot. Unless you convince me that you are a Sergeant in the RAF. Where were you shot down? How did you get to Chartres? Who helped you? If you don't answer my questions, make no mistake, you will face a firing squad. I will let you think about that for a while."

„Take him back to his cell," he instructed the guards. „Fetch the other Britisher."

Chapter 33. Prisoner Of War

November 1943

Chapman was brought back into the room and roughly forced back into the chair. The German officer slapped his swagger stick against his leather boots as he walked slowly around his prisoner. Chapman stared straight ahead, determined not to be intimidated by the interrogator. If he could stand flying directly into intense flak, he wasn't going to let some jumped-up Nazi scare him. Dealing with fear and facing death was his daily job. Every time he'd climbed into his aircraft, there was about a one in ten chance he wouldn't survive.

But, like all other aircrew, he'd volunteered. He'd felt scared, that was only natural, but he'd carried on regardless. This was no different. He certainly wasn't going to let this Hun get the better of him.

The German stood behind him and put his mouth close to Chapman's ear.

"So, have you decided to give me the information I need to confirm that you are an officer in the Royal Air Force or are you and your colleague to be shot? The choice is yours."

The interrogator walked back around the desk and took his seat facing Chapman. He took out his cigarettes and lit one, blowing smoke rings towards the bare light bulb that hung from the ceiling.

"Or do we make things less comfortable for you first?"

He nodded to the soldiers standing at the side of the room. They took places either side of Chapman and held his hands behind his back.

The interrogator took a drag on his cigarette and tapped it to remove the ash leaving a bright tip. He leant forward and held the glowing tip of the cigarette an inch from Chapman's right eye.

"Which is it to be? Will you tell me who helped you or will you lose one or both of your eyes?"

The German's ice-cold stare made it very clear that he would have no hesitation in carrying out his threat. But, if he gave away those brave individuals who had helped him, would certainly be tortured and executed. He didn't want to die himself or be blinded. Could he withstand the threatened torture? Or should he try to give the minimum information. The escape and evasion training they'd received had implied that few would be able to resist questioning and if that did become inevitable, they should, at least, try to hold out for a day or two to give those who had helped them time to go to ground – assuming that they knew they were at risk. Maybe he could give misleading information at first and just dribble out the truth gradually.

The cigarette moved closer to Chapman's eye but diverted at the last moment and was pressed into his cheek. The smell of burning flesh filled his nostrils as the pain hit but at least he wasn't blinded.

The German took another drag on the cigarette and held it close again.

"That was just to show that I am serious. It's your choice. Who helped you? Where was the farm?"

At that moment, the door to the corridor opened and a Luftwaffe Major entered the room. His empty right sleeve was pinned up and his face was disfigured by burns.

„What is going on here?" he demanded.

„I am interrogating this prisoner, as I am sure you can see."

„I understand that the prisoner is RAF. As you well know, RAF prisoners are the responsibility of the Luftwaffe,"

„He was arrested in civilian clothing and carrying forged documents. It is by no means certain that he is a member of the RAF."

„Really? I understand he has given you his name, rank and serial number. Is that not sufficient for your enquiries? You certainly have no reason to torture him."

„Perhaps you forget yourself, Major, in criticising me for carrying out my duties. We have friends in high places, you know."

„Don't you dare threaten me. You may be able to intimidate prisoners and some members of the Luftwaffe and the army but I have faced real danger. That's how I received these injuries. And, if you want to claim influential friends, it was the Fuhrer, himself, who presented me with this bauble." The Major fingered the rare Knight's Cross of the Iron Cross with Oak Leaves and Swords medal that hung around his neck.

The interrogator considered outstaring the Major but lowered his gaze after a few seconds.

„You can have him if you wish."

„There is a second man I believe? I will take him too."

„Prepare the paperwork transferring the two men to Luftwaffe responsibility, and bring Sergeant Ferguson here," the interrogator instructed.

Once the paperwork was completed, Chapman and Simon were left alone with the Luftwaffe Major.

"I am Major Bauer. I'm sorry you had to put up with the Gestapo officer."

Chapman and Simon glanced at each other. *Was this another ploy?* Simon wondered.

"Oh, don't worry, I'm not going to try to get information out of you. I don't need it. We already know your names, ranks and serial numbers. That you, Pilot Officer Chapman, were the pilot of Stirling P-Patsy, and you, Sergeant Ferguson, were the Flight Engineer. We know you attacked Mannheim and were then shot down by night fighters and bailed out over the Ardennes. As for the resistance workers who may have helped you, they are not my concern. Unfortunately for them, they are the Gestapo's business." Major Bauer grimaced as he said the name.

"We found the remains of your aircraft, by the way. There were three dead crew members in it. Air gunner Sergeant Hunter, Navigator Pilot Officer Stewart and Wireless Operator Sergeant Murray. We identified them from their identity discs. They have been buried in a churchyard near the crash site. We have also captured two other members of your crew: Sergeants Campbell and Webb. They were caught the day after you were shot down."

"I see, sir. Thank you for the information."

Bauer shrugged his shoulders.

"I would hope I would be given the same courtesy if our roles were reversed. You will now be taken to a transit centre where you will be assigned to a permanent prison camp. You have a long journey ahead of you. If you give me your parole, I can leave your hands free – otherwise, you will be handcuffed which will be far less comfortable."

"It's our duty to attempt to escape," Chapman pointed out, "so it would be wrong of us to give our parole."

"So be it. It's you who will be uncomfortable," Bauer said.

The two men were taken out to a canvas-sided lorry and helped to climb into the back where they sat on the hard benches on opposite sides near the cab. Two Luftwaffe airmen, armed with rifles, sat either side at the back of the lorry. A corporal and the driver lifted the tailgate and secured it before taking their positions in the cab.

As the lorry drove away from Gestapo headquarters, Chapman leaned towards Simon.

"I was worried there for a bit. I thought that bastard was really going to have us shot."

"Me too," Simon admitted. "I had hoped Campbell and Webb had got away but they clearly didn't do as well as we did."

"That, I think, was largely down to your experience and your French."

"Well, Skipper, much of what I learned was from an old poacher."

The lorry made its way eastward, passing through Versailles and by-passing Paris then on to Reims, reversing the route the airmen had taken by train. They drove for nearly twelve hours each day, stopping occasionally for the escorts to stretch their legs, go to the toilet behind hedges and refuel both the vehicle and the men. They made overnight stops at Luftwaffe bases where Simon and Chapman were secured in cells in the guardhouses.

At the end of the third day, they arrived at the transit camp north of Frankfurt. They drove through the double gates in a ten-foot-high fence and pulled up at the reception building. As they climbed down from the lorry, they looked around them. There were rows of wooden huts beyond a further barbed wire fence. Guards kept watch from towers around the inner compound. Simon and Chapman were jabbed in the back with the barrels of other guards' weapons and directed into a long concrete building. Inside they were pushed into individual cells and the doors slammed behind each man.

Simon looked around. There was a rudimentary bed with a single blanket. A bare lamp behind a protective grill in the ceiling lit the plain walls. There was a barred window six feet up in the wall opposite the door. He jumped up to try to see out of the window but the only view was of the wooden huts and the forest beyond. The only other item in the cell was a bucket which he assumed was his toilet. As it had been a long day and there wasn't much else he could do, Simon took off his shoes and stretched out on the bed. Apart from the brief periods while they were being interrogated in Chartres, it was the first time he'd been on his own for months. If he hadn't been in aircraft with the rest of the crew, they'd be in briefings, in training rooms, the mess or down the pub with others from the squadron. It was quite pleasant having his own space for a while – though whether he'd feel that way if he was in solitary for long might be another matter.

The next morning, a guard banged on his door.

„Stand clear of the door," he ordered. Although he didn't understand German, Simon quickly realised what was expected of him. The door opened a few inches and a plate with a lump of black bread and a mug of water were slid through the gap.

It was the first food Simon had had for nearly twenty-four hours and he ate it eagerly. He had barely finished the last crumb when the door was opened again and he was ordered to follow the guard to an interrogation room.

Despite Major Bauer's claims that they had all the information they might obtain from Simon and Chapman, the airmen faced further questioning. While in the lorry, they'd agreed on a story and descriptions of resistance members that they could eke out.

They claimed they hadn't known their precise location after bailing out but, as they'd previously said, knew that heading north of west would take them eventually to the Channel coast. Their escape map didn't have sufficient detail to identify their exact route and, as far as possible, they'd kept to paths within the forests and away from any towns or villages. When asked about the resistance members who had assisted them, they described the landlord and barmaids at the Royal Oak pub frequented by the crew when they were at Stradishall. Their portrayals of the locations where they'd been held were equally vague – but were consistent.

After several days, Simon was released from solitary confinement and loaded onto another lorry with other prisoners, driven to the local railway station and loaded into a cattle wagon for the journey to a permanent POW camp. In his case, it was to Stalag 344, which housed non-commissioned officers, near Lamsdorf, just north of the Polish/ Czechoslovakian border. Chapman was transferred the next day to Stalag Luft III near Sagan.

Chapter 34. Stalag 344

November 1943

A detachment of soldiers stood waiting for the train when it stopped at a level crossing. The guards opened each wagon in turn and instructed the prisoners to dismount.

„Raus! Raus! Schnell! Schnell!" the call went out along the train.

Simon was glad to be able to stretch his legs as he looked around him. The single rail track had crossed a small road – both arrow-straight as far as he could see. There were a few houses on either side of the road but no station buildings, just a slightly raised platform indicating the halt. The terrain was flat as far as the edge of the forest, about half a mile away.

A German officer chivvied his men who pushed the prisoners into line. Four of the guards mounted motorcycle combinations, their passengers taking hold of the machine guns fitted to the sidecars. Satisfied all was in order, the officer climbed into a Kübelwagen and led the column along the road with the remainder of the guards either side of the captives ensuring that none of them attempted to escape into the woods that closed in on the road.

The tall fir trees obscured what little light penetrated the cloud cover as the sun set. A cold wind blew from the east spraying the column with the remains of the rain that had settled on the branches. Finally, the gates of the prison camp appeared in a gap in the trees at the side of the track. Simon's heart sank as they entered the compound. This was intended to be their home as long as the war lasted.

The new arrivals were drawn up inside the wire while a roll call was taken to ensure no one was missing. Once they'd been processed, they were allocated to huts through the compound. Most of the new arrivals were RAF aircrew with a few soldiers who had been captured in Italy and the Dodecanese. The intake was split by service and rank.

Simon's hut was in the middle of the main compound. Walking to it, he could see the tall double boundary fences with guard towers and a trip wire marking the 'no-go' limit within the fences. Taking a step over that wire invited the guards to shoot.

The accommodation blocks were single-storey brick or wooden constructions set on piles of bricks to allow the Germans to look underneath and check for tunnelling and shallow-pitched roofs. Inside, each had two rooms fitted with two or three-level bunk beds for 130 men – plus ablutions. In spite of stoves, the huts were cold, not helped by missing panes of glass in the windows.

"Welcome to Hellsdorf," greeted a sergeant wearing an Air Gunner's brevet. "I'm Frank Stevens. That bunk there is free," he said, gesturing at a middle tier near the window. "I'd introduce you to the rest of this crew but I don't suppose you'd remember the names."

"Probably not," Simon admitted. "I'm Simon Ferguson." Looking around, he could see that all of the men wearing battledress tunics were aircrew sergeants – some with pilot's wings, others with brevets with initials to indicate their trade.

"So, what's your story, Simon?" asked one of the pilots. "I'm Ken Dean, also known as Dixie after Dixie Dean the footballer, though I prefer rugby to football."

"We bailed out a couple of weeks ago after a raid on Mannheim. We were making for Spain when we got picked up in Chartres."

"I assume from the civvy clothes that you were being helped by the resistance."

"I'd prefer not to comment on that."

"Quite right too. Walls have ears, don't you know."

"So, what's this place like?" Simon asked. "What's the routine?"

"Apart from having to assemble for appells, that's roll calls, twice a day, sometimes more, we're pretty much left alone. The conditions are diabolical, the worst I've experienced, and I've been in several camps. The food is rubbish. Thankfully we get Red Cross parcels once a week which makes a difference. The whole place is grossly overcrowded. But, apart from that, it's a holiday camp. Mind you, we're better off than the Russians and Poles in the other compounds. Their conditions are even worse than ours. The Germans do tend to observe the Geneva Convention most of the time for the British but not for them."

"What about work, Dixie? I know NCOs are only required to do supervisory work – so where does that leave us?"

"It's only really the pongos who have to work and the army has plenty of their own NCOs to supervise them so they leave us Brylcreem Boys alone. Some of the lads do nothing, others are taking the opportunity to study, then there's various clubs like amateur dramatics – there's a couple of professional actors from before the war here. And, of course, there's trying to escape or helping with escape attempts. If you have an idea for an attempt, you need to submit it to the escape committee."

Over the next few days, Simon considered what Dixie had said. The war could go on for several more years. He didn't think there was any doubt about the final outcome now that America was involved. The Germans had lost the battle of Stalingrad earlier that year, Italy had surrendered and it was inevitable that the Allies would invade Europe, probably next year if the build-up of equipment throughout the South of England was anything to go by. How long it would then take to finish the job was another matter. It could turn into another war of attrition, neither side able to penetrate the other's defences.

In the meantime, he had no intention of just idling away his time. Ideally, he wanted to escape but he knew that it wasn't going to be as easy as strolling out of the gate and walking home. Being on the run after bailing out had shown the importance of preparation. Of having appropriate papers, clothes and money and a clear plan of how to get out of German-occupied territory – though any such plan was likely to be changed once he was out. He realised that being able to speak French had been a major factor in getting as far as they had but they were now much further from freedom. Their journey to the camp had been mainly eastwards from Chartres – they'd been heading towards sunrises. One of the other sergeants had told him the camp was in Poland just north of the Czech border. There was no doubt, however, that being able to speak German would be a help if he did ever get out of the camp. That would be his first priority.

He'd also offered to help with any escapes already being organised. The escape committee had asked him to note any lessons he'd learned. He'd gathered that there were all sorts of tasks that might be involved from looking out for Germans searching the camp, known as 'Ferret watching', soil dispersal from tunnelling, to forging and map making. Keeping fit was also going to be important. It was a long way back to England and, if he did get out, there was no telling how much of it would have to be done on foot.

With that in mind, he left the hut and walked around the perimeter of the compound, staying inside the warning wire. He played over in his mind his attempt, with Chapman, to evade capture.

Back in the hut, he wrote down as much as he could remember about the journey to Chartres that might help other evaders. He recorded the steps that they'd taken, assistance they'd received, notes about buying train tickets. Things he'd noticed about how the Germans and French authorities had behaved – including the way they'd focussed at checkpoints on single or pairs of men in their twenties and thirties.

Perhaps there was an opportunity to increase their chances of success by changing their appearance. Maybe making himself look older, say fifties, maybe with a limp or something? Perhaps the professional actors in the amateur dramatics group could advise him? When he struck up a conversation with one of the group's members, whose name he could never remember, he found that any such help would come at a price: he'd have to join the company.

"I don't know anything about acting," he protested.

"Nor do half the others," he was assured. "You could always start by helping with the scenery."

"I guess I can manage that," Simon agreed.

"Good, the current production is based on Ralph Reader's Gang Show. Are you familiar with it?"

"Yes, he started them to raise money for a swimming pool at a Boy Scout camp and they've been linked to scouts ever since."

"That's right. I was involved in one of his early productions. Did you know he's now a Flight Lieutenant in RAF Intelligence – though most of his work is putting on shows around RAF Stations? I did think of asking him to put one on here but I don't think the Commandant would approve. Were you a scout yourself?"

"I still am, in theory. I was a Wolf Cub, Boy Scout, Senior and officially still a Rover Scout. I achieved my Kings Scout Award."

"In that case, you might want to join the chorus for the closing number Riding Along on the Crest of a Wave."

"Yes, I'd like that."

Simon was helping with the scenery one afternoon when Flight Sergeant Nigel Booth approached him.

"Simon, we have a problem with the show. Len West has been transferred and we need someone to take his place as one of the Andrews Sisters. You've got a good singing voice."

"You want me to go on as a woman?"

"Yes, is that a problem? There are several blokes playing women's parts. We don't exactly have much choice. No one thinks anything of it – well apart from Lawrence Bradshaw who was a female impersonator before signing up."

Simon thought back to the time when Lucy and his cousins had made him dress as a girl to join in their play. His initial embarrassment had vanished after the first few minutes and it might be interesting to see how he felt this time.

"Yeah, go on then, might be a laugh."

The show was presented in the camp theatre on Boxing Day. Simon and the other 'girls' came in for a bit of banter when they appeared in mock American uniforms with skirts to sing Boogie Woogie Bugle Boy; but were then forced to do an encore of Don't Fence Me In; which they aimed at the Camp Commandant sitting with the Senior British Officer watching from the front row.

Most of the audience joined in the final show number of Riding Along on the Crest of a Wave – then gave the cast a standing ovation and tumultuous applause.

Sitting at a mirror, removing his 'slap' after the show, Simon felt a pair of hands on his shoulder give a gentle squeeze. "You're a natural performer, girl," said Lawrence Bradshaw. "Your moves just flowed. Nick and Paul were OK – but you really looked born to it."

Simon wasn't sure whether he was pleased with the comments or worried about the implications.

Chapter 35. The Plan

New Year 1944

The new year was bitter. The temperature dropped to 22 degrees Fahrenheit at night and rarely got above freezing during the day. Icy winds blew in from the Russian Steppes and penetrated every gap in the walls of the buildings and around any padding used to try to seal broken windows. The compound and the roofs of all the huts were covered in a foot-thick blanket of snow, with much deeper drifts where it had blown against obstacles.

If anyone opened a door, there would be shouts of protest. Everyone wore all the clothes they could find in a desperate attempt to stave off the cold – thankful that there had been an issue of new uniforms, courtesy of the Red Cross, just after Christmas. Coal for the stoves had virtually run out and was severely rationed.

It wasn't just the prisoners who suffered.

Guards stationed in the watch towers, or 'Goon Boxes', had to be relieved regularly. They swung their arms and stamped their feet in an attempt to generate some warmth in their limbs while struggling to see anything through the driven snow. Those detailed to patrol the compounds did so in a cursory fashion – making use of any shelter they could find from the wind.

The covering of snow had also curtailed tunnelling as there was nowhere to dispose of the excavated earth – all available spaces were already full. Other escape activities continued. Uniforms were converted to civilian clothes. Maps were still copied – though identity cards had been put to one side as frozen fingers were no use for fine details.

Simon continued his German language practice; even talking to the guards in their own tongue and studying their accents. He wouldn't pass as a native speaker but he could now hold a conversation. He was also learning his lines for the next production by the Lamsdorf Players. They were doing Agatha Christie's Murder on the Orient Express. Simon was playing Mary Debenham, a twenty-six-year-old governess. He hadn't needed much persuading to take the role. He'd decided that he wanted to see how convincing he would be presenting as a female. Lawrence Bradshaw, who was playing Countess Helena Andrenyi, had agreed to pass on as many tricks of the trade as he could and constantly nagged Simon during rehearsals if he failed to display feminine postures or gestures.

As he entered the theatre for rehearsals one Monday there was a buzz of excitement. He grabbed one of the other players. "What's happening?"

"Haven't you heard? There's been a big escape from Stalag Luft Three near Sagan. They say nearly a hundred Kregies have got out."

"I heard two hundred," said one of the scenery painters. "This on top of the three that got home using that vaulting horse last year, the Goons must be going mad. I bet they'll have every man and his dog out searching."

Simon realised this was Pukka Gen. And, if something similar coincided with his own attempt, it would make it even more difficult. All he could do, however, was to try and anticipate as many problems as possible and find ways to avoid them and he continued to use every opportunity to benefit from other's experience of trying to escape.

By the end of the final performance of Murder on the Orient Express the week after Easter, Simon was quite certain that the key element of his escape plan could work.

It was now time to find a partner for the escape. One candidate stood out.

"It's not getting out of the camp that's the problem. Hundreds of men have escaped from the various camps: over, under or through the wire, jumping from trains, posing as Germans or other Axis personnel, pretending to be sick and a dozen other ways. But it's not getting out, it's staying out and not getting caught that's the issue." Simon listened to Warrant Officer Edward Baxter as they played chess one evening. Baxter tapped the ash from his pipe, put it in his pocket, then moved a bishop. "I think that's checkmate."

Baxter was a forger, specialising in Identity cards and travel documents. He shouldn't have been a prisoner of war, his role in the RAF was in photo intelligence, safely based at a bomber station in Lincolnshire. Before the war, he'd been an engineer. He'd blagged his way onto a mission to Bremen. It should have been a milk run but they'd been hit by flak after they'd dropped their bombs.

"Can we find somewhere quiet to talk?" Simon asked.

"By all means, let's go for a stroll around the wire."

They joined the circuit of men circling the boundary fences, leaving enough space to avoid being overheard.

"I've got an idea for an escape – and I'd like your views on it and, if you think it's sound, for you to join me on the attempt."

Baxter stopped and lit his pipe.

"Go on."

Simon explained his plan.

"As you can see, it requires multiple sets of papers, someone who has experience in engineering and a reason to have an interpreter. With those, we stand a good chance of travelling openly and avoiding too many questions. You're the forger, how feasible is it to create the documents?"

"That's not a problem. It's just a matter of getting originals to copy and time to produce them."

"So, are you interested?"

"There are a lot of specifics that need to be sorted out, but, in principle, definitely."

They met each day to hammer out the details, determined to follow the example of the men from Stalag Luft Three. Then, at the beginning of April, the excitement over the mass breakout was tempered by the news that fifty of the escapees had been murdered.

"Do we press on regardless, or wash it out?" Simon asked Baxter when they heard the news.

"Your choice, Simon. It's your scheme. I'm happy to have a bash."

"OK. Let's do it."

They then took the plan to the escape committee. One Warrant Officer and two Flight Sergeants sat at a table as Simon and Derek presented their scheme.

"As you know, one of the main reasons escapers are caught is language. Ferguson and I both speak fluent French. Ferguson also speaks passable German. Another reason is that after an escape attempt, the Germans are on the lookout for single men or pairs of men; especially those in their twenties," Baxter explained. "The third reason is that the escaper can provide no reasonable excuse for being where they are if they are questioned. They're often caught hiding in barns or walking off the beaten track and avoiding other people."

The members of the committee, Warrant Officer Cox and Flight Sergeants Clarke and Young nodded to each other in agreement with what Baxter was saying.

"Ferguson's scheme circumvents these factors. As I said, we both speak fluent French. We won't be travelling as two men in their twenties or thirties. I'm obviously considerably older and Ferguson will be dressed as a woman. You've all seen him perform female roles and there is no doubt that he can carry off the disguise. That means we can travel openly on trains and other public transport."

"Our papers will show that Warrant Officer Baxter is a French engineer involved in work for the Germans and my papers will show that I'm his assistant and interpreter. We can, if necessary, give the impression that I'm also his mistress – any officials questioning us might think Mr Baxter is a dirty old man but that's probably going to distract them if we are stopped," Simon added.

"So, you plan to swop roles with two soldiers on a work party at a factory that also employs women. Once there, you, Ferguson, will change into clothes brought in by one of the women workers then, with Baxter, you'll leave the factory and walk to the railway station. Is that right?" asked Flight Sergeant Young.

"Yes Flight. Baxter is producing appropriate documents to get us out of the works. We won't use those again away from the factory. Once clear, we adopt the second identities. Our papers will show us being transferred to the Channel coast to work on the Atlantic Wall or the U-boat pens at Brest. We will travel by train and stop, when necessary, in hotels."

"Your plan depends on getting help from one of the soldiers on the work party at the factory. How certain are you that he will agree and that he'll be able to provide what you need?" asked Warrant Officer Cox.

"The theatre group used him to obtain clothes for the play from women at the plant in exchange for food and cigarettes from the Red Cross parcels, Mr Cox. So, we know he can get what I need. I don't doubt that he uses some of the stuff from the parcels to bribe the guards to turn their backs and I dare say he takes his cut too."

"What else will you need from the committee?" asked Cox.

"I'll produce all the documents we'll need. I just need some materials. I'll need a civilian suit if possible," said Baxter.

"We also need any maps and railway timetables from Oppeln, and if you've got any cash that would be a help."

"We can manage some money and your suit, Baxter. We've used work parties as escape routes before so I'm happy that part will work. God knows how many soldiers we currently have posing as RAF aircrew now," Warrant Officer Cox confirmed.

Cox looked at Young and Clarke. They nodded their heads in approval of the plan.

"We'll be sorry to lose you from the forging team, Baxter but good luck with the scheme. Just one thing, Ferguson, is this why you've allowed your hair to grow so long?" Cox asked.

"Yes, sir. I hope it will help me to pass muster."

"Hmm. Not sure if you're aware of it, but what with playing female parts and being friendly with Bradshaw, there's been gossip about you which could get you into trouble. However, if it's only for the purposes of an escape attempt, that's another matter."

Simon and Baxter were elated as they left the meeting.

Chapter 36. Working Party

May 1944

First thing we need to do, Simon, is speak to Corporal Parker on Friday when he gets back from the working party," Baxter said as they walked away from the hut where they'd met the Escape Committee. "I can get on with producing some of the documents but we also need other originals to work from."

"I'll have a word with the scrounger, no sense waiting until Friday, Edward." It still felt strange for Simon to address his escape partner by his first name. It wasn't just the difference in their ranks or their comparative lengths of service. Baxter was old enough to be Simon's father and he'd been brought up to address his elders by title, but Baxter had insisted that they were at least equal partners in the escape attempt.

Between them, they confirmed what each would do over the next few days then separated.

'It really was going to happen,' Simon thought. The idea scared him. *'Could they really carry it off? What would the German's reaction be if he was caught dressed as a woman? Oh well, he was committed now; in fact, that wasn't strictly true. He could always pull out or find some insurmountable obstacle.'*

Simon was about to enter his hut when a goon pushed past him. The scrounger was in the corridor.

"He didn't seem happy," Simon observed.

"He wasn't. Seems he didn't like me asking him to get something for us."

Simon knew better than to enquire what the scrounger had asked for, or what pressure he'd brought to bear on the German soldier. The latter probably involved a threat to expose previous exchanges of contraband for items from the Red Cross parcels. The scrounger was an expert at making harmless requests for innocuous items in exchange for a few cigarettes or a bar of chocolate – then gradually increasing the demands.

"What can I do for you, Simon?"

"Any chance you can get hold of permits and travel documents for female French staff working for the Germans?"

"Planning to get out, are you? I wondered if that was why you were growing your hair."

Simon looked horrified.

"Has everyone picked up on that?"

"Don't suppose so for one moment. Most of them in here don't think about anything or take much notice of what's going on around them. They tend to just live in their own worlds, maybe play a bit of football or get absorbed in a hobby or studying something. Yes, I can probably help. There's a French interpreter in the Kommandatur who might be persuaded to lend me her documents. She's from the Alsace region and supported the German's appropriation. As you probably know, it's swopped between German and French control since the eighteen hundreds. Since Stalingrad and the Italian surrender, she's started to worry about her future when the Allies win so is being quite helpful. The only problem is, I can get them from her in the morning but she'll need them back before she leaves for the day. Is that long enough?"

"It'll have to be."

The next morning, Simon and Baxter met the scrounger again. He had a smile on his face as he approached them, a towel draped over his arm.

"You look pleased with yourself."

"I think I have a right to be. I didn't want to mention it, in case it didn't come off – but I've got something the escape committee has been after for quite a while. Let's go into Hut 40 and I'll show you."

Inside the hut, the scrounger took a set of papers out of his pocket.

"Is this what you were after?" he asked handing them to Baxter.

"Perfect! I'll take copies of it with the pin-hole camera."

"The what?" asked Simon.

"Pin-hole camera. It's a crude device but allows us to take copies of documents and use them as templates for our own copies. Sadly, it's not good enough for photographs for identity documents. The exposure time is too long. The paper and chemicals are courtesy of the German's own photographic section. We have to use them sparingly, if our contact takes too much, it might be noticed and he could get caught."

"Speaking of cameras, would this be any use?" the scrounger asked, his face displaying a smug smile and raised eyebrows as he held out a Leica 35mm camera and two rolls of film.

"Bloody Hell!" Baxter exclaimed, taking the camera and testing its shutter mechanism and aperture settings. "How the hell –. No, don't tell me how you got it."

"Actually, I'd better give the camera to the escape committee – but I'm sure they'll be happy for you to use it for photos for your identity papers. But I also wondered if this would be useful," the scrounger queried, pulling a railway timetable from his pocket. "We need to return this tonight with the identity and travel documents."

With that, he walked out of the hut whistling.

Baxter and Simon looked at each other for a moment, stunned by the prizes they'd been given.

Simon broke the silence. "I'd better make some notes on times of trains and routes that might be useful."

"And, I'd better get on with taking copies of the documents."

When they met again that afternoon to return the documents and the timetable to the scrounger, Simon told Baxter that he'd looked at a potential route for their escape.

"There's a train from Oppeln about nineteen hundred hours. Due into Breslau at twenty-one thirty. We could continue overnight but I suggest we stay in a hotel. The trains are likely to be less crowded and we're more likely to be questioned. Hopefully, they're less likely to wake up all the guests in a hotel."

"Good point. Even if they do investigate the hotels, they'll probably take until the next day to check papers."

"Exactly. We'll be fifty miles from Oppeln by then and, even if the Germans are searching for us, they'll be looking for two men. But I suggest when we buy the tickets at Oppeln we get them to Frankfurt. That way, if they have worked out our disguises, they'll still be looking in the wrong place."

Baxter nodded his head. "Go on."

"The next day, we make for Nuremberg. We should get there by evening. Again, I suggest we avoid travelling overnight. Day three, we get to Strasbourg and on day five make for Paris. How does that sound?"

"Fine so far."

"Right. Chapman and I stopped in a safe house in Versailles. I suggest we keep a watch near the road to it. They usually go to a bar nearby at lunchtime and I might be able to recognise someone. They may have all been rounded up along with the people who helped me in Chartres but, if not, they may be able to advise whether it's best to head for the channel coast, Brittany or Spain. We can keep watch from a bar opposite the one they use."

"Good idea. Now, I've had a word with Warrant Officer Cox and the escape committee is happy for us to use the camera the scrounger obtained to produce photographs for our documents. You'll have to be dressed as –. Actually, what are you going to be called?"

"Simone Delevigne from Andrésy in the Île-de-France region. A friend of mine's mother came from there and used to describe it so I might be able to answer a few questions if asked."

"It all sounds fine but do you think we need to have a contingency plan in case we can't find any accommodation in Breslau?" Baxter remarked.

"We could continue on our way. There's a train scheduled for twenty-three forty to Dresden. We can change there for Nuremberg."

"That sounds like a sensible option."

On Friday 26th May, Corporal Parker warned them to be ready to join the working party on the Monday. Their papers were all ready and they had some high-energy tablets made from sugar, oats and other ingredients from the Red Cross parcels and slabs of chocolate to keep them going if they needed them. They swopped places with two fusiliers who were listed for the work party on the Sunday evening and assembled with the rest of the men just after dawn on the Monday morning. The sentries herded them onto a lorry for the hour and a half's drive to the factory. The other members of the party ignored Simon and Baxter, it wasn't the first time RAF NCOs had changed places with other ranks; they were just jealous of the two who had been chosen to move into the RAF quarters and avoid the hard labour.

Simon and Baxter were allocated to loading bags of cement onto a hand truck then wheeling it to a train where it was loaded onto wagons for the journey to some construction site or other; perhaps even the Atlantic Wall that their papers showed them to be transferred to once they were out of the factory. If that had been the case, it might have been easy to just climb into one of the wagons and wait until it reached its destination.

An hour after they started work, Parker approached them. His frown told them his news wasn't good.

"The woman who was to provide your clothes is ill and not here today. You'll have to stay with the working party until she returns to work."

Simon looked at Baxter. "So, do we stick to the plan and wait for her?"

"Can't do anything else, can we? All your papers are in your female name."

"Well, you could get away on your own. Your papers are fine."

"No Simon, we're in this together. It's your scheme. We'll wait. Not looking forward to spending all day manhandling these bags of cement though!"

"Let's hope she returns to work in the next day or so then."

Chapter 37. Escape

30th May 1944

Y ou're set to go," Parker told them as they loaded sacks into the train. "Gabriela's back today and she has your clothes. She does laundry for some of the German soldiers so they're used to seeing her carrying parcels to and from work."

Simon and Baxter exchanged relieved looks at the news.

"I'll detail you to take some paperwork to the office during the afternoon. She will then show you where you can get changed. The two of you leave the factory separately. You then carry out whatever plan you have to get away. I don't know what that is nor do I want to know."

"Well, thanks for your help corporal and good luck for the rest of the war."

 The remainder of the morning dragged on but eventually, Parker came over to Simon after one train had pulled out of the sidings and handed him the records of materials loaded that day.

Simon walked through the factory yard to the office inside the main building.

"I'm looking for Frau Sendler."

"I am Gabriella Sendler," a young woman, about Simon's height and build announced. She took the papers from him and put them on her desk.

"There is a problem with one of the toilets. Do you know anything about them?" she asked.

"I can have a look for you," Simon replied.

Gabriella took Simon out into a corridor then showed him the female toilet with an out-of-order notice on the door.

"Your clothes are inside. I will come and collect you at the end of the day. I will knock like this tap tap – tap tap – tap. We will leave together."

Simon examined the clothes that had been left for him. They included a calf-length black skirt, long-sleeved blue blouse, raincoat, shoes with a small heel. There was also a small suitcase containing underwear and a nightdress.

Simon put his papers into the suitcase and changed into the female outfit. He'd purloined a few bits of make-up from the theatrical group and he applied it sparingly. Since planning the escape, he'd been plucking hairs from his face and neck with tweezers to avoid five o'clock shadow while travelling; thankful that, in any case, he'd never had much facial hair and what he did have was slow growing.

Just before six o'clock, there was the expected knock on the door. Simon opened it a fraction to check that it was Gabriella then slipped out into the corridor.

"Follow my lead. We are two friends chatting as we leave work, just nod as though you understand."

They left the factory building and walked towards the gate. Gabriella talking and Simon pretending to understand her Polish.

They flashed their identity cards at the bored guard at the gate who simply waved them through.

Baxter broke away from his working group before they were herded back into their compound. He'd removed his jacket while working so it was relatively dust-free. He then brushed down his trousers to make them as presentable as possible, put a tie around his neck, took a traditional Tyrolean hat from his haversack and put it on his head.

Taking a deep breath, he strode towards the exit gate, produced his identity card and presented it to the guard who gave it a cursory glance and waved him through.

He couldn't identify Simon from the back as he followed groups of women from the factory up the road and wondered if he'd been able to get out. As arranged, he continued to head for the railway station relying on Simon, or Simone now, to make contact with him. Their train was due to depart at nineteen hundred hours but they still needed to buy their tickets.

Then two of the women ahead stopped, apparently to say good night. As one turned sideways onto him, Baxter realised that it was Simone – '*he must only see her as that or he might make a mistake that could cost them dearly'* – he thought.

She had seen him and, as the other woman walked away, she waited for him to join her.

« Bon soir, Monsieur Vannier, » she said, using the name he had adopted.

« Bon soir, Simone. »

They continued along the road towards the station. Inside the booking hall, Simone was horrified to see a German officer from Lamsdorf camp coming off the platform. She hoped he wouldn't recognise her. *'Had he attended any of the performances where she'd appeared as female? She didn't think so. Would he recognise her through her disguise? She hoped not. Would he recognise Baxter though?'* All she could do was keep her fingers crossed. Baxter was pretending to study the rail timetables and she tried to keep her back to the guard as he walked past the end of the queue.

"That was a close one," Baxter whispered as she joined him with the tickets.

« It was, but we must only speak French from now on, even in private. »

« You are absolutely right, Simone, sorry. »

« The train is running eight minutes late, Monsieur Vannier. »

« OK, well we allowed for some slippage and we don't have any connections today so it's not really a problem. »

The train drew into the platform fifteen minutes late; Simone and Vannier climbed aboard and found two seats. They put the suitcase in the rack and settled back for the journey. Soon after they left Oppeln, officials demanded to see their papers and tickets.

„Why are you going to Frankfurt?"

„Monsieur Vannier and I are being transferred to work on another project. I'm his assistant and his interpreter. He doesn't speak much German."

„You are French?"

„Yes, Monsieur Vannier is an engineer."

„Where in France are you from?"

„He is from near Nantes, I'm from Andrésy, in the Isle de France region."

The official examined the documents, looked between the photographs on them and Simone and Vannier. Then handed them back.

« Merci Mademoiselle, » the inspector said as he stepped away and demanded the next passenger's papers.

Simone handed Vannier's papers back to him and put her own in her bag, giving him a quick smile and discreetly raising her eyebrow.

At Breslau, they left the station without any further checks.

« Hopefully, the fact that papers aren't being checked here means our absence hasn't been noticed at the camp, » Vannier remarked.

« I think you're right. Now, let's see if we can find a hotel for the night. »

After the fifth hotel had turned them away because they were full, Simone turned to Vannier.

« Looks like we revert to plan B. »

They returned to the station and booked tickets through to Nuremberg.

Chapter 38. Breslau to Nuremberg

31ˢᵗ May 1944

At the railway station, they checked that their train was running to schedule and which platform it would leave from; it was a few minutes late which was just as well as they'd spent a lot of time trying to find a hotel. Simone took their papers and bought their tickets to Nuremberg.

« We have to change three times, first at Dresden. There's a couple of hours wait there – more if the trains are delayed. »

Their papers received a perfunctory check at the barrier and they walked along the platform. The train pulled in and Simone and Vannier stood back while some passengers alighted then they prepared to climb aboard. As they did so, a smartly dressed middle-aged man stood to one side to allow Simone to enter first.

„After you, Fräulein,"

„Thank you, sir," Simone said with a smile, stepping up into the carriage followed by the polite man, with Vannier behind him.

It was a boost to her confidence that she had been treated as a woman. It helped confirm that her appearance was convincing.

She took a seat next to a window. The lighting in the carriage was dim and the windows covered with blackout material. The polite man took the aisle seat next to her. Vannier caught Simone's attention and raised his eyebrows. He coughed to attract the intruder's attention then noticed the swastika buttonhole badge he was wearing and decided not to make a fuss. He sat down in the window seat opposite Simone, a table between them.

„So, Fräulein, where are you travelling to?" the polite man asked.

„My manager and I are being transferred to France to work on the Atlantic Wall." She gestured towards Vannier.

„Is that right? And what do you do?"

„Monsieur Vannier is an engineer; I'm his assistant and interpreter."

„And how far does your manager expect you to go to serve him? "

„I beg your pardon, sir!"

„Oh come now, you're an attractive woman and assistant can cover many sins!"

Simone felt his knee pressing against her thigh. She turned slightly in her seat so her legs were away from his.

„Would you like a drink, Fräulein?" the man asked, proffering a hip flask. „It's excellent French cognac."

„No thank you, sir."

He poured a capful and took a sip.

„And where are you from, Fräulein?"

„Just outside Paris. A village called Andrésy on the banks of the Seine."

He took another sip of his cognac.

„And what work do you do for the Fatherland?"

„I'm afraid I can't tell you anything about our work. It's secret. Now, if you will excuse me, sir, I'd like to try to sleep. It's been a tiring day and we have a long journey ahead of us tomorrow."

„Of course, Fräulein, "

Simone rested her head against the side of the carriage and closed her eyes to try to discourage any further conversation from the man. In adjusting her position, she inadvertently moved her legs closer to his.

A few minutes later, she felt something brushing her thigh. The man next to her seemed to be dozing so she assumed it had been an accidental contact. Then his hand touched her thigh again. She pulled her legs away but he pressed her again, more firmly this time.

She didn't want to attract any attention by causing a fuss so turned to him.

„Excuse me, please. I need to use the bathroom."

He stepped into the aisle making it possible to squeeze past him. As she did so, he grasped her bottom, his fingers pressing between her buttocks. He then followed her as she walked down the aisle towards the toilet which was in the next carriage. In the vestibule between the carriages, he caught hold of Simone and tried to kiss her.

„What do you think you are doing?" she demanded.

„You flirted with me earlier and put your legs next to me and didn't object when I touched you. I thought you wanted some fun. You French girls are all alike."

„I did no such thing, now let go of me this instant." She was about to rake his shin with her foot when Vannier came up behind them.

« Do you need some help, Simone? »

« This man apparently misjudged my intentions. »

While Simone was significantly shorter and slighter built than the man, Vannier wasn't. He stood well over six feet tall, weighed sixteen stone and had played rugby for his RAF station. He stared at the man who shrugged his shoulders and walked back down the carriage.

Simone and Vannier returned to the seats and sat down together as the man disappeared through the door at the other end of the carriage.

« That was a close call, » Vannier remarked. « I was ready to throw him out of the door if he hadn't backed down. »

« Just as well that wasn't necessary, if his body had been found it might have caused problems. »

The remainder of the journey to Dresden passed without incident. They took turns to doze to ensure that one or other of them was alert and, if necessary, nudge the other if they started to mumble in their sleep.

At Dresden, they took the opportunity to freshen up and have breakfast in the buffet.

Simone glanced around to see if anyone was taking any notice of them. As far as she could see, no one was.

Shortly before their train was due, Simone and Vannier made their way to the platform. Dresden was a major transport hub at the junction of east-west and north-south routes and the station was busy even as dawn was breaking. Crowds jostled on the main concourse and each of the platforms. The clamour was bolstered by the sound of carriage doors slamming; guards' whistles signalling the footplate crews and their responses on the engines' own whistles, by steam engines' exhausts as the crew fed power to the wheels and by the clash of buffers between carriages colliding as the trains jerked into motion.

On the platforms, porters shouted warnings to passengers in their way as they wheeled carts of luggage or other goods and sergeants in charge of groups of men barked their orders.

Simone and Vannier passed through the barrier without issue and joined the passengers waiting for their train to arrive. When it did, they climbed aboard and settled into seats facing the direction of travel with Vannier in the aisle seat.

If the train ran on time, they were due into Nuremberg about half past six, more than twelve hours ahead.

As the train left Dresden, they passed marshalling yards packed with wagons carrying tanks and other military equipment.

« I wonder whether that's heading for the Russian front, France or Italy? » Simone whispered.

« Good question, let's hope the RAF or the Yanks don't choose right now to attack it! »

« Hmm, that would be a bit of a nuisance! »

« Perhaps we should try and remember what we see. »

« Absolutely. Mind you, I suspect it's going to be a few more days before we get home and I don't think we should write anything down or it could be construed as spying. »

The pair had to change trains twice more before they arrived at Nuremberg shortly after six that afternoon. It gave them a chance to stretch their legs, freshen up and get something to eat. They were now used to passing through barriers and confident in their documents.

At Nuremberg, they left the station and looked for a hotel. By the fourth regretful shake of the head from the proprietors, they were beginning to wonder if they would ever find somewhere to stay.

However, the fifth hotel, the Pension Hilde, little more than a bar with a few rooms to let, said that they had one room. The customer who had booked it hadn't arrived and it was after eight o'clock so it was his misfortune.

After signing the register, they climbed the narrow stairs to the first floor. The walls and ceiling were yellowed by years of tobacco smoke from the ground floor bar and the paint was peeling from the paintwork. Some of the windows were cracked.

„We can't get glass to repair the windows since the RAF bombed the city in March. Our gallant night fighters shot down nearly two hundred of their bombers," the proprietor told them. „Then the Americans came two weeks later in daylight."

Simone and Vannier had met some of a Lancaster crew who had been shot down while on the raid. They'd said that it had been a bloody affair and they'd seen several other Lancs and Halifaxes hit by flak and fighters. Whether the losses had been as high as the proprietor was claiming was unlikely – the fighters would almost certainly have overestimated their successes but it had clearly been an expensive mission.

The room was comfortable enough, certainly compared with the accommodation in the POW camps. There was a double bed, an easy chair, a wardrobe and chest of drawers with a mirror on top and an enamel bowl with a jug of water.

They freshened up, then went back down to the bar where they ordered beers and *Stammgericht* (the plate of the day).

The Pension Hilde's patrons were a mix of transient residents and local regulars. The latter grouped together at the bar drinking beers while most of the transient guests sat at tables eating *Stammgericht*. Two of the others who were passing through came into the bar together while the remainder seemed to be on their own. The individuals were, however, asked to share tables.

Simone judged that most of the locals were labourers or factory workers from their clothes while those passing through were slightly better dressed wearing suits or jackets rather than overalls. The regular patrons at the bar generally ignored those sitting at tables; while the travellers kept to themselves. Those sharing tables gave each other perfunctory nods of acknowledgement but hardly seemed to speak to each other.

At the end of the meal, Vannier lit his pipe and sat back while he finished his beer.

« Well, I've had worse meals, » he said quietly.

« True. I've also had a lot better. What I wouldn't give for one of my mother's rabbit pies! »

« Come on, it's probably better to talk upstairs in our room. »

Chapter 39. Nuremberg - Stuttgart

1st June 1944

Simone woke to find Vannier snuggled up to her back with his arm resting across her waist. She could feel something pressing against her buttocks and realised that Vannier had a morning erection. Laying there, she realised that the touch of his penis and his arm resting on her stomach didn't disturb her. She'd been living as Simone for more than thirty-six hours and it seemed totally natural to her. She no longer felt that she was acting as Simone, she *was* Simone. She wondered what it would be like reverting to Simon when they got back to Blighty. Not that there was any alternative, she could hardly stay as a woman.

She turned onto her back lifted his arm off her and nudged him with her elbow.

"What the–?" Vannier moaned, in English.

« French only! It is time to get up. »

 « I thought our train wasn't until gone eleven, » Vannier protested.

« It isn't but we still need to check out by ten. »

Vannier lay on the bed for a few moments while Simone washed her face, pulled on a pair of knickers, took off the nightdress she'd been wearing; put on her bra and padded out the cups with rolled-up socks then put on her dress.

« I used to watch my wife dressing. You really are very convincing. »

« That's all very well but you need to get a move on. »

Vannier got out of bed wearing just a pair of underpants. He crossed the room to the dressing table, poured some water into the bowl and took out his razor to shave.

« Don't you need to shave, too? » he asked.

« No, I've been plucking the hairs out using a tweezer. I started doing it once I knew I was going to be Simone. »

« Sounds painful! And very time-consuming. »

« It is, on both counts. But it leaves my skin smoother and avoids the risk of ending up with cut marks and five o'clock shadow that might attract attention. And, let's face it, I had plenty of time at the camp. »

« Good point. »

When Vannier had finished shaving, Simone used the mirror to add some lipstick and powder then turned to Vannier who had now dressed.

« Ready? » she asked.

« Yes. Let's go and get some breakfast. »

They descended the narrow stairs and went into the bar. Most of the other guests had already left for early trains. The proprietor served them some ersatz coffee, probably made from acorns, and some dry black bread with thin slices of sausage and cheese. They ate their breakfast, handed in their room key, left the guesthouse and walked to the station.

As usual, Simone bought their tickets to Stuttgart.

„Is the train running on time? " she asked.

„Which train. The next through train to Stuttgart is at fourteen hours ten."

„I thought there was one at eleven hours sixteen? "

„The eleven hours sixteen is a stopping train and does not go all the way to Stuttgart. You will have to change at one of the stations before and you will then catch the fourteen hours ten train. You can either wait here or at one of the other stations. It is up to you. The ticket is the same."

„I see, thank you. "

« What was that about? » Vannier asked when Simone re-joined him.

« The eleven sixteen doesn't go all the way, we have to change or we can wait here until fourteen ten and take it all the way from here. »

« Let's get on our way. We can break the journey and have lunch while we wait for the connection. »

« I think that's best. »

They joined the queue for their train and showed their papers, as usual, at the barrier. They'd only taken a score of paces along the platform when Vannier stopped and took hold of Simone's arm.

« What's the problem? » she asked.

« You see the chap by the sign for the waiting room? Wearing an overcoat and Homburg hat? He's a Flight Lieutenant from my station. His name's Price. He must be on the run like us. »

« Has he seen us? »

« Don't think so. »

« You know we have to ignore him, don't you? »

« Of course. I just hope he doesn't approach us. He could wreck our cover story. »

Their discussion was curtailed as the train pulled in – enveloping those waiting close to the edge of the platform with steam.

Simone and Vannier watched while Price joined the train then climbed into a different carriage. They'd taken their seats in the open plan coach when Price came through the connecting door and took a seat further down the carriage, facing Simone and Vannier.

« Damn, that's all we needed, » Vannier murmured.

« Not a lot we can do about it is there? Here, pretend to read the newspaper to hide your face. » She handed him a copy of Das Reich that she'd picked up at the station.

The train started with a jerk, the engine bellowing out clouds of smoke from the chimney and steam from the pistons, the huge wheels slipped then gripped the rails again and it gradually picked up speed. The station buildings and platforms were soon left behind.

As they entered open country, the ticket inspector and police entered through the carriage.

Simone looked at the policemen. What little hair he showed under his cap was grey, matching his moustache. She assumed all the younger, fitter members of the force had been conscripted into the army.

Confident that their papers had already passed inspection, Simone and Vannier handed them over. As before, they were questioned about their journey but their answers satisfied the officials. Vannier had, however, put down the paper while showing his documents.

« I think you've been spotted, » Simone whispered.

Flight Lieutenant Price was looking at Vannier, his mouth agape. When Vannier returned his look, he dropped his eyes and shut his mouth. The officials finished inspecting one set of papers and moved on to the row before Price.

« I hope his documents pass muster, » Vannier muttered.

The ticket inspector had reached Price. Vannier watched him hand over his ticket. He held his breath, praying there wouldn't be a problem in case Price involved him.

It seemed his ticket was fine. Then the police asked for his other papers.

Vannier watched the police officer put his hand on his pistol and draw it out of its holster.

Price protested as he was dragged out of his seat and forced down the carriage to the connecting door. The train had started to slow for the next station. As it pulled into the platform, Price broke free, knocking the policeman down. He pushed past the ticket inspector, opened the exterior door and jumped out. Simone and Vannier watched as Price fell to the ground, then picked himself up and started to run back along the platform. The policeman followed him onto the platform. He stood still and aimed his pistol at the fleeing Price and fired. Price was zigzagging to spoil his aim and the shot went wide. Two further shots also missed as Price lengthened the distance between them before darting out of sight behind the end of the train.

Simone, sitting next to the window, had the best view of a discussion between the policeman, the ticket inspector and the train guard.

« Can you see what's happening? » Vannier asked.

« The policeman is gesturing at the back of the train. The ticket inspector is pointing to the train and his watch. I think he's saying that the train has to get on the way but the policeman is objecting. The guard is also gesturing. Now the policeman is stamping his feet. »

« I hope we aren't held up too long, we don't want to miss our connection. »

« No, it's OK. The ticket inspector is getting back on the train and the guard is blowing his whistle and waving his flag. They're leaving the policeman behind. »

« Well, that was a bit of excitement, » Vannier remarked as the train pulled out. « I feel a bit guilty not trying to help Price, but there really wasn't anything we could have done, » he continued.

« Nothing at all. I suggest we leave swopping trains as late as we can – put as much distance as possible between us and any manhunt that the Germans might raise to find Price. »

Two hours later, the train pulled into the last station where they'd be able to switch trains.

« We've got about two hours before the Stuttgart service is due. Shall we try and find somewhere away from the station to get a meal? » Simone asked.

« Sounds a good idea to me. »

Their connecting train got them into Stuttgart shortly after seven that evening without any further incidents.

They were fortunate in obtaining accommodation for the night after only two refusals.

Chapter 40. Stuttgart - Paris

2nd / 3rd June 1944

The following morning, Simone and Vannier walked back to the railway station for the next leg of their journey. The first stage was from Stuttgart to Strasburg where they had just over an hour's wait for the express to Paris.

As the train pulled into Strasbourg, Simone felt a sense of relief. They were now in France rather than Germany. Not that it really made any difference. The Germans were still in control. But, at least, they could hope that the locals would be more inclined to help if the need arose. She then remembered that Strasbourg was in the Alsace region and had been part of Germany until the end of the Great War. It was likely allegiances would be split.

They used the hour between trains at Strasbourg to have lunch. They ensured, however, that they were well placed to board the Paris train when it arrived and were able to grab two second-class seats together. The places opposite them were taken by two Luftwaffe Obergefreiter, equivalent to RAF Leading Aircraftman, wearing gold collar tabs indicating aircrew, parachutists or ground crew.

„Guten tag," one said as he took his seat opposite Simone.

« Bonjour, » Simone replied.

„Sprechen sie deutsch?" he asked.

« Non, nein. I do not speak German, » she replied, not wanting to get into conversation with him. She opened a magazine she had picked up in Strasbourg.

„That is a pity," he remarked then turned to his colleague. „Stuck up French bitch."

„Some of them were keen enough to get to know us in 1940," said the other.

„How far is it from the station at Nancy to the airbase?" asked the first.

„Not far. Whether there'll be transport waiting for us or we'll be kept waiting is another matter."

„Do you know what we have based there? I was just told to pack my gear and get on my way. No other details."

„I don't think we should talk about it in public. That French woman or the man she's with could easily turn out to be members of the resistance!"

„Good point. Or, even worse, pretending not to speak German and actually Gestapo!"

„Scheiße, don't say that! We'll end up on the eastern front."

Simone kept a straight face and hoped Vannier would do the same if he was able to understand what the Luftwaffe airmen were saying.

As the train pulled into Nancy, they stood up and made their way to the exit doors.

« I was hoping you might pick up some information from those two, » Vannier whispered.

« At least they took us for French, » Simone responded.

The seats vacated by the Germans were quickly taken by two Frenchmen in their mid-twenties. They nodded and wished Simone and Vannier a good afternoon before talking quietly between themselves.

The train pulled into Bar-le-Duc, only half an hour late, for the final scheduled stop before Paris. A trolley was wheeled along the platform offering refreshments and Simone took the opportunity to buy some bread and ham and a bottle of wine; handing the money through the window. By the time the train pulled out again, every seat was occupied and almost every inch of aisle and corridor was full of bodies sitting on suitcases where they had them, or standing if they didn't.

« With luck, it'll be impossible for the police or ticket inspectors to get through these crowds to check papers. It should be about two and a half hours to Paris, » she told Vannier. « That would get us into Gare de l'Est about eight o'clock. I think we should try and get a hotel near there if we can. »

« That sounds bang on, » Vannier agreed.

An hour later, the train ran through Reims station.

« I came through here with the skipper with the escape line, » Simone murmured.

« The sooner we get to Paris the better, » Vannier remarked. « The atmosphere in here is stifling. »

« I don't suppose we smell any better. It's been a while since we had the chance of a shower. »

« That's a fair point. »

« In case we don't make contact with the people in Versailles on the first day, I suggest we book the hotel for two nights. »

« Whatever you think, Simone. »

The train was an hour late when it steamed into Paris Gare de l'Est. The final release of steam as the engine stopped just short of the buffers sounded like a runner breathing out their last exhausted breath after finishing a hard race.

Simone and Vannier had to wait while the aisle cleared before they could take their case from the overhead rack and make their way onto the platform. They walked quickly to get into the middle of the crowd. The ticket inspectors and police at the barrier couldn't spare more than a glance at any of the passengers' papers if they were to clear the crowd in time for customers for the train's return trip to access the carriages.

« I remember seeing some hotels down this road when we came through last time, » Simone said as they left the terminal.

The third hotel they found was able to offer them a room for two nights. The room was similar to the others they'd stayed in, adequately furnished, though the fitments had seen better days but with the shortages due to the war weren't likely to be replaced for some time yet. There was a bathroom next to their bedroom with a shower attachment over the bath that spat out a lukewarm spray. Simone was relieved to be able to have a full body wash instead of just a wipe with a cloth which was all that had been possible at the previous hotels.

The next morning, they left the hotel and took the Metro to Invalides station where they caught the train to Versailles. Remembering the route she and Pilot Officer Chapman had followed the previous year, Simone led Vannier along the side then across the front of the former town hall and past the main Post Office to the junction of Avenue de Paris and Rue des États Généraux. She pointed to one of the two cafés facing each other.

« That's the bar that the people from the safe house used when we were here. We'll wait in the one across the road. »

Simone and Vannier ordered a glass of beer each and settled down to wait at a table on the edge of the Avenue de Paris. It gave them a clear view down the Impasse des Gendarmes and they'd have plenty of time to see anyone coming from the safe house. They were on their second glass of beer when Simone sat upright.

« That's one of the people from the safe house coming now, » she whispered. « I think her name is Isabelle. »

Isabelle strolled up the road and went into the bar. She came back out a few minutes later with a glass of wine, sat at one of the outside tables on the pavement of the road to the safe house, took out a packet of cigarettes and lit one.

Simone turned to Vannier. « Wait here. I'll go and have a word with her. »

She stood up, crossed the road and approached Isabelle.

« Bonjour, Isabelle, may I join you? » she asked taking hold of the back of a spare seat at the table.

Isabelle stared at Simone and screwed up her eyebrows. « Do I know you? » she asked.

« We have met, though I doubt you'd remember me, » she replied as she sat down next to her.

« Who are you? »

Simone looked around to ensure that they could not be overheard. The adjacent tables were empty and any pedestrians were too far away and too focussed on crossing the road to take any notice of two women chatting.

« Do you still keep grounded swifts in the hay loft in the old coach house? » she asked, ignoring Isabelle's own question.

« What are you talking about? »

« Grounded swifts, creatures of the air that need help to fly again. That's what you and Yvette called your visitors, isn't it? How is Yvette by the way? Did she get away after the trouble in Chartres last November? »

« I don't know what you're talking about. You must have mistaken me for someone else. »

Simone leant closer to Isabelle and whispered.

« Yvette was escorting two RAF aircrew you'd had in the hay loft last November. Their names were Pilot Officer Bill Chapman and Sergeant Simon Ferguson. They were captured at the safe house in Chartres. That is, WE were captured at the safe house. I am Simon Ferguson, though at present I'm using Simone. I've escaped with a colleague who's across the road. I'm pretending to be his assistant and interpreter. We worked out that a man and a woman together attracted less attention than two men or a single man. We're after information. »

Isabelle sat open-mouthed for a moment then took a drag on her cigarette, finished her glass of wine and pushed her chair back from the table.

« Come back to the house. We can talk more freely there. Follow me at a distance. You remember the way? »

« Yes, I do. »

Isabelle stood up and walked back down the Impasse des Gendarmes. Simone signalled Vannier to join her and they followed.

At the bottom of the cul-de-sac, Isabelle opened the side door to the house and gestured for them to come in.

« You make a very convincing woman, Simone. I can see how you'd avoid attention. But what help do you need? »

« Mainly information. Édouard is one of the best forgers and he's produced our documents including some blanks in case we need to adopt different identities. Our cover has been that he is an engineer being transferred from work in Poland to the Atlantic Wall. That's given us an explanation for travelling our route so far. But we need to decide which way to head now. Is it possible to get across the channel or do we need to change direction and make for Spain? »

« Most of the coast from Holland down to the Cotentin peninsular is sealed off. It's impossible to get through and, even if you did, there are no boats available anywhere. You might be able to make it to the Brittany coast. There used to be an escape line through Plouha, but I'm not sure if it's still operating. There's a reseau in Le Mans who might be able to tell you if that route is still open. Go to the Café Nicole and ask for Alain. Tell him you have a package from Chantelle. Your current documents should get you that far then you can decide if you need to go south. »

Simone looked at Vannier who nodded his head.

« That sounds like a plan, » she said.

« So, what are your intentions now? » Isabelle asked.

« Return to the hotel. We booked for two nights in case we couldn't make contact today. »

« Is it possible for you to help us out? »

« How? »

« We need two identity cards completing. They need names printed on as though they've been typed. I was going to do them as our usual contact is unavailable but if your colleague is an experienced forger, I'm sure his work would be much better. »

« I'm more than happy to help, » Vannier said. While he worked on the identity cards, Simone and Isabelle sat in the garden with glasses of wine.

« I think I remember you now, Simone. We've had so many airmen through here, they only stop for a night or two and, to be honest, we try not to remember them. Yvette did get away from the ambush in Chartres. The Boches had found out about the safe house but not about the way escapees were taken there. She returned here without knowing you had been taken prisoner. »

« I'm glad to hear that. »

« How has it been, impersonating a woman? Do you find it difficult? »

« Surprisingly, it seems to come naturally. I had to lose masculine habits, of course, but there was a female impersonator in the camp who gave me a lot of tips. Then there is the way men treat women. I never noticed it before but it is very different – and that's without them trying to get you into bed! »

« So, have you had much trouble with that? I'd have thought being with Vannier would have discouraged any approaches. »

« There was one man on the train from Strasbourg to Paris. He tried to assault me, claimed I'd led him on. He even groped my bum. It was disgusting. Goodness knows what he would have done if he had found what I have in my knickers! Vannier got rid of him though. »

When Vannier had finished the identity cards, he and Simone left Isabelle and made their way back to the main avenue.

« Do we have time to walk up to the palace? » Vannier asked.

« I don't see why not; our room is already booked and we don't have anything we need to do this evening. I don't suppose it's open to visitors and even if it is, it'll mainly be Germans, but we can have a closer look at the outside. »

even if it is, it'll mainly be Germans, but we can have a closer look at the outside. »

Chapter 41. Leaving Paris

Sunday 4th June 1944

The Le Mans train from Montparnasse station was made up of a hotchpotch of carriages including one, at the back, in British Southern Railway livery with individual compartments and a guard's brake section.

« I wonder what this is doing here? » Simone queried.

« They brought some rolling stock over with the British Expeditionary Force in thirty-nine. It must have been abandoned after Dunkirk, » Vannier replied.

« I suppose so. Actually, this might suit us. There's no corridor or link to other coaches so there won't be any checks on documents on the way. »

« That's a good point. And, not having access to the buffet car might put others off from using it. There's another trick my girlfriend and I used to use to keep a compartment to ourselves. »

« What's that? »

« We pretended to canoodle. Everyone was too embarrassed to come in with us. »

Simone looked at Vannier. Was he trying to get to kiss her? Perhaps his arm being over her waist when he slept next to her wasn't just a force of habit from his marriage. Would she object if he did? She didn't mind feeling him next to her in the mornings. If anything, it was quite comforting.

« Well, I'm not sure about that! » she protested, reluctant to encourage him.

« We don't have to actually do anything, just sit side by side with my arm around you. »

« So long as that's all we do. »

They climbed aboard and settled into their seats next to each other. As anticipated, other passengers glanced into the coach but moved on. A handful did occupy other compartments in the same carriage but most continued along the platform to the connected coaches.

Just as the guard blew his whistle, a young woman opened the door and climbed in.

« That was close, » she said. « I thought I was going to miss the train. »

Simone looked at her as she removed her raincoat before taking the seat opposite. She wore a white blouse and a navy skirt. Her handbag matched her shoes, but it was the brooch pinned to her blouse that attracted Simone's attention. It was a gold oval about four by three centimetres set with eight garnets arranged as petals.

« That's a very pretty brooch you're wearing. A friend of mine had one exactly the same. Her grandmother gave it to her for her sixteenth birthday. »

The woman looked at Simone. She screwed up her eyebrows, her eyes becoming slits through which she stared intently, her chin dropped and her mouth opened.

« It was during a visit to her just before the war. She lived in Andrésy. Do you know the village? » Simone continued.

Vannier sat silently during the exchange listening and wondering what was going on.

« Do I know you? You look vaguely familiar, but I can't place you. But this was given to me by *my* grandmother who lives in Andrésy. That's too much of a coincidence. Who are you? » the woman demanded.

« I'm not surprised you don't recognise me, Lucy, or are you using a different name now? But you were the first person to dress me like this and give me my name. »

Lucy's eyes opened wide as she realised who was facing her.

« Simon, Simone! But what are you doing here and why are you dressed as a woman? » Lucy squealed as she jumped up and threw her arms around her.

« We're on the run from a POW camp. My old skipper and I were trying to get back home after being shot down last year and noticed that women and couples attract far less attention than single men or pairs of men, so I came up with this scheme. Vannier's papers say he is an engineer and I'm his assistant and interpreter. More to the point, what are you doing here? Last I heard, you'd gone to London to serve with the FANYs. » Then the penny dropped. « You're with the SOE, aren't you? I did a couple of flights taking agents and equipment into France. One drop wasn't far from here. Just west of Chartres. »

« When was that, Simone? »

« Middle of October; 11th I think. »

« You're joking! That was when I was dropped in. It was a Stirling. Registration letter S-Sugar, I remembered it because it was your initial. »

« Well, I'll be… Anyway, what do I call you, I'm sure you're not using Lucy, are you? »

« My papers say Eloise Dubois, my code name is Lynx. »

« Anyone care to tell me what's going on? » Vannier asked.

« Sorry. This is a friend from home. We've known each other since we were children. In fact, we went out together for a while. It was her mother that I tried to impress by learning French. Seems I was Flight Engineer on the mission to drop her into France last year. » Simone explained. « So, what are you doing on this train Eloise? » she continued.

« I've been alerting a group in Paris to expect some personal messages on the BBC over the next day or so. Their wireless operator was captured a couple of weeks ago and I delivered a new radio for them. Now I'm going back to Sablons. Where are you going? »

« Our papers showed we were being transferred to work on the Atlantic Wall. But we're now using some that redirect us to the submarine pens at Brest. That gives us a reason to be anywhere along the routes from Paris to Brittany. We made contact with the escape line the skipper and I used originally and they said it may be possible to get out through Plouha. They gave us a contact in Le Mans who might have up-to-date gen. »

« If that's the Café Nicole, it's fortunate that we bumped into each other then. It was blown last week. You'd better come with me and we'll see what we can find out for you. I think the invasion might be imminent. It's the only reason I can think of for warning different groups to listen out for personal messages on the BBC. If it does happen soon, you might be better off waiting for the front line to pass over you. It all depends on where it happens. »

« You think it'll be that soon then? »

« I really don't know. The Germans seem nervous and are putting a lot of work into the beach defences all along the coast. As far as we can gather, they seem to think the most likely location will be the Pas de Calais. It's the shortest crossing point. But the Allies must realise that the Germans will be expecting them there so maybe they'll try somewhere else. Who knows? Apart from Churchill, Roosevelt and Eisenhower, that is. »

« No doubt they'll be trying to mislead the Germans wherever they plan to invade. »

« Absolutely. And that's why they'll have groups such as mine sabotaging railways, bridges and telephone lines all over the place. I think the messages we've been warned to expect will be the instructions to start the attacks. That's why I believe it'll be very soon. »

« What do you think? » Simone asked Vannier.

« She certainly makes sense. And, if we've lost the contact in Le Mans, the other options seem to be gambling that we can make contact with the escape line through Plouha or turning south for Spain. If we go south, our cover story isn't as strong and goodness knows how long it would take us to get to the border and find a guide to take us across. I'm for sticking with your friend. »

« Fine. We get off the train at Nogent-le-Rotrou. That's the third stop. You said you had tickets to Le Mans, is that right? » Eloise asked

« In fact, they are for Brest. »

« Fine. Now I know you can ride a bicycle Simone, but what about you, sorry, what was your name? »

« Édouard Vannier. Yes, I can ride a bike. »

« Good. It's about nine kilometres from Nogent to the safe house. We will need to borrow bikes from Henri, a local mechanic. There's a porter at Chartres station. He should be looking out for me to collect a package. I'll get him to telephone Nogent for us. »

Eloise looked again at Simone and shook her head.

« I can't believe this. So, tell me what you can about what you've been doing since I left to join the FANYs. How are Grace, Daphne and Mary and your mother and aunt and uncle? »

« I haven't heard from the family since I left on my last mission. As you know, I joined the RAF, they didn't need any more pilots, so I trained as a Flight Engineer on Stirlings. My original crew was shot up on one mission and

I was seconded to S-Sugar while the skipper recovered and the aircraft was repaired. That's when I did the SOE flights from Tempsford. What about you? »

« As you guessed, my job with the FANYs was cover for the SOE French section. »

« But weren't you too young to join them? »

« Ah. Well, I don't know if you're aware, but I had a sister who died as an infant – before I was born, obviously. I used her birth certificate to pretend to be older than I was. »

« That explains it. »

« My French heritage, speaking the language fluently and having spent a lot of time over there made me a prime candidate. I still had to complete all of the training, of course, but I finally passed out as an operative. I was dropped in with a wireless operator, as you know, last November. Our team leader returned to England six weeks ago and I was promoted from courier to take over from him. I was allowed to wear this brooch because it was French. »

« You're incredibly brave to be doing that work. »

« Phht! I had to do something, just like you. Hopefully, if the invasion happens soon, our work will be finished before long. »

At Chartres, Eloise got off the train and spoke quickly to the porter who had been looking out for her and handed over the package. « That's arranged. He'll phone Nogent and get a message to Henri to organise three bikes for us. »

As the train left Chartres, the twin spires of the Gothic cathedral towered above the surrounding buildings until they were lost to sight in the gloom. The town gave way to flat open countryside that reminded Simone of the area around the airbases where she'd trained on Stirlings and later operated from. A storm was building and rain lashed the windows of the carriages.

« It's not going to be a pleasant cycle ride, I'm afraid, » said Eloise ruefully. « This is dreadful weather. Heaven help anyone at sea in these conditions! »

« You said you think the invasion is imminent? » Vannier enquired.

« I'm basing it on the warning for all groups to listen out for personal messages on the BBC – they're codes for each group and the only reason I can see for the alert is because of the invasion. Mind you, if the weather is as bad as this on the beaches, maybe they'll have to postpone their plans. »

« I'm glad it's not my decision, » Vannier replied.

Chapter 42. Resistance

Sunday 4th June 1944

Eloise walked ahead of Simone and Vannier as they left the train at Nogent. Out of the station, they crossed the square to a garage where several bikes stood chained to a post. A catch on the top of the door rang a bell as she opened it. A stocky man emerged from a back room, he was around one point eight metres tall, eighty kilos in weight and about forty years old. His wrinkled, ruddy, face had two-day-old stubble and below a bushy walrus moustache, a Gauloise cigarette dangled from his lips. His overalls were so dirty, with grease marks all over, it was impossible to say if they'd originally been green or brown. He wiped his hands on a piece of cloth.

« Bonjour, Henri. Are you well? » Eloise asked, offering her hand to be shaken.

« Fine, Lynx. Are these the friends who need bikes? »

« Yes, Henri. Your best ones, please. »

Henri grunted, then wheeled three bikes out of the shop.

« These should suit you. There's a rack on one of them for your suitcase. »

Vannier looked at the bike he was being offered. It was very basic, just a single gear but the tyres seemed in good condition. He hoped he'd manage; it had been years since he'd ridden.

Fortunately, the route was mainly flat and, although it was raining, the wind was behind them and helped them along.

About a kilometre before Sablons, they left the road which had been following the rail line and took a rutted track to a farm. The main house was on the left-hand side of the yard. Built from traditional stone, the steeply sloping roof was covered in dark grey slate with three dormer windows that lined up with two other windows and the front door on the ground floor.

Beyond the farmhouse stood an enclosed stone barn and facing the house across the yard an open-sided Dutch barn used to store implements and bales of hay and straw.

Eloise led them to the stone barn.

« Bring the bikes inside, » she told them as she opened the door.

Several men were sitting on benches, cleaning weapons. They looked up as Eloise brought Simone and Vannier into the room. One of the men spat out the cigarette that had been hanging from his lips.

« Who are these people, Lynx? You know better than to bring strangers here, especially at this time, » he demanded.

« Relax, Jules, » she told him. « They're RAF aircrew who have escaped from a POW camp and want to get back to England. »

« Since when did the RAF have female aircrew? And how do you know that are telling the truth, they could be Gestapo plants for all you know. »

« I've known Simone since we were children. We played together in England. She is actually a man – pretending to be a woman as part of their escape plan. »

Jules was mollified by Eloise's explanation. The other men returned to their tasks.

« I must say, Simone does make a convincing woman, » Jules remarked.

« Thank you, Jules, » Simone replied. « We were fortunate to meet with Lynx on the train. We'd planned to go to Le Mans. We'd been told there was a café there where we might have been able to get information. »

« The café Nicole, » Eloise said. « I told them that it had been blown. So, what is going on now? Do we have any more news? I delivered the radio to the Reseau Candide in Paris and gave Gaston his package on the way back. »

« I don't think we'll get confirmation of the invasion orders tonight with this storm. I hear it's even worse at the coast. In the meantime, my men and I are getting ready. Alouette is out with her radio to listen for any further messages from London. »

Eloise turned to Simone and Vannier.

« Jules leads the resistance group here; this is his farm. I act as liaison with London and link with other groups in the region. It should be done by a courier but I'm having to cover both roles at the moment. Alouette is my wireless operator, she was dropped with me last year. »

« Is there anything we can do to help? » Simone asked.

« Not at the moment. I think Jules' men have just about finished checking their weapons. We've been over the plans a dozen times so everyone knows what they have to do. If we get the message to execute them, you can join us if you want – but, if you do, you'll lose the protection of being Prisoners of War. »

« I'm game, what about you Édouard? »

« Hell, yes. I was sitting on my backside in the camp for far too long. » Vannier replied. « In any case, after the execution of those poor sods from Stalag Luft Three, who's to say we're safe as POWs? »

« In that case, we'd better go over the plans with you, » Eloise told them. She spread out a map and pointed out the route they'd be following to their target.

« We're going to blow up the railway bridge over the river here. As you can see there's one road that crosses the railway, about two hundred metres from the bridge. It's actually a dead end so if there are any German patrols, they'll have to come from the main road. The alternative is along the railway itself. So, Simone, if you keep watch from this point and you, Édouard from here, you should be able to give us warning. »

« How do we warn you if we see anything? We can hardly shout out and something like a whistle would be too obvious. » Vannier said.

« Use these duck callers, » Eloise replied. « Signal with three short followed by one long whistle. »

« Morse code for V for victory! I like it, » enthused Vannier.

The door opened and a girl entered the barn.

« Papa, Mamam said to tell you dinner is ready. »

« Thank you, Sylvette, we'll be over shortly. Let her know there are two extras, » Jules remarked.

The farm kitchen had been designed to cater for the workers and the farmer's family so the table was large enough to fit Jules' resistance fighters, Eloise, Simone and Vannier and Jules' wife and daughter.

Prudence, his wife, placed two large casserole dishes on the table together with two freshly baked Pains de Campagnes and dishes of golden yellow butter.

« Eat, » she commanded.

After dinner, with little more to do, until listening to the BBC News followed by the personal messages at nine-fifteen, they all relaxed. Vannier joined in a card game with three of Jules' men in the main barn while Eloise and Simone found a quiet corner in the Dutch Barn, where they could speak privately.

« So, Simone, are you and Vannier a couple? »

« Certainly not. What gave you that idea? »

« The way you were sitting next to each other in the train carriage with his arm around your shoulder. »

« That was to discourage anyone else from entering our compartment. Nothing more. »

« Are you sure? You looked very relaxed and I've seen the way Édouard looks at you. He's definitely interested in you. »

« Ridiculous. We are just with each other to try to escape! »

« If you say so. Anyway, tell me, how are you finding life as a woman. Are you comfortable or is it awkward to pretend to be female? Do you worry about being recognised as a man? »

« I'm used to it now. I was very anxious at first but I knew that if I showed any nervousness, that would attract attention. I had to concentrate on avoiding masculine gestures and postures but, now, it seems quite natural. »

« I'm not really surprised. You quickly got into the role when we put you in a dress for that play. I actually thought you should probably have been born a girl, you certainly fitted in as one. »

Simone looked at Eloise with hooded eyes.

« I'm not sure whether that's a compliment or an insult, » she protested.

« It's not intended as either, just a statement of fact. I think it was seeing your inner femininity that attracted you to me. But you kept it well suppressed when we were going out together. »

Simone wasn't sure how to reply. She knew there was a lot of truth in Eloise's remarks. She had felt comfortable when her cousins and Lucy had dressed her as a girl for their play. In fact, if truth were known, she was disappointed that they hadn't insisted that she dress up again to join in any of their other activities. She'd protested when she was cast as Mrs Ramsbottom for a skit at the scout campfire when she was eleven – but only to avoid appearing too eager – and had done the same at Lamsdorf camp. Was it really because couples attracted less attention than men on their own that had driven his idea of presenting as a woman for the escape? Or did some inherent drive create the plan to satisfy its own need?

« Even if what you say is true, it doesn't mean Édouard is attracted to me or me to him. We did agree that it might help our cover story if I also pretended to be his mistress but that hasn't been necessary; well, apart from sitting next to each other on the train. We've had to share a bed when stopping at hotels to save booking two rooms – and nothing has happened between us. »

« No? »

« No! OK, his arm usually ends up around my waist and he spoons up behind me. But he does that in his sleep from habit. »

« That's what he tells you, is it? And, how do you feel waking up with him pressed against you and his arm around you? »

« I don't mind. »

« You don't mind? »

« No, I don't mind. »

« That's all? This is Lucy you're talking to! »

« OK. If you must know the truth, I quite enjoy it. It feels comforting. »

Eloise looked at Simone and smiled.

« And? »

« And what? »

« You know. »

Simone realised that Eloise was forcing her to face up to how she really felt.

« I imagine what it would be like to be a woman waking up next to her husband. I also wonder what it would be like to make love as a woman. Is that what you want to hear? »

« I only want you to be yourself. There's nothing to be ashamed of. It's what I had to realise when I accepted that I preferred girls to men. Are you shocked to hear me say *that*? »

« No. I'm not shocked. So, are you telling me we might have a chance of getting back together if I'm really a woman? »

« I might, if you were keen on women – but I think you're attracted to men. »

« If I was, I can hardly do anything about it with the bits I have. And, as far as I know, there's nothing I can do about those. »

« Well, that's not entirely true. First, there are ways that you can be with a man even now but there have been cases where individuals have had surgery to change their genitals. There was a Danish person who had operations before the war. Sadly, she died of complications but the Nazis have been carrying out other operations and may have improved techniques. Not that they've done that to make things better for the individuals but for their own despicable reasons. »

« Is that supposed to encourage me? »

« It's intended to make you aware of future possibilities. But, perhaps the first step might be to see how you feel about being with a man, and Édouard is certainly interested in you and I think you're interested in him despite your protests. »

« I've already told you I have no interest in Édouard; apart from anything else, he's nearly twice my age. »

« So, if he was younger, you might have been interested? » Eloise responded with a twinkle in her eyes.

Simone stared at Eloise. She knew Eloise's last remark was to tease her, but she had given her a lot to think about.

« It must be about time for the BBC news, » she remarked to avoid any further discussions.

They went back to the main barn where the others gathered to listen to the radio. There were no action messages for them from the BBC.

Alouette returned as the BBC broadcast ended. She handed Eloise a message.

« London now wants us to monitor this junction for troop movements tomorrow. Do you have anyone you can spare Jules? » asked Eloise, pointing it out on the map.

« Not if they want us to also keep watch over the other locations, » Jules replied. « Unless Édouard and Simone can help. »

« Fine by me, » Simone agreed.

« And me, » Vannier confirmed.

« Right, well, Simone can go with André and Édouard can take his place with Jacques, » Jules decided.

« Good idea. Simone and André can take the bikes, it's about four kilometres. If I remember the location, there's a hay barn about a hundred metres from the junction which should give them cover. Right, well, if that's all, I suggest we all get some rest. »

That night, Simone struggled to get to sleep thinking about what Eloise had said, how she felt about it – and the consequences.

Chapter 43. D-1

Monday 5th June 1944

After a good breakfast, provided by Prudence, and with a basket containing bread and ham and a bottle of wine, Simone and André set off for their traffic watch. They took backroads as far as possible to avoid encountering any German convoys and reached their observation post without any problems. Their target was a junction just before a narrow bridge over a river.

They hid their bikes out of sight and created a nest at the edge of the barn from the straw to observe the traffic without being seen by casual bystanders. They took it in turns to use the binoculars provided by Eloise to watch the traffic and identify the number and types of vehicles, number of personnel and their unit badges while the other wrote the details down in a notebook.

There was an almost constant stream heading northeast towards Rouen.

« They seem to be transferring troops to the area north of the Seine estuary, maybe to the Pas de Calais, » said Simone.

« Looks that way, » André replied.

« Let's hope that's *not* where the invasion is planned then. »

The two of them lay next to each other and kept watch most of the day.

« You have known Lynx a long time, I think, » André said during one lull in traffic.

« Yes, since we were children. She was a friend of my cousins. I was staying with them because my mother was having a difficult pregnancy. »

« You saw a lot of her, did you? »

Simone rolled onto her back and looked up at the sky.

« Not at that time. Once my sister Mary was born, I went home. It was only when my father was killed at Dunkirk that we moved in with my aunt and uncle and I got to know her better. In fact, she was my girlfriend for a while. »

« I am sorry to hear that your father was killed. » André rested a hand on Simone's arm.

« Thank you. It's a long time ago now and many of us have lost family and friends. What about you? What's your story? Do you have a family? »

« Oh yes, I have two sisters. They are thirteen and twelve years old. My father is doing forced labour in Germany, my mother does what she can to keep us fed and clothed. »

The sun gradually made its way across the sky, when the clouds broke sufficiently for it to be seen, and the two of them lay side by side continuing to share experiences. Simone was surprised how easy she found it to share her story, including how she'd come to be dressed as a woman, with André.

« You are very convincing as a woman, » André told her.

« I had a lot of help from another prisoner at Lamsdorf, » she said. « He was a female impersonator before the war. »

« When the Germans invaded Paris, I was working in a revue bar on the Place Pigalle. We had several female impersonators working there and I got to know the girls well, especially Yvonne. One night there was a group of drunken German Officers in the club and one of them made offensive remarks about the girls. He said he worked at a camp where they knew how to deal with such degenerates and boasted that they made them wear pink triangles and carried out operations to see the effect of castrating them. »

Simone shuddered at the thought.

« He said one psychiatrist's experiments involved creating vaginas then forcing homosexual men to have sex with the ones they'd operated on to monitor their reactions. He laughed when he said it took several attempts before they had workable results and most of the subjects died as a result of the operations, » André declared angrily.

« That's horrendous! » said Simone.

« Yvonne waited for him in the toilets and slit his throat. We hid him in one of the cubicles. We had to get away from the club before he was found. That's when I came here and joined the resistance. »

« What happened to your friend? »

« Sadly, she was arrested and shot. »

Simone rested her hand on André's arm.

« I'm so sorry to hear that. »

« Well, as you said, we've all lost friends and family. The sooner we can finish this war, the better. Come on, it's time we were heading back to the farm. »

After dinner, everyone gathered in the barn to listen to the personal messages from the BBC.

« Blanche envoie ses amitiés à Marie Louise. Je répète: Blanche envoie ses amitiés à Marie Louise. »

« Les fauteuils d'orchestre sont dix-huit francs. Je répète: Les fauteuils d'orchestre sont dix-huit francs. »

« A pleine Vitesse il ne faisait que cent kilomètres à l'heure. Je répète: A pleine Vitesse il ne faisait que cent kilomètres à l'heure. »

« Blessent mon cœur d'une langueur monotone. Je répète: Blessent mon cœur d'une langueur monotone. »

« Dans la nuit étoilées du quatorze Juillet. Je répète: Dans la nuit étoilées du quatorze Juillet. »

« So, this is it! Invasion. » Jules looked at Simone and Vannier.

« *Blessent mon cœur d'une langueur monotone* was the message for us to activate our plans. It means the invasion will start within forty-eight hours, » he explained.

He addressed his men.

« You all know your tasks. This is when we start to liberate our beloved France. We don't know yet where the invasion will come. But that doesn't matter. Our job is to hinder the movement of German reserves and disrupt their communications. Sadly, many French men, women and children will also die over the next few days. Liberty has its price. So, my friends. Bon chance. »

He turned to Eloise.

« So, Lynx, are you and your friends ready? »

« We are, Jules. »

Chapter 44. D-Day

Tuesday 6th June 1944

Simone and Vannier kept watch while Eloise led the remainder of her team to the bridge over the river. There, they scraped ballast from underneath the rails, planted explosives, connected the detonators and led the wires to a position upstream from the bridge. When the clouds didn't hide the full moon, they could see down the track to a slight curve.

The silence was broken by the call of owls hunting, the wind blowing through the trees and the burbling of the river as it flowed over rapids. Eventually, the background noise was drowned by the sound of a steam engine.

« The train is coming, » Eloise warned. She could now see it emerging around the bend.

She checked the connections on the plunger one last time and gripped the handle.

« Get ready, » she ordered.

She watched as the engine approached, she could see one of the crew peering out of the side of their cab, lit by the glow from the firebox as they fed more coal. As the front wheels reached the edge of the bridge, she pressed the plunger down and flattened herself against the ground.

The explosion ripped the rails from the sleepers and the engine veered to one side, off the bridge and into the river. Momentum drove the following wagons after it, some slewed one way, some the other as they concertinaed in slow motion. Guards in the rear wagons, alerted by the explosion, jumped off the train. Eloise's team shot them as they fell to the ground.

The locomotive boiler exploded and fire spread to the wagons.

« Time to get out of here, » Eloise yelled.

Her group faded into the trees on either side of the track while the German guards took cover behind and under the wagons that had come to a stop on the tracks. They fired wildly at any shadows before they realised that the fire was spreading among the wagons.

„Get away from the train, it's going to blow up," a Hauptmann shouted.

They needed no second warning. The first of the wagons that had caught fire exploded, catching many of the guards in the open. Other soldiers got clear before the next wagon blew up. They could only watch as each wagon exploded in turn.

Down the track, Simone and Vannier could see the cloud of black smoke and the sparks of exploding munitions from their lookout positions.

As arranged, they met up with Eloise and her group.

« Anyone missing or hurt? » Eloise asked. « No? Well, let's get out of here. I think we may have company before long. »

Back at the barn, they were in high spirits as they heard that the other teams had also been successful. Three lines of telephone cables and a petrol dump had been destroyed. Their exhilaration was increased later that morning when the BBC Home service announced that D-Day had come and that the Allies had started landing troops on the northern coast of France.

Everyone cheered and embraced each other.

Jules produced some bottles of Champagne.

« To liberty! » he toasted.

The initial fervour gradually subsided.

« Do we know where the invasion has taken place yet? » Simone asked.

« The news said northern France, but that could be anywhere from the Pas-de-Calais to Brittany. We don't even know if this is the main invasion or a feint. Now I suggest you get something to eat then rest. »

When Simone woke again, Eloise and several others were gathered around the radio.

« Any more news? » she asked.

« Nothing on the BBC – though we've heard from other groups that the invasion is along the Normandy coast. We're hearing that there are thousands of ships off the beaches. It seems there have also been parachute drops. Some near Ouistreham and some on the Cotentin peninsular. Ah, here's Alouette. Maybe she has news from London. »

The wireless operator joined Simone and Eloise.

« We have some messages, I'll just decode them and let you have them, » Alouette said.

« Fine, I'll get you some coffee while you do that. »

When Alouette handed Eloise the decoded messages she called Simone and André to join her.

« London wants us to keep up the pressure, » Eloise replied. « They also still want us to monitor movements. How do you and André feel about returning to your observation post? »

« Fine by me, » Simone replied. André gave a gallic shrug of the shoulders but there was a smile on his lips.

« By the way, Simone, do you want Alouette to notify London that you are with us? They can then pass the information to your units and your mother. Vannier has asked that his information be sent, » Eloise said.

« Yes, please, that would be great » Simone agreed.

« Fine, I'll add the information to my next schedule, just give me the details, » Alouette said.

Simone and André's observations showed an almost constant flow of vehicles through their junction. It was split by traffic heading north and northwest towards Normandy and northeast towards Rouen for roads to the Pas-de-Calais.

« The Germans don't seem to have a clear idea of where the main attack is going to come, » André remarked.

« Very true, » Simone replied. She and André were lying close together, their bodies touching at hips and shoulders. Neither was inclined to give the other more space; they were more than happy with the physical contact.

Chapter 45. D-Day +1

Wednesday 7ᵗʰ June 1944

Simone and André had been back at their observation point for an hour on the day after D-Day. A German motorcycle combination stopped near the junction and the crew dismounted. Simone watched as they stretched to ease their muscles then walked around before standing and urinating at the edge of the field containing the barn.

« Damn, » she exclaimed.

« What's up? » André enquired. He raised his head and looked towards the enemy soldiers. One of them was looking straight at the barn. He lifted his arm and pointed in their direction nudging his comrade. They walked up the slope towards André and Simone.

Simone rolled onto her back and pulled André on top of her. « Make it look as though we're just a couple making love. Hide the binoculars under the straw. »

Simone pulled her skirt up her thigh and tugged her blouse from inside the skirt waistband.

André put one hand on her bare thigh. She wrapped her arms around him and looked into his eyes.

« Kiss me. Make it look real, » she whispered.

He needed no encouragement and pressed his lips to hers. He caressed her thigh and slid his other hand under her shoulder.

Simone responded instinctively to his kiss. As she felt his tongue pressing between her lips, she opened her mouth to let it in. She pressed her fingernails into his shoulder as he squeezed her thigh. He lifted his head and looked over hers; the Germans were about fifty metres away and walking directly towards them.

« They're nearly here, » he murmured before kissing her again.

„What are you doing here?" one of the Germans demanded.

« I'm sorry, I only speak very little German, » André replied as he and Simone got to their feet doing their best to look embarrassed. « Do you speak French? »

„Your papers," the German demanded; holding out his hand.

André and Simone handed over their documents. Then Simone coyly refastened her blouse buttons and straightened her skirt.

„Leave them, Karl. They're just having fun; lucky beggars. It'll only cause us more work if we take them in. They're no threat to us."

„You're probably right," Karl agreed, handing back Simone and André's papers. „Give her one for me, you lucky devil," Karl added winking at André. As they walked away, Simone and André watched, their arms around each other's waists, maintaining the image of a couple.

At that moment, there was a roar from the sky as two Typhoon fighter bombers shot overhead and fired a salvo of rockets at the vehicles crossing the bridge. André dragged Simone to the ground and lay on top of her.

The roar of the Typhoon's engines grew louder as they dived again to fire four more rockets each at the German vehicles. They climbed away again to return a third time to strafe the convoy with their cannons having expended all their rockets.

Lying flat on the ground, André and Simone couldn't see the battle but they could hear the sound of different weapons as the German column fired back at the attacking aircraft. Once the aircraft had flown off, André sat back on his haunches and looked down at the junction.

« There are several lorries on fire blocking the road and the bridge over the river. The troops can't get close at the moment. Wait, they're bringing up a half-track to push the wreckage out of the way. »

Before the half-track could reach the first burning lorry, its cargo exploded. Sparks flew in every direction for several minutes and a plume of black smoke rose from the remains.

André was still sitting on his haunches, his knees either side of Simone's legs.

« I don't think we need to pretend to be making love any longer. The Germans are going to be far too busy to worry about us for a while, » André said, although he made no effort to move.

Simone's hands were resting on his thighs. She could see a growing bulge stretching the crotch of his trousers. What would it be like to see his penis, perhaps to hold it, fondle it even?

André could see where she was looking and was conscious of his erection. He looked at her face and she lifted her eyes to look into his. She licked her lips.

« Who was pretending? » she whispered.

He leaned forward. She slipped her arms around his back and pulled him down onto her again. With their lips fastened together, Simone inserted one hand inside André's waistband. André undid her blouse buttons and lifted it and the bra underneath clear of her chest. He took the nipple between his teeth and flicked it with his tongue.

Simone squirmed and moaned, her fingers searched inside his trousers, found his penis and wrapped themselves around it. She wished she had a vagina so she could take him inside. Maybe the future that Eloise had predicted would allow that to happen if she was to remain a woman. Was that possible? Was it what she wanted? She really didn't know – but she knew what she wanted right now and recognised André wanted the same.

As they lay side by side afterwards, André's arm around Simone's shoulders and her hand cupped over his spent penis, Simone knew she'd released a genie from the bottle and it could never be put back.

Simone and André returned to the farm in time for dinner. As they entered the barn, Eloise approached them.

« How did it go? » she asked.

« Well. There was a bit of excitement when two Germans spotted us and came to investigate but we convinced them we were lovers finding somewhere to be alone. Then two Typhoons shot up the convoy we were recording. We've got the list of the vehicles here, » Simone said, handing over her notebook.

« Great, I'll give it to Alouette to send to London. So, you had to pretend to be lovers, did you? And was it hard to pretend? » Eloise asked Simone as André took the bikes to rest them against the wall.

« I think we were convincing. And that's ALL I'm going to say. » Simone replied.

« OK, I won't ask anything else. »

Chapter 46. D-Day +2

Thursday 8th June 1944

At the end of their fourth day monitoring traffic at the barn, Simone lay next to André. Traffic had tailed off through their junction and they had lots of time to talk – and enjoy each other's bodies.

She wondered where she was going to go from here. When they made love, she *was* Simone, not Simon playing the part of a woman – and definitely not a man with another man. Her penis and chest may say she was male, but she was totally comfortable presenting and behaving as a female. Perhaps, she reflected, it was like the bible said – that there was a difference between the soul and the body. It seemed to her that her soul was female even if her body was male – even if her uncle, the Reverend Bartlett, would say that the soul has no gender.

« A sou for them, » André said as he leaned over and kissed her.

« Pardon? » she replied, screwing up her brow.

« For your thoughts. Do you English not say a 'penny for your thoughts'? Only in France it would be a sou, or a centime, if you prefer. »

« Oh yes. » she rolled onto her side to face him.

« I was wondering what I can do in the future. I will soon have to get to the Allied lines and return to England. I'll have to go back to being Simon. And, I'm not sure that I can. »

« You are saying that Simone is the real you? I think that is probably true. »

« It may be true, but how can I live as Simone? I'm still a sergeant in the RAF and there is a war to fight. I can't just disappear. »

« Well, you *could* just vanish. There must be thousands of missing people and unidentified bodies. One more wouldn't be noticed. »

« Perhaps not, but I couldn't do that to my family. And it wouldn't solve the problem of what I'd then do to live. »

« You could live with me. After the war, we could get jobs at a club in Pigalle like I had before. »

« How do I explain this to my mother, sister and especially my uncle. I told you he's a priest, didn't I? » Simone asked, gesturing at the clothes she was wearing.

« You don't think they'll understand? »

« I doubt it. I'm not sure I understand it so how can I explain it to anyone else? Then there is the law in Britain. Homosexual acts are illegal between men. »

« But, you're not really a man, are you? You've just said, deep down, you are female. »

« That's how I feel – but it's not how the law will see it. »

« Perhaps things will change after the war. »

« Perhaps, but I wouldn't count on it. »

« Then come back to France. The law is different here. »

« First, we have to survive until then. »

« We will. I am sure of it! »

Simone looked into André's eyes. They were unblinking but she could sense a sadness.

« Of course we will. » She kissed him then sat up. « Come on, we need to get back to the barn. »

They made their report and gave details of movements to Alouette to transmit on her schedule that evening.

« There has been a message from London about you, Simone, » Alouette informed her. « Eloise has the details. »

Eloise came over to Simone.

« London wants Vannier back as quickly as possible and are sending a Lysander tonight to pick him up. It's bringing a new courier and a replacement wireless operator to take over from Alouette who is going back with Vannier. They also want someone from another group. As you probably know, the Lysander can only take three passengers, and even that's a tight squeeze, so I'm afraid there's no room for you. They do want you to get back as soon as possible without taking any significant risks. »

When Eloise had mentioned a pick-up, Simone assumed she'd be flying out in hours. She was relieved that she had more time with André.

« So, what do they suggest? Head for the coast and try to get through the lines? »

« Effectively. Our information is that the German forces are concentrated around Caen and to the east of the Orne River around Ouistreham. Your best bet is probably to make for somewhere between Caen and Bayeux. » She pointed to the area on a map spread on the table. « Your soundest route is probably along back roads through Falaise and Villers-Bocage. »

« On my own or with someone else, if Vannier's flying back? »

« I thought André might go with you. Are you happy with that André? »

« Absolutely, » he replied, smiling at Simone.

« Good, if that's settled, I'll leave the two of you to sort out the details. »

« That's fine, Eloise. Do you need us for tonight's pick-up? »

« No, Jules' group is sufficient. You get some rest; you've got a long ride ahead of you tomorrow. »

Simone stepped over to Vannier.

« So, Édouard, this is goodbye. Seems photo interpreters are needed more than flight engineers. Thanks for all your support and good luck. » She held out her hand for Vannier to shake.

Vannier tapped her hand to one side and took her in his arms to hug.

« It's me that should be thanking you. Simone. It was your brilliant plan, and your fluent French, that got us out of Lamsdorf and to here. I couldn't have done it without you. I won't be taking any more joy rides to see what it's like at the sharp end. I'm probably in enough trouble as it is! You look after yourself. And the very best of luck in the future. I suspect you're going to need it. » He kissed her on both cheeks. Simone wasn't sure whether it was a French 'bise' or a more affectionate English kiss.

The reception committee arrived at the landing field and prepared for the arrival of the Lysander from Tangmere on the English south coast where it had refuelled. They set out three landing lights in an inverted L shape. The first lamp was positioned at the base of the landing ground, the second 150 metres upwind and the third 50 metres to the right of the second lamp.

Jules stood, torch in hand, listening for the aircraft. When he heard it, he flashed the pre-arranged Morse code which was acknowledged by the aircraft blinking its light. The aircraft flew around and lined up with the landing lights. The single-engine black aircraft touched down by the first landing light, its strange shape, with high wings and fixed undercarriage, almost pre-historic. It slowed as it headed towards the second light – then turned and taxied back to where Jules, Vannier, Alouette and the third passenger waited. The pilot swung the Lysander around again ready to take off as the first of the passengers climbed down the ladder attached to the fuselage. The second incoming passenger passed down a suitcase radio and other luggage before climbing out themselves. Alouette, Vannier and the other passenger boarded and closed the cockpit cover as the pilot opened the throttle and set the Lysander off down the improvised runway. The entire process from touchdown to the aircraft leaving the ground again had taken just over three minutes.

Jules's team collected the landing lights and led the newcomers to a waiting car to take them back to the farm.

Chapter 47. D-Day +3

Friday 9th June 1944

Rain was falling steadily as Simone and André rode away from the farm.

Their initial route took the same path as their road watch trips but then continued to the northwest towards the Channel coast. The eastern end of the Allied beachhead, near Caen, would have been closer, but the limited information they'd been able to gather indicated that the Germans were strongest in that area.

At the end of the first day's journey, they reached a house owned by one of Jules' cousins. Built from local stone and at least two hundred years old, it was set back from the road. There was a stable block and a coach house to the rear. They rode into the yard before dismounting and knocking on the kitchen door.

Their call was answered by a statuesque woman, about fifty years old, her immaculately groomed white hair framed a perfectly made-up face. She wore a string of pearls around her neck and matching earrings over an elegant purple calf-length dress.

« You must be Simone and André. Jules has told us about you. I'm Hortense. Put the bikes in the stables, then come in and dry off; you look like drowned rats! » their hostess declared. She waited at the door for them to return.

« Good, hang your coats in the boot room and leave your shoes in there. Now, do you have a change of clothes in your case? You need to get out of those wet things. Here, take these towels to dry your hair. »

« We only have spare underwear, I'm afraid, » Simone said.

« No matter, Simone, I'm sure we can find something for you both. André is about my husband's size. You're slimmer than I, if not as tall, so I'm sure I can find a skirt and jumper that will suit for the time being. Ah Eugene, » she said to her husband who had just entered the kitchen. « Can you find André here something to wear while his own clothes dry? »

« Of course, my dear. Come with me, André, » Eugene replied.

« And you come with me, Simone. How was your journey? Apart from the rain. Hasn't it been dreadful? Who would have thought it was summer? »

Hortense led Simone out of the kitchen into the front hall then up a wide staircase to the first floor and her bedroom. She opened a wardrobe and selected several skirts and jumpers.

« Right, how about these? The jumpers may be a little bit big on you but it's the best I can offer. »

Simone picked up each item in turn and held them against herself.

« These look perfect. Thank you, »

« It's nothing, my dear. Let me show you to your room. We weren't sure if you were sharing with André or not – but from the looks between you, I suspect you are. »

« Yes, that would be perfect. »

« Fine, now, would you like a bath? If so, the bathroom is at the end of the corridor. There's a robe on the bed. »

« That would be lovely. »

« Fine, I'll leave you to it. We'll be in the drawing room when you're ready. It's to the right at the bottom of the stairs. There's coq-au-vin in the oven for dinner so there's no hurry. Give me your jumper and trousers and I'll hang them to dry. »

« You're so very kind, » Simone said.

« It's nothing. The count and I are too old to run around blowing up trains and the like – but we can provide hospitality and shelter to those who do. » With that, Hortense gave Simone a hug.

It was tempting to soak in the bath while the water relaxed her muscles and the warmth penetrated back into the bones that the rain had frozen; but, despite Hortense's assurances that there was no need to hurry, it felt rude to spend too long getting changed. When she returned to the bedroom, André was finishing knotting a tie.

« You look very smart, darling, » Simone remarked.

« And you make me wish I hadn't already dressed, » André replied taking her in his arms.

« Plenty of time for that later. Come on, we don't want to keep Hortense and Eugene waiting. »

« The Count and Countess, you mean, » André said. « Eugene told me their family used to be lords of the manor around here and this is the ancestral home. Fortunately, they were only minor nobs and actually supported the revolution, so escaped the guillotine. »

Simone turned her back so André wouldn't see the appendage hanging between her legs as she pulled on a pair of knickers. She'd be very glad to be rid of it; if that was ever possible. She then put on the skirt before fastening a bra, stuffing it with spare socks, and pulling the jumper over her head.

« Ready? » she asked.

« I've been ready since you came back from your bath! »

« Come on then. »

As her own shoes were drying in the boot room, and Hortense's were too big for her, Simone walked barefoot down the stairs. They entered the drawing room where their hosts were waiting.

« Ah, there you are. Did you have a good bath? Oh, you have no shoes. Are your feet cold? Would you like some socks to keep them warm? Eugene, could you fetch a pair of your socks for Simone? Now, would you like a glass of wine or would you prefer beer? »

« A glass of wine would be perfect, thank you, » Simone replied. « And, yes, a pair of socks would be fine. »

« Could I have a glass of beer? » André asked.

Hortense turned to ask Eugene to get the drinks then remembered that she'd already sent him on an errand to find socks for Simone. She gave each of them a drink then waved towards chairs around a log fire.

« Do sit down, I know it's June but it's so chilly, I thought it would be good to have a fire this evening. »

Eugene returned a few minutes later and handed Simone a pair of grey woollen socks.

« There you are, my dear. Now, tell us about your adventures or as much as you can. I gather you escaped from a prison camp, Simone, » the countess said.

« Shall we take our drinks through to the dining room? I'm sure our guests must be hungry, I know I am, the coq-au-vin must be ready by now, » Eugene suggested.

At the end of the evening, Simone and André retired to their bedroom.

As soon as they closed the door behind them, André took Simone in his arms and she surrendered to his kisses. He undid her skirt and it dropped to the floor. She undid his tie and shirt buttons and slipped it off his shoulders. he then lifted her jumper over her head and reached behind her to unfasten her bra. She sat on the edge of the bed and pulled him to her, undid his trousers and pulled them down. His underpants then followed revealing his erect penis.

Simone lay back and swung her legs up onto the bed. André lay next to her and fastened his lips onto hers. She took his penis in her hand and cupped his balls as his tongue penetrated between her lips and entwined with hers. He reached down and rubbed the outside of her knickers then took hold of the waistband.

Simone held his hand with hers to stop it going any further.

« Please don't touch me there, » she said. « I want to be your woman, but if you touch my dick, it ruins the illusion. You can do anything else but not that, please. »

He removed his hand.

« I'm sorry, I didn't realise. »

« I know it's probably silly but it's how I feel. »

« Is this OK? » he asked as he took a nipple between his fingers and tweaked it.

« Oh yes! »

« How about this? » he asked then took the nipple in his mouth and flicked it with his tongue. Simone moaned.

« That's fabulous, but the other one is feeling neglected. »

« Can't have that, » André replied as he transferred his attention.

Simone fondled André's penis. She could feel the veins as it stiffened. André felt behind her and slid his fingers inside the back of her knickers. She pulled his head up so they could kiss; his tongue flicking hers as it darted in and out in time with his finger probing below. Anticipation of what was to come made her wriggle and press her body against his.

Spent from making love, they lay in each other's arms.

« This is much more comfortable than the barn, » Simone remarked.

« Certainly is. No need to pull bits of straw out of various places. »

They then both fell silent. André felt Simone trembling in his arms. He looked at her face and saw that she was crying.

« What's wrong? »

« Nothing, just ignore me. »

« You don't cry for no reason. In fact, I can't remember you ever crying. »

Simone said nothing.

« Come on darling. What is it? Surely you can tell me. »

« Where do I go from here? Who am I really? If Simone is the real me, it's going to cause massive problems. The RAF certainly won't want me as Simone. They're likely to think I'm trying to get out of being aircrew and classify me as LMF 'lacking moral fibre'; cowardice in other words. They'll demote me and put me in prison before dishonourably discharging me. Then there's my family. What would my mother say? What would my sister Mary think? And my uncle. He'll worry about what his parishioners say. But I really don't think I can carry on as Simon. »

Simone sobbed.

« But, if I did continue as Simone, what would I do? I know you've said we could be together and get jobs in a club in Pigalle. But would that work? I'll still legally be male. God, it's a mess. And, I'll still have to live with this damned deformation between my legs. Might be much better if I don't survive. »

« Don't say that! We will sort something out. The war can't go on much longer now the Allies have invaded. It could be over by Christmas. Maybe the RAF will consider your belief that you are female as a mental breakdown as a result of being a prisoner of war. Perhaps they'll offer treatment. I know it's not ideal but it's probably better than being assessed as lacking moral fibre. Or maybe you can play the role of Simon for a few months; at least while working. I know it wouldn't be easy but you've had to play a number of roles while escaping. As for your family, perhaps they will understand when you explain it. »

« Are you suggesting that I'm mad claiming to be female? Thank you very much! »

« No, that's *not* what I'm saying. Haven't I proved that I accept you completely – that I love you, Simone? »

Simone looked at André's sad face and recognised the truth of what he was saying.

« Yes, I know, darling. I'm sorry. It's just that everything has come to a head. I don't want to lose you – I love you too but I'm going to have to get back to England soon. Forgive me? »

« Of course. I do understand. Look, there's not much we can do to solve the dilemma now is there? We need to just take one step at a time not try to cross our bridges before we get to them, isn't that what you English say? »

« You are right. Ignore me. I'm just being stupid. »

Simone wrapped her arms around André again and snuggled up to his chest. Maybe things would work out, somehow.

The next morning, after thanking their hosts, the pair set off again. The rain had eased but it was still cloudy.

Simone wondered if that reflected her own situation. There were certainly problems ahead – but, perhaps, they could be resolved.

The road became hillier and gradually rose several thousand feet as they approached the coast. They stopped near Falaise that night with another resistance contact and reached Nogers-Bocage the following afternoon. They planned to spend the next day reconnoitring the area.

Chapter 48. Contact

Monday 12th June 1944

The priest of a small village near Noyers-Bocage had allowed Simone and André to sleep in the church crypt overnight. The next morning, they climbed the stairs to the bell tower. From there, they could look out over the rolling countryside and the fields and hedgerows to other villages. They tried to identify clues as to where the front line between the Germans and the Allies lay.

« It's difficult to know how close they are now. We've been hearing shooting since Tuesday. First it was artillery and tanks but for the last two days, we've also heard machine gun and rifle fire. »

« Thank you, Father, » André said.

« I'm concerned that either the Germans or the Allies will use the tower as an observation post and it will then be attacked by the other side, » the priest continued.

« There are some German soldiers at the edge of that field over there but the fact that they haven't taken over the tower suggests the front line is still some distance away, » André remarked.

« I pray you're right, my son! Now, if you will excuse me, I'll leave you here. I have some parishioners I must visit. »

Simone and André watched the priest leave the tower then returned to scanning the countryside around the church.

« I think there are some tanks in that wood. I saw a plume of black smoke for an instant. The sort you get when starting an engine. There's another! » Simone said.

She wasn't the only one to have seen the puffs of smoke. It had attracted the attention of a flight of Typhoons overhead acting as a cab rank to be called on to attack targets on the ground. Two of the aircraft peeled off and dived towards the wood. They each fired salvos of four rockets at the far edge of the trees; climbed then returned for a second run. The explosion of the rockets was followed a few seconds later by a larger explosion, flames shooting up from the trees.

« Looks like they hit an ammunition or fuel dump, » Simone said.

« That'll keep the boche busy! » André replied.

As they watched, they saw artillery shells exploding about half a mile north of the church and along a line east and west of the initial bursts.

« I wonder if that's to soften up German infantry before an attack, André? »

« Seems very likely. »

The fire from the Allied artillery was answered by salvos from German guns south of the church, the rounds flying overhead.

« Hell, we may be closer to the front line than we originally thought. »

« You're right and I imagine it's going to get a bit hot around here soon. I suggest we withdraw. »

The two of them climbed down the stairs, left the church and dashed to a nearby barn.

« How are we going to break through the lines? » André asked.

Simone sighed.

« I thought we could hide up in a building and wait for the Germans to retreat past us and let the Allies overrun our position. The danger is the Germans might occupy the same building and find us. Even worse, the Allied soldiers might see it as a potential observation post and shell it just in case. That might happen even if the Germans didn't occupy it. »

« What about a damaged building? »

« Wouldn't ruins would be just as attractive as cover and as likely to become a target? »

« Very true. So, where does that leave us? »

« I suggest we wait until nightfall to try to sneak through the German lines. We can find somewhere to hide between them until daylight, then make ourselves known to the Allied forces. »

« Why not just keep going once we are past the Germans, Simone? »

« It could be pushing our luck not getting observed by lookouts on both sides. I don't want to be shot by our own troops! »

« OK, but where do you suggest we try to break through? »

« I'm not sure. There are bound to be some spots where their line is thinner. The problem is finding them. »

« How about riding our bikes along the lane that ran down past the woods where the tanks were? Maybe we'll get a better idea of where the Germans are that way. »

« Good idea, André. Come on! »

They recovered their bikes and set off down the road. They'd gone about half a mile when a German soldier stepped out in front of them from a gap in the hedge.

„Go back. It is not safe here!" he commanded.

„We need to get to Saint Pierre. My grandmother lives there. She's ill and needs help"

„No matter. You cannot pass here. The Amis are down there. "

„Is there another way?"

„I don't know. Now go back!"

They turned their bikes around and cycled away. Once they were out of sight, they turned off and rode parallel to where they thought the front lines were then tried again to ride through with the same result. The next road was also blocked.

« Let's try the other side of the first road. »

« Whatever you say, Simone. »

The tracks in the other direction were also blocked.

Back at the church, they reviewed their position. The priest had brought them some bread and cheese and Normandy cider.

« We're not going to get through in daylight, André. We'll have to wait until dark. »

« I agree, hopefully we won't be spotted. »

« The moon is in its third quarter and I think moonset is about four forty-five, that's an hour before sunrise. If we lay up short of the German lines by four thirty, we can use that hour when it's dark to creep past. Remember the ditch near the fourth road we explored? It's not deep enough for them to use as cover but if we stay right down, we should be able to get past them. »

« OK, but then what? »

« There's a stream running the same way not far from the ditch. It passes under the road between Tilly and Fontenay. There's a bridge you could hide under, » the priest told them.

Simone and André looked at each other.

« That's it then! We'll have to leave the bikes here, I'm sure you can find a use for them, Father, » André said.

« Most certainly, my son. Perhaps you'd both like to say a prayer for your mission? »

« Absolutely, Father. »

They left the church just after three and crept as close to the German positions as they dared before lying on the ground. They'd checked each other for any items that might rattle or rustle and for anything that might catch on twigs or branches in their path when they crawled along. Clouds were covering the moon as it set and the rain fell steadily.

« This will help us, the sound of the downpour will hide any noise we might make and discourage any lookouts, they'll be wet and miserable after several hours on guard duty if I know soldiers. »

« You're right André, come on, let's make the most of the cover. »

They crept along, inching their way just metres away from where they thought the German guards were. Simone stopped when she smelt tobacco smoke and heard a cough to her right.

„Do you think the Tommys will come tonight, Hans?" she heard one of the guards call to his comrade.

„Not until the morning, Erwin. They always attack at first light. We don't have to worry until then."

„The paratroops didn't wait until dawn. They dropped at night."

„Yes, but that's different. The attack on the beaches was at dawn and that's when they'll start here. If they come at all."

„I need a shit, cover for me will you?"

„ I told you that meat looked bad, Erwin. Be quick, we don't want the Hauptmann putting you on a charge for leaving your post. "

„Huh! he'll be wrapped up in his sleeping bag!"

While the guards were distracted, Simone and André edged their way along the ditch. After three hundred metres the stream that had been running parallel to the ditch, swung left across their front and the furrow discharged into it. They followed the bank of the stream until it turned right again to pass under the bridge the priest had mentioned.

« Damn, the tunnel is flooded, there's no place for us to rest. »

« All this rain has swollen the stream, André. I think we can still get through to the other side. Maybe we can find cover there. »

As the first light of dawn broke, they could see the ruins of a cattle byre about fifty metres away. A gate next to it led onto a farm track. There wasn't much left of the building, the roof was missing and one end wall had collapsed; the others were little more than three feet high, most of the original stones scattered around.

 « We might be better off in the byre, » Simone suggested.

« I thought you said even ruins might be targeted in case they were being used. »

« I did, but we can't stop here. We'll be in full view of the German lines if we stay out of the stream and freeze if we stay in the water. »

« Come on then, before it gets any lighter. »

They got to the ruins and sat with their backs to the wall.

« It'll protect us from small arms fire, if not anything larger, » André said.

« At least we're out of the wind and the rain seems to be easing. »

« How far do you think we are from Allied lines? »

« I wish I knew. It could be a hundred metres; it could be a kilometre. »

André turned away from Simone and stared over the remains of the wall.

« Listen, did you hear that? » he asked.

They sat there, neither of them speaking; holding their breath. Then the sound of an engine and clattering of metal grew louder.

Simone scrambled across to what remained of the far wall and peaked over the rubble.

« It's a Sherman tank! It's got a star on the front. It must be American. » she cried. « Quick, it's coming along the track. Stand the other side of the wall, so we can be clearly seen. If we try to hide, they may mistake us for Germans. »

The tank grew closer. Simone could now see soldiers walking behind it, using the armoured vehicle for cover.

« Wave, André. Make them think we're French civilians. »

As the tank passed, one of the supporting infantry raced over to Simone and André.

"You are in danger here, take cover." « Vous êtes in danger, ici. You comprenez? » the soldier said in broken French.

"Yes corporal, I understand completely. Where are your headquarters?" Simone replied.

"Blimey, you speak good English, Miss. I've no idea where our HQ is. Hell, I've no idea where we are. All I do is keep marching in the direction I'm told. Maybe the sergeant will know. Hey Sarge, these two civilians want to know where our HQ is."

"Tell them to keep heading north towards the coast, they'll find it somewhere up there."

"Which unit are you? I thought when I saw the star on the tank, you were Americans but you're obviously British," Simone asked.

"We're Sherwood Rangers, Miss, Nottinghamshire Yeomanry."

"Ask if they've seen any Germans up the road," the sergeant shouted.

"Yes, there are some about five hundred yards up there," Simone replied. "There were also some tanks in the wood about half a mile to the west but they were attacked by Typhoons yesterday."

"Thank you, Miss," the sergeant called.

Chapter 49. Parting

Tuesday 13th June 1944

As the tank and its accompanying infantry drove down the track, Simone and André stood with their arms around each other and watched.

« What are you going to do now, André? Stay in France and try to get back to Jules' group or come to England? »

« If we could stay together, it would be a difficult choice. But we can't be together in England, can we? And you need to re-join your unit, don't you? »

« Yes, I do; and see my family. Maybe after the war, we can be together, but, for now, it would be impossible. »

« I understand. I know no matter what you choose to do, someone may be hurt. »

« Whatever happens, I'll never forget our time together. You've let me see there could be a future as Simone. Sadly, it's likely to come at a high price. »

« So, who is going to report back to your side, Simone or Simon? »

« It has to be Simon, much as I hate the idea. »

« Well, the clothes you are wearing aren't exactly feminine; those trousers, boots, jumper and waterproof jacket could all be male or female – it's the padding that produces the shape. »

« Yes, I'll have to get rid of the bra and find some male underpants. God, the thought of that makes me cringe. I should be able to get some uniform items even if they are army rather than RAF. I don't suppose they have any ground forces over here yet. »

« You'll have to do something about your hair, too. And your make-up. »

« Damn, yes. I can try to hide most of my hair under my beret at the moment. »

« Shall I wait while you get changed? »

Simone looked at André and paused before answering.

« I'd prefer it if we said our goodbyes before I change. André. As I said before, I need to be dressed as a female to act like one. I don't consider myself to be homosexual but if I'm Simon again, that's how it will seem to me. I'm sorry but I can't change that. »

« I understand. As far as I'm concerned you are female regardless of how you look. Come and find me again after the war. Jules will know where I am. » He took Simone in his arms and they kissed. « I think I'll try and catch up with those soldiers. Look after yourself. See you after the war, » he said then turned and trotted down the track where the tank had gone.

Simone watched him until he disappeared round a bend then trudged into the remains of the byre, wiping a tear from her cheek. She removed her make-up, took off the jumper and removed her bra, which she left in the ruins of the byre. Then Simon pulled the jumper back over his head, tucked as much of his hair as he could under his beret and strode out in the opposite direction to André.

After an hour and a half walking along country lanes, Simon reached a junction with a two-lane road. The signpost pointed to Bayeux to the left and Caen to the right. He'd just started walking towards Bayeux when he heard a vehicle approaching from behind. He turned around and saw that it was a British Army Bedford lorry. He stood at the edge of the road and tried to wave it down but the lorry sounded its horn as it drove past. Other vehicles passed him in both directions but none of them were prepared to stop for what appeared to be a French civilian, especially one in muddy clothes from crawling along a ditch.

Another hour brought him to a major junction on the outskirts of Bayeux. British Military Police had set up a control point with a sergeant and three MPs. Simon approached the sergeant.

"My name is Sergeant Simon Ferguson, RAF. I'm an escaped prisoner of war."

"Do you have any identification on you?" the MP Sergeant asked.

"No, I lost my identity discs after bailing out from my aircraft."

"I see. Right, well, who won the FA Cup final in 1943?"

"Don't play games, Sergeant. There hasn't been a cup final since the war started. I'm a Flight Engineer on Stirling bombers. We were shot down after attacking Mannheim last November. I was held in Stalag 344, Lamsdorf in Poland. My service number is 10927... ."

"OK, never mind that, I believe you. How did you get this far? It's a hell of a trek."

"Mainly trains, bicycles and walking. Look, I want to get back to England. And, it would be I need a replacement uniform. Can you help?"

"There's a transit camp the other side of Bayeux. They should be able to get you to one of the RAF advanced landing grounds and your own mob should be able to help you from there."

"That sounds good. I hadn't expected the RAF to be over here yet. Can you get me to the transit camp?"

"I don't see why not." The sergeant turned to one of his men. "Williams, take this man to the transit camp. Don't take too long about it. It's only ten minutes each way so I'll expect you back in less than half an hour." He looked back at Simon. "That suit you?"

"Perfect, thanks."

"Yeah, no sweat mate. Sounds like you've had quite an adventure."

"You could say that!"

Simon had to repeat his story in more detail to a lieutenant at the transit camp. The officer had initially been sceptical but decided it would be easier to let the RAF sort it out. There was a lorry in the camp heading for Advanced Landing Ground B3 at Sainte-Croix-sur-Mer and he instructed his corporal to put Simon on it.

"This is one of yours, lad," the corporal told the RAF driver. "Says he's an escaped POW, wants to get back to Blighty. Your lot can sort him out."

"Right, well climb in the cab," the driver told Simon. "We're already loaded and ready to go."

As they drove out of Bayeux, the driver offered Simon a cigarette. "Do you smoke?"

"Not for me, thanks."

"So, what's your story? Escaped POW the corporal said. Is that right?"

"Yes. I was in Stalag 344. I got away from a working party with a colleague."

Chapter 49 Parting

"Strewth! So, what are you? Aircrew?"

"Yes, Flight Engineer. We were shot down on a raid. I'm Sergeant Ferguson."

"My name's Miller so I'm usually called Dusty. Came over on D plus three."

"So, what is this Advanced Landing Ground?"

"You'll see it soon. They started constructing it the day after D-Day. At first, it was a dirt airstrip for emergencies but there's a square-mesh-track runway as well now. Went operational three days ago. It's very basic, tents for accommodation and the like. There are squadrons of Spitfires and Typhoons based there. Anywhere in particular you want dropping?"

"I imagine there's an orderly room or equivalent."

"Of course. Wouldn't be an RAF station without one, would it?"

The driver pulled off the road and into the entrance to the ALG where an RAF Service Policeman stood guard. The SP lifted the barrier and let the lorry through and Miller drove to a cluster of marquees and tents with lorries with aerials behind them.

"They'll probably be able to help you in there," he told Simon.

"Cheers, Dusty, much obliged."

As Dusty drove off down the temporary roadway, Simon entered the most likely-looking marquee. He approached a corporal sitting at a desk and coughed.

"Can I help you?" the corporal asked.

Simon explained who he was and related his story yet again. At the end, he added "Is there somewhere I can get a uniform? And I don't suppose for one moment there's a barber here. It's been a while since I was able to get a haircut."

"Damned right it must be," a voice shouted in his ear.

Simon turned around to come face to face with a stern figure wearing the coat of arms badge of Warrant Officer on his sleeve. "What are you doing here?"

Simon sprang to attention. "I'm Sergeant Ferguson, I escaped from Stalag 344 with a Warrant Officer Baxter. We met up with some French Resistance near Chartres and Mr Baxter was picked up by Lysander. There wasn't room for me so I've been making my way by bike and on foot. I want to get back to England to re-join my squadron, sir."

"I see. I knew a Baxter in Photo Interpretation. What was his Christian name?"

"Edward, sir." Satisfied that Simon was who he claimed to be, the Warrant Officer's attitude softened.

"Right. Corporal Dawes, do we have any gash uniforms you can kit Ferguson out with? Sergeant Hunt was about Ferguson's size. Wasn't LAC Lane a barber before joining up?"

"Yes, sir, I believe he was."

"Well, see if he can do something about Ferguson's hair. He looks like a woman. Sort out the uniform and accommodation for him in the sergeants' mess. How do you feel about talking to our pilots about your escape? I suspect they'll be interested in your experience."

"No problem, sir."

"Fine, Dawes will take care of you then."

Simon was kitted out with a replacement uniform which had belonged to a member of the squadron who, Corporal Dawes told him, had been shot down the previous day. The rough battledress blouse and trousers contrasted with the silk skirt and cashmere jumper Hortense had leant Simone just a few days earlier. He accepted that, for now, Simone had to be hidden and this was his lot.

"Are you a pilot, Sergeant Ferguson?"

"No, I'm a Flight Engineer."

"By rights, you should remove Hunt's pilot's brevet then. Not sure if we have any Flight Engineer's badges. Don't get too many of them operating out of here. In fact, I think you're the first we've seen. Oh, the hell with it, you're aircrew. Keep the pilot's wings 'til you can get the right badge! Just don't tell anyone I said to do it."

"Don't worry, mum's the word!"

"OK, let's find LAC Lane for your haircut. Or would you prefer something to eat first?"

"Barber first, I think. My hair seems to attract too much attention!"

While they were walking to Lane's section, a Dakota landed and taxied up to a large marquee bearing red crosses.

"I thought this was a fighter field, Dawes."

"It is, but they're also using it to fly casualties back to England."

"Any chance I can get a lift on one of those flights?"

"I doubt it, they're crammed to capacity with casualties and crew. You'll have to ship back by boat. We'll take you down to 'Port Winston' tomorrow."

"Port Winston? Where's that? I've heard of Cherbourg and Le Havre but not Port Winston."

"We brought it with us. They've created it off the beach at Arromanches."

"You're having me on!" Simon protested.

"No. On my life. They sunk old ships and towed over huge concrete blocks to act as breakwaters then built floating piers out to jetties where ships can unload," Dawes replied. "I saw them with my own eyes when we were coming over."

Chapter 50. Back to Blighty

Tuesday 13th June 1944

Simon could have wept when he saw the result of the haircut Leading Aircraftman Lance had given him. It had taken him months to grow his hair long enough to create a feminine style. Now all he was left with was a 'short back and sides'. But he knew it had been essential if he was to hide his true self and the alternative didn't bear thinking about.

Corporal Dawes pinched out the cigarette he'd been smoking.

"Ready Sarge? I'll take you over to the mess tent for some grub now. Then we'll sort out accommodation."

"Fine, I could certainly do with something to eat."

As they were finishing their meals, Simon recognised a pilot entering the tent. Bob Butler had been part of the same intake when he'd enlisted.

"Give me a minute, Dawes," he told the corporal.

He walked over to the other man who recognised him as he approached.

"Simon, my God, what are you doing here? And what's this?" he asked, prodding the pilot's wings above the breast pocket on Simon's battledress. "You made it as a pilot, after all, did you? Well done. Didn't I hear that you were a POW though?"

"Good to see you, too, Bob. No, I didn't make pilot, I'm a flight engineer. And yes, I was captured but I escaped. Managed to get through the lines and here I am. Obviously, I didn't have my uniform and this was the best they could sort out for me here. What are you doing, didn't you go onto multi-engine kites? So, what are you doing at a fighter base?"

"I'm flying Dakotas. Just came in with some supplies, they're offloading now then we'll take on some casualties and take them back to Broadwell. They'll be in hospitals by the end of the day. Hopefully, give them a better chance of pulling through. Our nurses – we call them the Flying Nightingales – will load the injured and look after them. They're real heroines. It'll be another thirty minutes before the aircraft is refuelled so I'm grabbing a meal while my co-pilot looks after things."

"Is that your Dak outside then?"

"It is. So, what are your plans now? Do you need a lift back to England?"

"That would be wizard. I was told your flights are full and I'd have to go back by boat."

"You don't want to do that! Have you seen how rough the Channel is? You're only a little one, won't add much to the all-up weight, let's face it. Mind you, it's standing room only."

"Great!"

Simon went back to the corporal.

"The Dakota's pilot's a friend of mine. He's giving me a lift back to Broadwell. I won't need any accommodation after all, thank you corporal."

"No problem, Sarge. I'll leave you to it then."

Simon walked out to the Dakota after Butler had finished his meal.

As with all of the aircraft Simon had seen over the last week or so, the Dakota had black and white stripes around the fuselage and wings.

"I'd have thought if you were carrying casualties, you'd have red cross signs on the aircraft."

"We can't because we bring in supplies on the outward trip. But don't worry, the Luftwaffe doesn't bother us very much these days. The odd Messerschmitt or Fokker Wolfe gets through but our fighter umbrella gives us almost total dominance."

At the aircraft, an RAF nurse wearing sergeant's stripes reported.

"We're just about ready, Bob."

"Thanks, Phyllis. This is Simon Ferguson, a friend of mine. We're giving him a lift back to Blighty. Seems he didn't like the accommodation the Germans gave him, no sea view, or some such complaint so he's been making his way to the coast. Right scoundrel, didn't even pay his hotel bill when he left." He turned to Simon. "Phyllis is in charge of the nurses. Just keep out of their way on board, please. They all deserve medals for the work they do. We don't even allow them parachutes – if something does happen, they're expected to stay with the plane to deal with any casualties if we crash."

The two men climbed aboard and made their way to the front of the aircraft. Bob slipped into the left-hand seat, turned to his co-pilot and introduced Simon.

"I did warn you, it's standing room only. I suggest you sit on the floor with your back to the cockpit bulkhead during take-off, Simon."

"Fair enough."

"Pre-startup checklist please, Barry."

The two pilots ran through the checklist and, satisfied all was well, started the engines in turn. A few minutes later they taxied to the eastern end of the airfield, turned into wind and lined up with the twelve hundred yards of square mesh track runway. The co-pilot pushed the throttles to their take-off settings and, once the engines had settled at their required revs, Bob Butler released the brakes.

Simon steadied himself as well as he could, remembering the previous times he'd taken off – watching his gauges or sitting next to the pilot and helping with the controls. He was relieved to be on the final stage of his journey back to England. He wondered how his family would react to his return. No doubt they'd be pleased to see him. But would they recognise the changes in him since they'd last met?

The Dakota gradually built up speed as it bounced down the track. The tail lifted off the ground, leaving the aircraft running on just the main undercarriage. The bouncing diminished as the wings provided more lift until they were airborne.

"Undercarriage up, please," Bob instructed.

"Two green lights, Skip," the co-pilot advised.

Butler banked the aircraft gently to starboard to set course back to England, trying to keep the Dakota as stable as possible to minimise problems for the Flying Nightingales and their patients.

"Come and have a look at this, Simon," Bob called.

Simon stood at the entrance to the cockpit and looked out. They were leaving the coast, flying over a village.

"That's Arromanches down there. And that is Port Winston. This is Gold beach, just one of the five invasion beaches. Over to the west are the two American beaches Utah and Omaha and, to the east, the Canadians at Juno and another British beach at Sword."

Simon could see a semi-circle of massive concrete blocks extending out from the beaches to the east and west of the village, providing a breakwater.

Within the protected area, several floating roadways ran out from the sandy beaches to piers at which ships were already unloading supplies. Lorries drove along the roadways and straight off the beaches.

"That's incredible. How the hell did they manage to build that already? Amazing, just amazing."

"I'm told Port Winston is as big as Dover and I can believe it. They reckon it should last long enough for us to capture a permanent port like Cherbourg or Le Havre. There's another one down the coast in the American sector," Bob told him.

"I can't get over how many ships there are down there."

"They say there were seven thousand ships used on D-Day. And more than eleven thousand Allied aircraft."

"Staggering. I was surprised to see they'd already got airfields set up over here. The planning that went into this is stunning."

"Well, if we don't win now, I don't know what it would take."

With its unpressurised cabin, the Dakota stayed at a few thousand feet to limit the effect of altitude on the casualties. Overhead, they could see the contrails of higher-flying bombers and fighters.

"Isle of Wight ahead, Simon. That's where we cross the coast."

"Great, good to be back!"

"Another half hour and we'll be on the ground at Broadwell. It's important that we keep out of the way while they offload the injured."

The familiar patchwork of green fields and woods of the British countryside passed below the Dakota as it flew on towards Broadwell. Simon finally felt he'd made it home.

"Andover down to port, Simon, didn't you say that's where you were born?" Bob asked.

"Well, just outside the town. That village to the west. You can make out the forge by the crossroads."

Simon thought back to when he and his father had worked together, when everything had seemed so simple. They'd get up, have breakfast then go out to the forge where his father would shoe horses or mend farm implements and he'd repair engines. A great deal had changed since then –

even though it was only four years. There were even more changes to come and they wouldn't be easy.

Ten minutes later, Bob lined the Dakota up for the final approach. Simon had taken his position on the floor by the cockpit bulkhead. The aircraft had hardly come to a halt before ambulances backed up to it, the large cargo doors were opened and the first of the casualties were taken off. Once their charges were on their way to hospitals, the nurses gathered outside the aircraft and lit cigarettes.

Simon could only stare at them in awe.

"I don't know how you do what you do," he told them.

"Why not? You bomber types climb into your aircraft night after night, knowing that there's a good chance that one in twenty of you won't be coming back. And you've got to do thirty trips to complete your tour. Don't you think women can face the same issues?"

"No, not at all, I mean yes of course I think you can do the same. That's not what I meant. I just think it's incredible. Oh hell, I'm not expressing myself well."

"We can do everything men can do. So why shouldn't we?"

"I'm not saying you shouldn't. I've worked with ATA girls and I've seen women working with the French underground and, now you nurses. There's no doubt that you are as capable as any man and deserve to be treated as equals."

"That'll be the day! This is a man's world, run by men for the benefit of men. You aren't going to give up control easily."

"You're probably right. But I'd support you."

"Come on Simon, we need to check in. Then we can see about accommodation for you for the night. You can buy us a beer in the sergeants' mess."

"More than happy to!"

Simon then noticed a familiar Avro Anson sitting on the apron.

"That's the ATA bus. Someone must be delivering or collecting an aircraft," he told Bob.

As they walked past the Anson, a pilot climbed out of it. Simon recognised her as one of the regular visitors to the Civilian Repair workshop.

"Hello, Pam, fancy meeting you here."

"Hello Simon, haven't seen you for ages. I heard you'd joined up. Pilot's wings too, I see, well done."

Simon explained why he was wearing wings when he was a flight engineer.

"Quite an adventure then!" she remarked.

"You could say that. So, are you delivering or collecting?"

"Chrissy is delivering a Dakota, she's due in a few minutes. I'm here to pick her up then we've got to collect Thelma from Chedburgh, she's dropping off a Stirling."

"Chedburgh? That's where I'm trying to get to."

"Fine, I can give you a lift,"

"Sorry, Bob, looks like I'll have to owe you that beer."

 "It's been your lucky day, hasn't it? I bet when you got up this morning you didn't expect to be back home by the end of it."

"You can say that again. This time last night I was still behind German lines."

Chapter 51. Home

Tuesday 13th June 1944

Simon climbed out of the Anson and stood for a few minutes looking around at the Stirlings out on their dispersals. It had been nearly seven months since he'd left on the raid to Mannheim. He wondered if any of the crews who'd been active at that time were still around. It seemed unlikely. Some would have completed their tours and been rested, perhaps used to train new crews or given other duties. Some would have been shot down and taken prisoner and others killed. He was one of the lucky ones.

"Brings back some memories, I guess, Simon."

"Certainly does, Pam. A lot has happened since I took off from here last November."

"Well, I'd better get over to the Watch Room and sign in, see if they've got any news of Thelma."

"Yes, give her my best and thanks again for the lift. See you around sometime. Best make my number with the Adjutant."

Simon walked between the hangars, past equipment stores and briefing rooms to Station Headquarters. A corporal opened the hatch between the corridor and the Orderly Room.

"Yes, Sergeant, can I help you?"

"Is the Adjutant around?"

"Not at this time, it's gone nineteen hundred. He's probably over at the Officers' Mess. What did you need him for?"

"I've just returned to the station after a mission. I'm a bit overdue so need to sort a few things out."

The Duty Sergeant overheard Simon's remarks and came over to the hatch.

"Bloody hell. I thought I recognised that voice. What are you doing here, Simon? Last I heard, you were a guest of the Luftwaffe." It was Ian Cole, a sergeant Simon had played chess with in the mess.

"I was, Ian, but I got out with another POW."

Chapter 51 Home

Simon explained how he'd crossed Germany and France and his lifts back to England then with the ATA to Chedburgh.

"This time last night, I was still behind German lines," he said.

"Well, I suggest the best thing is to get you to the Sergeants' Mess. We'll organise accommodation and something to eat then a few drinks. I don't suppose you've had a decent pint of beer recently, have you? You can come back here tomorrow morning and sort out everything else. No doubt the Station Intelligence Officer will want a word; the MO will also want to check you over. I guess you'll need new kit too."

"Yes, I'm wearing everything I own at the moment and even this was from the gash store at the ALG. What about cash? I take it my pay has been accumulating. I reckon there should be about £70 due."

"We can't do anything about that until tomorrow. And don't forget tax and other deductions – including what you got from the Germans."

"What money from the Germans? We didn't get anything from them."

"Sorry, but they were supposed to pay you for work done and the Air Ministry assumes you got it and deducts it from your pay."

"Bloody hell. That's ridiculous." Simon took a breath. "OK, Ian, I know it's not down to you."

"So, what are your plans now you're back here?"

"Bit of leave then, hopefully, get back on the squadron."

At the mess, the first thing Simon did was to borrow a few pennies and phone the Rectory at Elmdene to let his mother, sister and the rest of the family know he was safely back in England.

He gave the operator the number.

"Is this call of urgent national importance?" the operator demanded.

"I'm RAF aircrew, just escaped from a Prisoner of War camp in Germany, letting my mother know I'm safely back in England," Simon told her.

"Please put a shilling in the slot," the operator instructed.

Simon could hear the phone ringing and then being answered.

"You're through, caller, please press button A."

"Elmdene Rectory,"

Simon recognised his sister's voice.

"Mary? It's Simon."

"Simon, but you're in Germany. How can you telephone us?" Simon then heard her calling to her mother. "Mum, quick, it's Simon on the telephone." His mother rushed to join Mary and share the handset.

"I'm not in Germany. I got back to England today. Is Mum there?"

"Yes son, I'm here. What do you mean you're back in England?"

"I escaped from the camp and got back home today. I've got to sort things out at the aerodrome but hope to get some leave in a few days and come home to see you all. I just wanted to let you know I was safe."

"That's such a relief. Did you get the parcel we sent?"

"Yes, look, I can't speak for long but I'll see you all soon. Love to Aunt Ida and Uncle Geoffrey."

After the phone call, Simon was allocated a room then re-joined Ian and walked into the dining room. He recognised some of the ground staff but none of the aircrew. Other members of his old squadron were sitting down to their post-operational meal of bacon and eggs. Simon ate his, then sat back with a cup of tea before they retired to the bar where he had his first pint of bitter for two hundred and ten days and he was questioned about his experiences. The first pint was followed by a second and a third and fourth. He wasn't sure how many rounds he'd signed for or how many drinks the rounds had comprised. No doubt he'd have a shock when he was presented with his mess bill. Not that he'd been the only one in the chair. Others had also stood their rounds.

About midnight, Simon decided he needed his bed.

Washing his face, he looked at the reflection in the mirror. It didn't seem to fit. He no longer recognised who he saw looking back at him. He felt like he was looking at a childhood photograph. It was someone he used to be – but not who he now was. Just where his future lay needed to be sorted out.

In spite of the drink, his thoughts were lucid. He contemplated the reaction of Pam, the ATA pilot to any suggestion that women weren't able to do everything that men could – not that he had intended to imply any such thing. He knew they could; that Simone could do anything. But he also knew that he'd have to work at least five times as hard to get half as far as Simone as he would as Simon.

That thought didn't deter him.

The End

Can I ask a favour?

If you enjoyed this novel, would you be kind enough to leave a review on any appropriate websites? They really do make a difference.

Thank you

Helen

Glossary

Item	Description
ALG - Advanced Landing Ground	Temporary airfields to provide close air support
Air Transport Auxiliary	Civilian organisation that transported aircraft from Factories and repair bases to RAF (and Navy) squadrons
Angels	Thousands of feet of height
ARP	Air Raid Precautions. ARP wardens were civilians; mainly volunteers
ATA	Air Transport Auxiliary
BEF	British Expeditionary Force sent to France in 1939
Big City	Berlin
Blitzkreig	Lightning war
Blood wagon	Ambulance
Boche	German
Boys anti-tank rifle	Anti-tank rifle designed to penetrate 25mm of armour plate. By the time war broke out, tanks had thicker armour and the weapon was ineffective.
Bren	Machine gun
Brevet	Badge worn above left pocket to indicate aircrew role. Pilot's brevet comprised wings either side of a crown over the initials RAF. Other brevets had letter designating role and one wing.

Item	Description
Brownings	Main machine gun used in aircraft gun turrets
Brylcreem boys	RAF men
Butts	The area on a shooting range where the targets are managed
Cab rank	Flight of aircraft patrolling above front line ready to be called into action by forces on the ground.
Chain Home	Original name for British radar system

Glossary

Char	Tea
Chiefy	Flight Sergeant - eg in charge of ground crew for an aircraft
Churchwarden	Lay official usually part time volunteers help run a church
Civilian Repair Organisation	Coordinated civilian workshops which repaired military aircraft.
Coned	Lit up by more than one searchlight
Dak	DC3 Dakota transport. Designated C47 by American forces
D-Day	Date of the invasion of Normandy - 6th June 1944
Dicey	Dangerous
Dixie	either nickname for men named Dean or large cooking pot
DZ	Drop Zone
Elsan	Chemical toilet
Erks	Lowest rank in RAF
FANYs	First Aid Nursing Yeomanry. Often used as a cover for women serving in other areas such as SOE
Ferret	Member of German search teams
Flak	Anti-aircraft artillery
Flying Nightingales	Nurses on casualty evacuation aircraft
Form 700	Form signed by captain of aircraft taking responsibility from ground crew
Gardening	Mine laying mission
Gen	Information
Geordie	Someone from Newcastle upon Tyne
Gibraltar Farm	Base at RAF Tempsford used by SOE
Go for a Burton	Killed in action
Goodwood	Maximum effort
Goons	German POW camp guards
Got some in	Get some experience before telling others how to do something
Ha'penny, farthing	Half a penny, quarter of a penny.
Happy Valley	Rhur Valley
Hexamine stove	Solid fuel stove

Ink dry on 1250	1250 was RAF identity card; if the ink hadn't dried, you hadn't been in long
Khazi	Toilet
Kite	Aircraft
Kregies	Prisoners of war from Kriegsgefangene
Kubelwagen	German equivalent of a Jeep
LAC	Leading Aircraftman
Lack of Moral Fibre	Aircrew unwilling to continue on operations were classified as LMF - and considered cowards
Lee Enfield	Standard British rifle
LMF	Lack of Moral Fibre
Mae West	Life jacket
Met	Meteorological
MI9	Military Intelligence 9: developed schemes to help escapers / evaders
Milk run	Easy mission
MO	Medical Officer
MP	Military Police
NCO	Non-Commissioned Officer
Panzer	German tank
Pongos	Members of the army
Port Winston	Harbour build at Arromanches
Press on regardless	Showing willingness to continue in spite of difficulties
Puka	Genuine
RDF	Range and Direction Finding (Radar)
RER	Réseau Express Régional - Suburban railway network
Resau	Resistance group
Rhubarb	Low-level fighter sweep, typically pairs of aircraft, seeking targets of opportunity
Ringway	RAF Ringway now Manchester Airport
Scrounger	Member of escape committee whose job was to obtain required items by whatever method they could employ

Glossary

Service Police/ Station Police	RAF equivalent of Military Police
SHQ	Station Headquarters
Sidesman	Shows members of a church congregation to their seats, distributes prayerbooks & hymnals, takes up collection
SNCF	Société nationale des chemins de fer français. French national railways
Snowdrop	RAF police from the white covers to their caps
SOE	Special Operations Executive - provided agents to support resistance movements
SP	Service Police/ Station Police
Spam	Canned pork meat
Special Operatons Executive	Provided agents to support resistance movements
Stalag 344	POW camp near Lamsdorf; originally numbered Stalag VIII-B
Stalag luft iii	POW camp for air force personnel. Site of several famous escapes including "The Great Escape" and the "Wooden Horse"
Stammgericht	Dish of the day
Tempsford	RAF Tempsford off the A1 south of St Neots. Used as the base for special operations flights including SOE missions
Tommy cooker	Solid fuel stove using hexamine tablets
Top of the line	Perfect condition
Tour	Series of operations. Bomber crews were required to do a tour of 30 missions
Typhoon	Ground attack aircraft
U/S	Unserviceable/ damaged
Very cartridge	Signal flare used in Very pistol
WAAF	Women's Auxiliary Air Force
Wash it out	Cancel
WI	Women's Institute
Window	Strips of metal foil used to confuse radar
Wizard	Excellent

About the Author

Helen identifies as female with a transsexual history - her pronouns are she/ her. She grew up as a RAF Brat and dreamed of being a pilot herself but failed the medical due to having had hay fever (the RAF considered it risky trying to land an aircraft and sneezing at the wrong moment).

Throughout her childhood and early career in PR, advertising and marketing and getting married and having a family, she concealed the secret that she was transgender.

In 1998, Helen accepted that she needed to transition. Losing one job as a consequence, Helen joined Greater Manchester Probation as IT Help Desk Manager in 1999. As the first openly trans employee nationally she provided awareness training for probation and prison staff (and others) and became the de facto lead on trans issues.

Helen persuaded the then Lesbian and Gay staff association (LAGIP) to extend its membership criteria to include trans and bisexual members and spent several years as chair. She also helped to found a:gender - the UK pan-Civil Service trans support network and was made an honorary life member when she retired in 2015.

She served on local and national diversity boards and chaired a trans charity in Manchester as well as training as a counsellor. Her work was recognised with several awards including a Butler Trust Award presented by HRH Princess Anne at Buckingham Palace.

Since retiring, Helen continued to present workshops on trans issues and provide counselling for trans individuals. She also became a volunteer with

Diversity Role Models - going into schools and talking to students about homophobic, transphobic and biphobic bullying.

Overall, Helen estimates that she's met well over 1,000 trans individuals who would previously been described as transsexual and many more who do not plan to transition permanently including cross-dressers, gender fluid, non-binary, drag artists/drag queens and some who identify as she-male. The discussions she's had with all of these individuals mean she has a huge wealth of information to draw on for her stories to ensure that they are authentic.

Helen started writing short stories for Cross Talk, Northern Concord Trans Support Group magazine, in the mid/ late 1990s — and started to write a novel while she was 'between contracts'. That novel was put on hold when she started working for Greater Manchester Probation in 1999.

After surgery in 2000, she joined Spice, a social activity group, in Manchester and did a number of adventurous events with them. This led to her colleagues asking, on Monday mornings, what she'd done at the weekend.

Typical answers were driving a tank, flying a jet, sailing a yacht, riding a quad bike or a hovercraft. Her colleagues told her that she'd led such an interesting life, she should write her autobiography — so she did.

While recollecting memories for it, she recalled an incident when she was 19 and living in London. She'd taken the train to Bournemouth, changing in the toilets at the end of the carriage and crossing over to Studland Bay and sunbathing in a bikini. She realised that she was being watched so left quickly.

But what if she hadn't noticed the guy?

What if he hadn't minded that she was trans?

That struck her as a possible start of a novel — which became 'Summer Dreams'.

Since retiring, Helen has been a member of the Manchester Women's Writers' Group which has provided valuable feedback on her work.

Check out Helen's website: www.helendaleauthor.info

Also by Helen

Fiction

Summer Dreams

"Summer Dreams" is an authentic story of the transgender community and illustrates the wide range of trans people's experiences, the problems, prejudices and fears that they face (and some of their own prejudices) — and the fact that being trans is just one facet of their lives. It was inspired by a true incident when the author was about 19.

But let Vicky tell you about Summer Dreams:

I was David, but now I'm Vicky.

I was sunbathing in sand dunes near Bournemouth in 2003, when Roger found me and changed my life. After spending a heavenly holiday with him as Vicky, I just couldn't face reverting to David. I knew, though, that becoming Vicky permanently was impossible.

There was only one option, I tried to kill myself.

Roger saved me then showed how life as Vicky was possible.

Summer Dreams tells of my transition journey, coming out to family and friends and their reactions, some of which were very difficult to deal with, especially Peter my twin brother's and the abuse we faced from him and others.

But being trans is just part of who I am. Roger and I have a normal life too.

But is it too good to last?

Summer Dreams is an adult novel with explicit sex scenes

It is set in 2003-8 when the terms transvestite and transsexual were commonly used.

ISBN

Paperback   978-1-9996329-3-9

What other readers have said:

"Brilliant"

"LGBT meets Howard's Way"*

"A page turner"

"Informs about trans issues without pushing it down the readers throat"

"It's a really good introduction to transgender issues and a romantic novel very well written"

"It's proper steamy"

"John didn't put it down beginning of lockdown, kept saying his glasses were steaming up"

"I really liked how Vicky was kind, caring and non-judgmental. Even though she's lucky, she still offers her help to Mia. Even though things seem to go smoothly, the book still shows the after thoughts and insecurities."

"An interesting viewpoint in the life of someone transgendered, the difficulties faced in life, and also in transition, many of which I had not considered. The basic storyline is sound, though I did find it a little 'wordy' in places, especially with the smaller details in regards to sailing, flying, and of routes to various places which seemed unnecessary to the story. Having lived in and around Southampton for 45 years I did enjoy, and imagined precisely, descriptions of pubs and places and I have been to. A good effort though for a first novel."

"Romance ... and some sailing! This short novel follows Vicky as she falls in love with a man who seems too good to be true. But Vicky faces obstacles that you don't often read about in romance. She's a trans woman and we follow her through surgery, through the process of coming out to her family, via various yachting incidents, right through to... well you'll have to read it to find out.

Also by Helen

'Helen Dale has written a sexy, exciting novel as seen through the eyes of five well-rounded main characters. I especially liked John Ives who had to ask himself some very searching questions when he discovered he enjoyed dressing as a woman - although this did come in handy on more than one occasion.

''Changes' is a thrilling page-turner with a heart-pumping finale. I read a huge chunk of it during a long plane flight and I couldn't wait for the return journey so I could immerse myself in it again.

woman? Or was the urge he describes as being 'innate' and 'part of me' always going to prove too strong?

I thought the chapter headings were clever. They reference different aspects of 'food and drink'. And the fun-times Christine has with her new friends in the restaurants and clubs of Canal Street are often juxtaposed with Christopher's participation in barbecues and picnics with his family and long-standing neighbours at home.

These two lives are as different as you could possibly get, and Christopher's heartfelt dilemma makes for a fascinating read.

Imposter

Peter Holmes, leader of Action 4 England, and his deputy, Tommy James, recruit one of their members to set off a bomb on a train carrying delegates to the Conservative Party Conference in Manchester – making it appear to be an Islamic terrorist attack.

Michelle Hartley has been working in Dubai but is travelling to Manchester to take up a new Project Manager role.

Glen Hargreaves is Australian; having delivered a yacht from the Caribbean to UK, he is visiting the Northwest to see where his family originated.

Jeff Shaw is transgender; he's been looking for a way of transitioning without causing financial problems for his family. He is travelling to Manchester to spend the weekend as his alter ego, Yvette.

When the bomb explodes, the train derails and Glen and Michelle are fatally injured. Neither has family or friends to miss them and Jeff realises this is his opportunity for his male identity to be 'killed' in the accident and for him to reappear as Michelle.

But where did Michelle's substantial bank balance come from — and will it bring consequences in the future?

Can Holmes and James get away with blaming an Islamic group for the bombing – or will **Khalid Ali** of the Habbani Intelligence Service discover the truth and bring them to justice?

What other readers have said:

of national leaders have on their everyday lives. A real page turner - I couldn't wait to hear what happened next and it kept you guessing to the very last page."

"Transgender avengers form a crack team to take down a corrupt and authoritarian US president before he causes more harm to their community. Good action-adventure romp with wish fulfilment for all those who have watched in despair over the past years as our hard-won trans rights are attacked by governments worldwide. Thoroughly enjoyed it."

Cross-over
Transgender Tales
Adventures and Misadventures on
a Journey from Transvestite to Transsexual

An online diary Helen kept between 1997 and 1999 when she first moved to Salford. She chatted to lots of other trans people online, many of whom had never been anywhere "dressed" so Helen invited them to visit and go down Manchester's Gay Village. This tells the story of those trips and others that she made with Vanity Club UK — a TV/TS club.

It also tells of her thoughts over that period when she started by identifying as transvestite but began to wonder if she was actually transsexual and if she would eventually need to transition permanently

There are descriptions of how Helen came out as trans to two of her oldest friends, at work and to her family — and the consequences of those steps.

It also includes:

- three stories that she wrote at the time for Northern Concord's magazine "Crosstalk" under the name Helen Williamson,
- A poem "Can You Tell Me What I Am?" which was written when I was questioning if I was TV or TS
- other humorous anecdotes from the period.

Also by Helen

ISBN

Paperback   978-1-9996329-1-5

What readers say:

"Some great short stories about the dilemmas of being a TV in the early 80s 90s. The diaries reveal a hidden community proudly remembered for its peer support, mentoring and deep friendship. full of spirit and life."

Non-Fiction Books

A Tale of Two Lives

A funny thing happened on the way to the Palace

**Inspirational story of award-winning trans activist,
writer, trainer and counsellor: Helen Dale.**

Having grown up as a RAF Brat and keen scout, dreaming of being a pilot in the RAF, she concealed a secret for decades before accepting, in 1998, that she needed to transition.

Losing one job as a consequence, Helen joined Greater Manchester Probation in 1999. As the first openly trans employee nationally she provided awareness training for probation and prison staff and others and became the de facto lead on trans issues.

She persuaded LAGIP, the then Lesbian and Gay staff association, to extend its membership criteria to include trans and spent several years as chair. She also helped to found a:gender - the UK pan-Civil Service trans support network and was made an honorary life member when she retired in 2015. Helen served on local and national diversity boards and chaired a trans charity in Manchester as well as training as a counsellor.

Her work was recognised with several awards including a Butler Trust Award presented by HRH Princess Anne at Buckingham Palace.

"A Tale of Two Lives" tells how she came out to family and friends and how that might have been handled better! It also covers her life after transition, embarking on a range of activities learning to scuba dive, qualifying as a yacht skipper, fire breathing, diving with sharks - including Great Whites - and holidaying around the world as part of a group or on solo trips showing that being trans is no barrier to living a full life.

Now available with colour Illustrations

A Tale of Two Lives is available as a paperback (with b/w illustrations) and as a hardcover with colour illustrations (depending on original photo).

ISBN

Paperback: (b/w illustrations):978-1-9996329-7-7

Hardcover (colour illustrations):   978-1-9996329-9-1

What people have already said:

"an excellent read and filled in some of the gaps in your eventful life. It was a brave thing to write it but I would not expect anything less from you"

"I've read the book and found it very interesting, down to earth, no holds barred, and for me personally extremely helpful in understanding a close relative in a similar situation. Well done, I look forward to the next one."

"A book about journeys and self-discovery and how to weather life's ups and downs. Fascinating insights into Helen's transition story richly peppered with the fullness of family, friendship, work and really living life to the full. Yes, Helen you have made a difference"

"I really enjoyed this book which covers the very interesting life story of Helen.

"It's a really good read and keeps you interested as well as explaining more about the TV/TS community and the struggles they can face. Highly recommended"

"I loved this book and as my son is experiencing some of the same issues it gave me insight. I also bought the book for him which I think helped, though he has chosen not to transition. He chose instead to tell his closest friends and felt able to do that."

Understanding Gender Variance

Helen Dale has been involved in the trans community for more than twenty years; initially providing support on the internet then training as a counsellor and counselling supervisor; chairing trans and LGB&T support groups and providing workshops on trans issues to a range of audiences — and has won several awards for this work.

This guide has been developed from those workshops and her personal experiences supporting other trans individuals.

It is intended to be easy to read keeping jargon to a minimum and explaining terms in simple language. The information is laid out in logical sections — with a comprehensive contents section to find relevant details easily.

With the number of individuals identifying as trans, intersex, non-binary or gender fluid doubling about every five years, if you haven't previously met or had dealings with a trans individual, you may well do before long whether as a manager or support worker friend or family. It will help you to identify the questions that you need to ask and how to avoid common mistakes. It will also be a valuable resource for anyone who identifies as transgender, intersex, non-binary or gender fluid.

The book is aimed at anyone dealing with trans people:

- Counsellors / Help-line Operators/ Befrienders
- Support/ Social Workers
- Union Staff
- Teachers and Lecturers

- Citizens Advice Bureaux
- Samaritans
- Criminal Justice System staff including
- Equality and Diversity Practitioners
- HR staff
- Other Managers
- LGBT+ organisations
- Family & Friends
- And Trans Individuals themselves

Contents include:

- Definitions
- Causality
- Social Transition
- Transsexual Journey to Surgery
- Travelling on: Post Transition / Surgery
- Trans Issues in Counselling
- Partners and Families
- Case Studies
- Legal History
- Discrimination & Hate Crime/ Incidents
- Employment
- Trans People in the Criminal Justice System
- Bibliography

Hard cover version includes colour illustrations; paperback version illustrations are black and white.

ISBN

Paperback (B/w illustrations):   978-1-9996329-3-9

Hardcover (colour illustrations):   978-1-9996329-8-4

What readers have said:

"Your books were the first thing I found that made sense from a human point of view instead of science and big words."

www.ingramcontent.com/pod-product-compliance
Lightning Source LLC
Chambersburg PA
CBHW051138190726
48290CB00006B/1896